the drink worth more than gold

a novel

the drink worth more than gold

a novel

Casey,

Thank you again for the support! I truly appreciate it & hope you enjoy the book! Keep in touch! All the best,

J. S. Loving

J. S. LOVING

BEAVER'S POND
PRESS

Edited by Kellie Hultgren

ISBN 13: 978-1-59298-709-2
Library of Congress Catalog Number: 2017900209
Printed in the United States of America
First Printing: 2017
21 20 19 18 17   5 4 3 2 1

Cover design by Alban Fischer
Interior design by Athena Currier

 Beaver's Pond Press, Inc.
7108 Ohms Lane
Edina, MN 55439–2129

(952) 829-8818
www.BeaversPondPress.com

To my parents, Scott and Teresa, for always believing in me to accomplish this dream.

Prologue—June 14, 1940

Joshua

I watched them walk into the city without opposition. The way they marched with discipline and honor, their boots clapping against the open road, made me shiver.

Fear came over me.

I gripped my mother's hand; my brother held the other.

I was seventeen, but in that moment, I felt more like a child of five living in a nightmare.

It was so quiet, I remember, as we all stood on the sides of the road as if watching the Bastille Day parade making its way through the city. I trembled as the ground shook when the tanks rolled by us. This was not a parade; it was an invasion.

"Are they going to kill us, Mother?"

She had a gentle voice when she spoke. "No, Petyr, they will not kill us, just invoke fear. They are barking, but they will not bite."

She gripped my hand. I gripped back. Even though she didn't say anything more, I could hear her trembling voice saying, *I am terrified.*

I am too, Mother.

The Nazi flag that hung from the Arc de Triomphe mocked us all as we stood waiting for our sentence to be carried out. My mother was reassuring, but deep down I knew we were going to be killed.

"*Cela aussi passer*," my mother whispered as she gripped our hands tight within hers. She was a religious woman, able to recall verses from memory when needed.

This too shall pass.

I recited the phrase in my head multiple times, yet I did not believe it in my heart. Mother would have been proud that I memorized the words so well; God hated me because He knew I was lying when I recited it.

This would not pass. This was just the beginning of it all. The end.

On that day, June 14, 1940, I watched as my freedom was stripped away till nothing remained. I was naked while still clothed. I was alone while surrounded by thousands. I died on the inside while still living on the outside.

And I thought in that moment, *There is no God.*

Part 1—August 16, 1940

Eliza

"Bolt the door behind you," I said to my sister as I put the small burlap sack onto the kitchen table.

It was awkward to carry; my tender skin itched where the rough fabric had slipped into the gap between my gloves and coat. Red splotches had developed on my wrists from my constant scratching. It was a habit, much like my grandfather's drinking after he lost his business to the Germans a few months ago.

"You can't run your shop here anymore," the soldiers had told him. "It is not right for a Jew to have so much wealth while others have so little."

They took most of our money, and the little we had left was spent on alcohol and tobacco that came in a small polished box with a sliding lid. When my grandfather smoked it, I had to leave the room so I didn't gag to death.

To provide the food, I had begun working at a corner shop, selling fresh vegetables to the civilians and soldiers walking by. I slipped a few coins at a time into my jacket—nothing that would raise suspicion—whenever a customer bought a tomato or turnip from me. My boss, Mr. Lazkovitch Sr., did not seem to mind when I took a few coins, but then again, he might not have been the smartest man.

"Bring me a drink, girl," Grandfather slurred.

I ignored him and opened the burlap sack.

A sudden hand on my back made me stiffen.

He grabbed a strand of my hair and sniffed it slowly.

"*Napój, teraz,*" he said firmly, pointing to the wine bottle on the counter.

"Papi," Isabella said, tugging his faded brown jacket.

Papi turned and smiled. "One moment, angel."

She nodded and ran to the back room where the three of us stayed together, one bed for Papi and me, Isabella in a small drawer on the floor.

"Do not do that again," he growled.

This too shall pass.

"Prepare supper, and pour me a drink."

He left me alone in the kitchen and joined Isabella in the bedroom.

I reached into the burlap sack and pulled out a potato. The knife cut easily into the thin brown skin. It was relaxing.

Bang.

The knife slipped, and I cut my thumb wide open. They were here.

Germans.

Claire

"Won't you at least take Leo with you? He has wanted to travel to the south for so long."

I shook my head as I placed the wooden panel over the boxes of wine hidden in the bottom compartment of my cart.

"He is not ready," I said.

"You are too young to go alone."

"I am nineteen."

"And that is too young to be traveling by yourself. What if the Germans find you and take you in for questioning?"

I chuckled as I climbed onto the front of the wagon. The leather reins felt smooth in my hands. "Then I will have to fight them all off!"

Dmitri did not smile. From his bag, he pulled out a lumpy white cloth. "Take this, at least," he said, handing it to me.

I took it. It weighed more than I expected. I opened the cloth and stared at the polished black pistol. My stomach churned.

"You won't have to use it," he reassured me.

I knew he was lying, but I did not say anything. I smiled and thanked him. "I will be back soon," I promised.

He nodded and backed away from the cart as I snapped the reins against the horse's broad back. It jumped to life, and the cart rolled forward, rattling as the wheels turned.

I sat back against the leather backrest that I had installed after the last trip southward from the outskirts of Pairs. I was tired, my eyes heavy, but I knew this was more important than sleep. Rumor had spread like wildfire across the countryside of the invasion of Paris; the country and its people were on edge.

Be brave.

I told myself the lie daily. It gave me hope that I would survive. I was a warrior at heart.

I drove for about an hour until I rounded a bend and froze. My heart seemed to stop. The world around me seemed to stop. I felt fear wash over me. In the middle of the road before me was a parked car; three men stood around it, smoking.

I pulled my reins. The cart slowed, but I could not turn around. They looked down the road, and one of the men waved and walked to the middle of the road, beckoning me.

I stopped.

Gabriel

The cigarette tasted bitter in my mouth as I sucked the smoke into my virgin lungs. I coughed, nearly vomited.

The other men laughed at my misery. They took long draws on their own cigarettes as they watched me struggle.

"Take another, Gabe," Izaak yipped.

I wiped my watering eyes and took another puff. This one was not as terrible, but the taste of the smoke in my mouth was unnatural. I hated it, but I had to be one of them. The Wehrmacht.

They were all fearless. Fighting until the last breath. I longed to be one of them. I wore the uniform, but I was not a true Wehrmacht—not yet, at least.

I was the first to notice the wagon on the road. A young girl, maybe a few years older than I sat on the front of the cart. She was beautiful. Blonde hair, long and healthy, fell down over her shoulder in a loose braid.

I walked to the middle of the road and lifted my arm to stop her. The others watched me and then noticed the wagon approaching. They waited by the car. That made me nervous.

I looked to them, but they said nothing. I licked my dry lips and tasted nicotine. I wanted to throw up, but I held it down. I had to prove myself to my superiors.

Acceptance. It was what I had always wanted. I longed for it daily, but no matter how hard I tried, it seemed to move further away still.

"*Stoppen sie*, Gabriel," Izaak motioned at the cart.

I nodded and walked toward the stopped cart, arm still held high above my head. The weight of my gun caused my shoulder to ache, but it was necessary to keep it close at all times.

I lowered my hand and patted the massive beast. It whinnied as I passed.

"*Guten tag*," I proclaimed with a broad smile.

She did not answer.

I felt sweat beginning to collect upon my brow, but I did not wipe it away. I continued to smile as I spoke again.

"*Wohin gehen Sie?*"

"South," she mumbled, not taking her eyes off me.

Her German was poor, and so I tried to talk to her in French instead. My mother had taught me, from a young age, both German and French. We lived on the border, so it was helpful when trading in Metz or Strasbourg.

"*Ce qui est dans le dos?*" I said, pointing to the cart.

She shrugged and replied, "A few crates of food and blankets for trade."

I nodded and rubbed my sweaty neck. I looked back to my superiors and switched back to German.

"She just has a few supplies for trading purposes in the south. Should I just let her go?"

Izaak frowned. "Check the back! She may be lying!"

I looked back to her, and that is when I noticed it sitting on her lap, slightly covered by a white handkerchief. She was so calm when she spoke.

"You will check the back and report to your superiors that there is nothing, else I will shoot you in the head."

I knew that if I said anything, she would shoot me, and then she would be killed too. A life for a life—but she was not a threat to anyone. She was an enchantress as she sat upon her seat as if it were a throne, her gun the spell by which she convinced me to do whatever she wanted.

I complied.

We walked to the back of the cart, and I looked inside. There were eight crates in total that I could see, all of them labeled *Food* on the top hatch. A woolen blanket had been stuffed against the far wall at the front of the cart, and a small knapsack lay beside it.

I felt the barrel on my lower back as she pressed it into my uniform. I wanted to cry, but I held it back.

"Now," she whispered into my right ear, "I am taking your pistol as well."

"You can't," I whispered as to not raise suspicion. "They will kill me if I lose it."

"Better you than me, then."

I gulped as I felt her free hand grab the butt of my gun and wiggle it free from its holster. She withdrew the other gun from my back and asked me to face her.

She was sweaty as well, but beautiful. I tried to speak, but words seemed to escape my mind at the moment.

"You saw nothing," she repeated.

I nodded and led her back to the front of the cart, keeping my shoulders back and posture perfect as I had been taught. I helped her back onto the seat, but before letting go, I squeezed her hand tight in mine.

She turned and frowned.

"What is it now?"

I gulped. "May I at least know your name?"

She pulled her hand free, grabbed the reins, and chuckled.

"My name is Claire," she said with a smile. "Don't forget it."

She snapped the reins, and the massive beast moved forward with powerful haste, leaving the three of us behind.

I scratched my head and watched as the small wagon rolled down the dirt road toward the south, her final destination unknown to me.

Claire, I thought with a smile. *I will never forget.*

Joshua

The lines for food were the worst. Small pantries had been opened up across the city, where civilians could collect their shares of food and supplies. I was the one sent to grab our food because of Petyr's condition.

I waited in the line, sweating like a pig baking in the sun. Others had brought small stacks of paper that they folded together to make fans. I was not as fortunate.

The German soldiers were fair to the majority of us. We were able to live as if they had not occupied France, and most encouraged us to live normally. It was not as easy as they made it out to be, however, and most French civilians did not even talk anymore. It was as if we were all walking corpses.

I thought about my father often. He was on the front lines in Belgium, fighting the Nazis, last I had read from his letter:

> *Dearest Cecilia,*
>
> *I dream of you each night and long to be in your arms soon. The war rages on around me, but inside my heart wages war against myself to keep pushing forward to one day see you again. I long*

*to see your auburn hair that falls in graceful curls,
the taste of your tender lips like a sweet wine in the
summer evening.*

*The men are growing restless here, longing to
go home and not fight this war. I agree with them,
but I still serve faithfully. We march for Brussels
soon, within the week. I am confident in our efforts.
The Germans will be stopped!*

Vive La France!

I will write soon.

I love you,

Pierre

Mother cried the entire night after receiving it. Letters had been
hard to come by in the past couple of months, so communications
with Father were quite sporadic. Yet we still waited for those crisp
brown notes to turn up under the golden mail slot in the lower
center of our door. I was usually the first to grab the mail when I
got home, so when we received a letter from Father, I tried to peer
into the contents using the lights in the living room until Mother
came home to open it for herself.

In a way, it was the only intimacy she had experienced since
my father went to war. She was angry about the war, but more
than that, she longed to be held by my father again. I didn't
understand intimacy; all I knew was that my parents cared about
and loved each other, and for me that was enough.

"Excuse me," a young girl said to me as I waited in line, a
miserable look on my face.

I looked down at her. She was covered in soot from head to
toe, her once blue dress was covered in black and brown splotches,
and her hair was unkempt.

"Do you have a few coins to spare?"

I felt a knot in my stomach. I had just enough for my family's daily ration, but nothing to spare. I looked around to see if anyone was paying attention, but no one seemed to care about the little girl asking for loose change.

"I am sorry, I don't."

She frowned. "I understand. I am alone and haven't eaten in three days. I just wanted to know if you could spare a few extra coins that you don't really even use in the first place."

"You don't have a family to go back to?"

"No, they are gone now. Taken away from here—not sure where, though. They said they'd write to me, but I haven't received any sort of letter or telegram from them."

"Do you know where they were going?"

"Mother said somewhere out east. Father was taken a few days before my mother. I am unsure where they are now."

The knot grew tighter within my gut. I didn't know what to say to the girl; not even a sorry would do justice to the situation she was going through. I plunged my hand into my pocket and fished out a few extra coins that I had found on the way here. It was nothing of significance, but when I handed them to the girl, she beamed with delight.

"Thank you! Thank you!" She bowed and held the coins tight in her hands. I watched her skip away to a small bread shop. She soon walked out with a stale loaf nearly as long as her forearm.

I smiled as I waited for my turn at the ration department. I knew our earnings would not get us as much as we had originally planned, but to me it was more than worth it to give up some money to help that girl out.

I had only wished I had asked her name.

Eliza

The soldiers passed by me without a second glance. They busted open the back bedroom door and began shouting in German. I dropped to my knees and put my hands on my head out of complete fear. My sister screamed as they dragged my grandfather out of the bedroom, his pants at his ankles and his underwear halfway up his thighs.

When they pulled him across the floor, his pants caught and tripped him as he attempted to fight back. He was so angry, his face red and eyes wild like a rabid dog's. He shouted at me, but I didn't care to decipher what he was saying. I was focused on not making any sounds in the hope that I would go unnoticed.

The soldiers brought my grandfather to the stairs and then out of the building; his voice echoed in the stairwell until they were outside. When he was gone, the entire room fell silent. It was eerie and, for a moment, peaceful.

Yet even peace shatters within a few seconds.

"Eliza?"

I opened my eyes and saw my sister standing in the doorway of the bedroom. Her hair was tangled, and her dress was unbuttoned along her side, causing it to sag off her shoulder. Tears welled up in her eyes, and without thinking, I moved to wrap her into a hug.

I didn't hear the soldiers reenter the room. They were not as forceful now as they had been with my grandfather. One of the two soldiers merely cleared his throat as he stood by the entryway. I turned around and stared directly into his blue eyes.

He knew Polish, but it was unnatural and choppy when he spoke. "Will you please come with us? We do not wish to hurt you."

His voice was gentle, but I knew that he was a soldier, and men of the military had no true feelings for the jobs they did.

"Please, don't make this more difficult than it needs to be, dear," the soldier said. He put his hand on my shoulder, and I shuddered.

"*Proze*," I whispered as I stood to face him. My sister clung to my legs, giving me uneven footing. I switched to German so that he could understand me better.

"*Wir sind allein, keine Familie.*"

The soldier winced and looked to his partner. He was not much help; he just shrugged and turned away from my sister and me.

The first soldier rubbed his neck and then nodded slowly in agreement. His voice was hoarse when he spoke. "The man we took downstairs, he was your father?"

I clenched my fist in anger, but I soon released it as I took a deep breath. "No," I said, trembling. "He is our papa. My father was taken from us a few weeks ago."

The soldier nodded and rubbed his neck again. It was a habit, I could tell. The skin was chafed along his collar. "And what of your mother?"

I wiped the tear that was beginning to form underneath my eyelid. "Dead."

The word was short and cold, like my mother's death. We never spoke of it after it happened. It was a hit-and-run: the man was drunk, and the police had never found the culprit. I was sixteen, my sister barely even three. When Mother died, my father nearly went over the edge himself, but he held himself together for Isabella and me. For that I was grateful.

A few seconds later, two more soldiers walked into the small apartment; their presence seemed to make the entire area cramped.

"What is taking so long?" one of them barked. "Grab the younger girl and let's go!"

The young soldier frowned at his superior but then in one swift movement grabbed my arm and mouthed to me, "I am sorry."

For a split second, I believed the man, but that was before I felt the gun against my chest. The hammer cocked, and he pressed it firmly into my chest, his eyes fixed on mine.

I held my breath.

Claire

As the cart rumbled down the road, I continued to think about that German soldier. He was so naive—just a boy, but a charming one nonetheless. I turned over in my mind the idea of seeing him again. What if the war were not raging around us? What if things were different? Would he actually give me a chance to prove myself?

I am French; he is German. The two simply do not mix. We are like water and oil.

I sighed and pushed the thoughts out of my mind, but still they nagged at me.

As my cart crested the next hill, I looked across the expansive, open countryside. It was so *calm*. Farms stretched as far as the eye could see, and I knew that among them were families nestled in their homes, probably eating an early breakfast before the morning chores. The vineyards were France's most prized possession. In the outskirts of Paris were hundreds of different vineyards.

I was moving into Bourgogne country, the main vineyards that dominate the east-central area of France and hold some of the world's most expensive wines. Father had always thought it necessary that I work in the vineyards with my brothers during the harvest seasons. We worked on a farm in the northernmost regions, Chablis. It was a 100 percent white-wine vineyard located on the banks of the Serein River.

During the summer, my brothers and I worked in the fields during the morning, and then after lunch we all went to the river and swam for nearly five hours a day. It was where I learned every type of swimming technique; it was also where I learned the difference between a flop and a proper dive.

The happy memories of those summer days flooded into my mind. It was a simple time in my life, one full of laughter, love, and a carefree mentality. The war had taken many things from me, but the memories would never be taken away.

In the distance, I heard a low hum that grew in intensity. I had heard the noise many times before; it was the sound of a thunderous caravan making its way to the capital from the east. I had already passed two smaller caravans since my run-in with the German boy, but neither had paid me any attention. I ignored the noisy hum and focused on my slow crawl southward atop the covered cart.

It wasn't until I saw the sleek black convertible that I began to sweat a bit more. Two significant Nazi flags on the front fender of the car waved violently against the opposing wind. This caravan was not like the previous ones of mere soldiers bringing supplies; this was an official procession, meaning that someone of importance was coming to the capital.

I tensed as the four cars drew ever closer to my lonely cart. I lowered my head so as to not draw attention to myself, but before I could rid myself of the impending encounter, the cars slowed and eventually stopped. I did not lift my head until I was at the driver's door of the last car. I sighed, thinking that I was safe from the inspection, but then a crisp voice rang out in High German.

"Madam!" one of the officials called from the second car. "May I speak with you a moment?"

I only understood parts of his German, but I knew I was in serious trouble if they found my wine stash, let alone the two guns I was carrying with me. I didn't get down from the cart, however, and instead called back to the stranger in French, "I am sorry, sir, I have nothing to sell!"

The German officials laughed among themselves. I gulped and felt my stomach jump into my throat. I reached down to my small pack and patted it softly.

Still there, good, I thought as I straightened up in my seat. The click of a car door made my skin crawl. Boots on gravel made my heart beat faster. It was as if a thousand eyes were waiting to see what was about to happen next. I bit my lip and stared straight ahead at the uneven road.

The man rested his arm on the side of my cart with a lazy stance. I did not look at him, but his presence demanded to be noticed. "You speak much too quietly, madam," he said in a voice that was as smooth as silk. "Do you not wish to look upon my face? Are you afraid you might fall in love?"

The other men in the cars laughed, and the man standing also started laughing at his own jest. I did not even crack a smile. I was terrified.

"Are you afraid, girl?" he whispered as he leaned in closer. I felt his hand find my left knee. I tightened my muscles and turned slowly to meet his face.

He was smiling. His hair was pitch black and slicked to the side of his face. His eyes were narrowed, as if he were searching for some weakness that he could expose. His lips curled as he squeezed my leg, causing his small, square mustache to lift slightly.

"Tell me," he said, squeezing my knee tighter, "what are you hauling in the back of your cart?"

I opened my mouth but caught myself before answering. "Blankets and clothes for my family in Orléans."

He nodded and withdrew his hand. At his gesture, three officials jumped out of the car with swift quickness and began to rummage through the back of the cart. I waited in silence, not breaking eye contact with the menace before me.

A few seconds later, the three men jumped out of the cart and reported that I was telling the truth about the supplies. I smiled in agreement; for the moment, I thought I had won.

The man with the black mustache sighed and turned on his heel. His steps were long and determined. He began to shout in German, and within a few seconds he walked back to the front of the cart with one of the hidden bottles of wine.

"What is this?" he demanded.

"A personal gift to my uncle and his family," I said.

"And what of the others?"

"More gifts."

I felt a sudden urge to grab the pistol on my right. It would be so easy to shoot the man, here and now. I knew him, I recognized him from somewhere, but I couldn't figure it out. I knew he was important, though—someone from the German nobility, perhaps.

Suddenly, one of the men called from the back of the cart, "Führer, we must go."

The man licked his lips and nodded.

The other man, the one in the car, had called him Führer. *This man is Hitler.*

I moved my hand to the small lump to the right of me and reached underneath. My fingers wrapped around the wooden stock of the German-issue pistol. I pulled it free from its hiding place just as the tyrant began turning around to face me. I moved without hesitation and prepared to aim, but just as I was about to draw forth my pistol, a sharp blow to the back of my head knocked me to my knees.

A burst of shouts and cocking of guns filled the air as they pulled Hitler away from my cart. The gun clattered to the floorboards, and before I could regain my balance, four soldiers were subduing me, one for each limb.

I failed to kill the monster.

Gabriel

I leaned against the car and picked my nails with my military-issue knife. Each of us received one when we joined the cause. It was nothing special: a wooden hilt with a medium-length silver blade. It was my own, though, the only thing I really owned. It felt good to hold a possession that was actually mine in my hands. I had never had such luxuries growing up. My family was poor; most days we did not eat.

My stomach growled at the thought.

I grabbed my knapsack and opened it to reveal a small heel of bread wrapped in a torn piece of cloth. The other two soldiers sat on the hood of the car, smoking cigarettes and reciting their favorite stories from their youth; they did not know I had the bread. Better that they didn't. If someone found out, I could be in big trouble. I broke off a small piece and put it into my mouth, allowing it to dissolve on my tongue.

It was dry, but it was at least food. I swallowed the piece and opened my mouth, trying to generate more saliva, but knowing I needed some water to quench the dryness.

"Engelchen," one of the soldiers called from the front of the vehicle. It was their nickname for me, but it was not a sign of endearment.

"What?"

The first soldier turned and raised an eyebrow. "Little Angel has a temper today, it seems. Is it because the girl is gone now? I know you fancied her."

I closed my pack and dropped it to the ground, attempting to ignore him. "I'm just tired."

He scoffed. "Tell me, Engelchen, who did you have to bribe to get drafted for the war? Puny arms and courage like a mouse. You are supposed to represent the grand army of Germany, but clearly you are more a mutt than anything."

I wanted to yell, throw my knife at him, do something, but instead I clenched my fist and walked away from the car, leaving the two to laugh between them.

I could hear them calling after me, "Little Angel. Little Angel. Come back, Little Angel."

I walked until their voices were mere whispers on the wind. I sighed, dreaming of home. I missed my family. I enjoyed sitting in the kitchen as my father recalled stories of the Great War. He was a valiant man, one with honor and a sturdiness about him that was unmatched by the common man.

I stopped and looked up at the vast blue sky. In my mind, I dreamed of being like my father, but in my heart, I knew I hated the country I served. The things we were doing to these people, the stories of the torture and imprisonment of innocents across Europe . . . I knew the truth, and it made me ashamed to wear the badge on my arm.

The rumble of a distant car caught my attention. I turned and saw the black cars processing up the road toward us. The crimson flag with the Nazi swastika flapped in the wind. I gulped and walked toward the front of the parked car.

"Who's this, then?" one of the soldiers said in a quiet voice as he straightened his shirt and tucked it into his pants. The other soldier threw away his cigarette in haste.

The cars slowed to a crawl as they approached us. The back-seat window rolled down on the first car, and a man with a small mustache saluted us. His chiseled face and slick black hair made him look handsome. My heart sank as I erected my arm outward from my body and recited the common phrase among the soldiers, "Heil Hitler!"

I had never seen him in person, only heard stories from other soldiers explaining how mesmerizing and captivating the man was. I didn't see it; in fact, I felt sick to my stomach as I met his eyes. He searched me as he rolled past, but never stopped smiling. I felt naked before his gaze.

The car sped up slightly, and the others followed in close pursuit of the lead car.

"They must be holding a meeting in the city square to honor his victory over the French," one of the soldiers whispered as he stood as still as a statue.

I was about to answer, but as the last car passed I caught glimpse of a figure in the window. Her head was downcast, causing her blonde hair to fall in front of her face. The same beautiful girl I had encountered at our checkpoint.

"Claire."

Eliza

I heard the gunshot before I felt the bullet pass through my chest. It didn't hurt at first, it just burned, as if someone had pressed a burning coal to my flesh and didn't let up. I gasped and grabbed the soldier's arm to support myself. The world seemed to slow down around me. I could hear a ringing in my ears, my vision was blurry . . . I tried to hold on to the soldier's arm, but my hand was weak, and I fell.

I was on my knees as I watched them take my sister from the room. She fought them the entire way. I think she was screaming for me, screaming my name to make them stop, but they didn't. She disappeared down the stairwell. I knew they would shoot her outside, if not in the stairwell itself, and then dump her body somewhere. Most of the soldiers had already left the room. Only the soldiers who had broken into our apartment remained.

They spoke, but I only heard the low droning of their voices in my ears, like the groaning of an old wooden door that needed oil on its hinges. They spoke to me, I could tell, but I didn't understand. The one who shot me, the man I had thought to be gentle and trustworthy, looked to his partner and ordered him out of the apartment. The soldier shot him a look of anger as he waved his pistol in my direction, but exited the room, leaving my soon-to-be killer alone with me.

He dropped to one knee and lifted my chin slightly. I read his lips when he spoke to me.

"I'm sorry."

He frowned and then stood up. He turned to the door, but just before he walked away, I grabbed his leg and gripped it with the remaining strength that I had. He tried to kick me away, but my grip only tightened. Again he tried to push me away, but I pulled harder and lifted myself off the ground slightly.

"Get off!" he shouted as he slapped me with the back of his hand.

I fell to the ground as a sharp pain ran through my chest where the bullet had passed through. I wanted so badly to stand and fight the soldier, but the strength was draining from me with each passing second. He shook his head and left me alone in the apartment.

I cried out to him to come back, but no one came. I was alone, I was dying slowly, and my world was crashing down around me at a rapid rate.

I pulled myself to the wall and rested my back against it; the wound stung like a plunging knife.

Closing my eyes, I prayed in a quiet voice to the last person I thought could save me. But even as I prayed, the God I had trusted so much was silent too.

Claire

The car rolled to a stop outside the large, ornate Senate building. Nazi flags flapped in the wind as the sun set in the western sky. The door opened, and a soldier grabbed me by the arm, yanking me out of the stuffy car.

The city seemed to be dead. There was a curfew in effect now. Everyone was to be in his or her home by sundown or else be arrested. I was an exception today. As the general in our car put it, "You are a guest of honor to Hitler himself. You should feel honored."

It was a lie. I was not a guest; I was a prisoner of the enemy. I'd had a chance to kill the vile monster, but I'd hesitated, and millions would die due to my lack of courage to pull the trigger.

Two men scrubbed the steps leading to the main doors. They were young, like me—probably tried to break curfew but were stopped without resistance. This was a minor punishment, but a punishment nonetheless.

Two soldiers stood on either side of the doors, and as Hitler was about to enter, the statue-like guards shot their arms out in salute to their fearless ruler. He smiled and returned the gesture. I didn't understand their infatuation with the man; he was ruthless and vile, yet they saw him as a savior and a god among men.

I had seen the Luxembourg Palace many times prior, but never had I entered. The outside was a cream color, with two wings that stretched outward from the building like two arms enveloping the center. In the center, at the very top, was a silver-colored dome with the lonely French flag still waving its merciful surrender. The lackluster sight dampened my spirit. Below the dome, the clock read 6:23.

The entrance hall was ornate, with white walls and velvet rugs leading from the main doors to side rooms. At the end of the small stretch of hallway was a larger opening that led to the "Grand Staircase." Nazi soldiers had replaced the typical French guard along the flanks.

I was nervous. The air seemed to thicken as we moved deeper into the palace, as if it were a slumbering beast and I was delving into its bowels with each step. I watched *him* closely. Watched his every move, every mannerism, every time he acknowledged a new soldier, entered a new room; I wanted to know him, the way he worked.

"You are quite observant," a soldier whispered in my ear as we followed the processional upward into the upper deck of the palace. His breath smelled like onions and smoke. "He is blind, you know; Hitler puts on a charade of being confident, but behind closed doors, the man is paranoid, always looking over his shoulder. He is a coward."

I glanced to the right, where the soldier followed close behind.

"He will fall soon," I whispered back. "He knows it."

"A girl speaks with such confidence. Why?"

I wanted to confront the man, but I knew that if I stopped, I would die.

"He hides in his alcove while his closest allies plot to overthrow him."

The man grabbed my shoulder and stopped me on the stairs. The rest of the party moved along, taking no notice of our abrupt stop.

"My name is Henning," the soldier said in a sly voice. His face was pointed like a fox's snout. He had thin blond hair, receding from his brow, and deep blue eyes. He was quite handsome, but something about him made me uneasy.

"Is it wise for you to be talking to me alone?" I said.

"I am a general staff officer, so if anyone questions me speaking to you, I will call them off," he said as he took my hand into his. Looking into my eyes, he murmured, "I tell you this, young one, because there is a change on the wind. A new day will dawn soon, but most do not see it yet. I, however, see it in the near distance. Much like you, I do not agree with Hitler's rule, but the time to dethrone him is still far off. Strike too early, and you will anger the beast into action. Strike too late, and the beast will find and consume you."

"Why are you telling me all this?" I said, pulling my hand away. "Why do you care about *me* so much?"

He smiled with thin red lips. "I will tell you the truth, my dear. If Churchill can induce America to join the war on side of the Allies, we will eventually be crushed and overrun by the material superiority. After, the most that will be left to us will be the Electorate of Brandenburg, of which I will be chief of the palace guard."

"You are confident, Henning," I said as I folded my arms across my chest. I was trying to be confident, but in reality, I was terrified. "That confidence might get you killed one day."

He smiled and opened his arm to direct me up the stairwell once more. "Come, young one, we shall speak more of this in time."

I let him lead me up the stairwell. I did not speak the rest of the walk, but in the pit of my stomach I felt an ache to trust this man—not just any man, a *Nazi*.

Joshua

The sirens rang across the city, signifying the start of curfew. It had been put into effect after the Germans took over. No one went out after dark anymore. Sometimes I heard rumors of people sneaking out into the city, trying to avoid the soldiers, as if it were a game. My mother had the eyes of a hawk and the ears of a fox, however, and she would know if I tried to leave.

"The curfew does not even work," I said as I stared at my plate.

"Joshua," she said with a sharp tone, "the curfew is not a game. It is law now. If you are caught, you will be punished with severe consequences. Please do not put me through such turmoil."

"I don't think you will ever have to worry about me sneaking out, Mother," I lied as I ate my supper with a broken fork.

We were eating a small meal that evening: a thin slice of ham, one for each of us, with a half a loaf of bread—stale, of course. I put the piece of flavorless ham into my mouth and immediately drank some water to wash it down.

"Is the food running out, Mum?" my younger brother, Petyr, said from across the table.

She shot me a quick glance, a warning not to tell my younger brother the truth.

"No, Petyr, there is plenty of food for all of us. We just need to be sparing with our portions is all."

He frowned. "You are lying to me. Why do you always lie to me? I'm nearly eight; I'm a young man growing fast!"

She stood and then walked to his side, where she knelt. She brushed his hair out of his eyes and kissed his forehead with her tender lips. Tears rolled steadily down her cheeks as she tried to keep her composure.

"Life is hard, Petyr, but we must endure through even our trials. God will provide."

I slammed my fork into my plate, chipping it slightly.

"Damn it, Mum! Stop lying to him! Did you not hear that he understands what is going on? We are in the middle of a war, and you just sit here and tell us everything is all right!"

My mother snapped her fingers and pointed at me. Her nostrils flared, and I could see the rage building up within her.

"Don't you ever use that language in my household again," she said through gritted teeth.

I stood up and kicked my chair from beneath me. "Why don't you tell Petyr the news, Mum? Why don't you tell him the letter you got in the mail today?"

She lowered her hand and tried to speak, but words became mumbles.

I was on the rise now; anger and resentment flowed through every inch of my body.

"Mum?" Petyr said with wide eyes. "Mum, what letter is Joshua talking about? Was it about Daddy? Is Daddy coming home?"

I opened my mouth to shout again, but my mother cut me off before I could get another word out.

"Get out of my sight!" she bellowed, shaking where she stood, tears running like waterfalls down her cheeks. Her face was red, bright red, and her eyes burned with anger and fear.

I snatched up my piece of bread and stormed out, back to my room, where the letter lay open on my bed, signed by my father's field marshal. I grabbed it and sank to my knees as I read the short typed-out paragraph over and over, trying to convince myself that it was a mere trick, a ruse to turn me against the ones I loved, but the words were clear and concise.

My father would not be coming home alive after all.

Gabriel

I was anxious. I hated being anxious. My mother said it was a problem I'd had since birth. I had pulled strings and convinced my superiors to allow me to take guard duty outside of the French government building that evening because I knew that was where Claire was being held. Naturally, I kept that reason to myself.

I stood near the palace and looked up at one of the windows on the third floor. Its light was on, the curtains pulled back, revealing an ornate bedroom. Soon, a woman came to the window and peered out across the quiet city. My heartbeat quickened, my breath drew thin—it was she.

I moved in desperate haste until I was underneath her window. I grabbed a few pebbles from the road and began tossing them at the lit window. The first three missed, but just as she was drawing the curtains for the night, my pebble found its target. She stopped and looked down at me.

She looked confused, but still she opened the window latch and leaned out from the room.

"What do you want?" she said.

"It's Claire, isn't it?" I replied. "The one who was on the road with the cart earlier today."

She frowned. "Why are you here?"

I did not expect that. I tried to find the words to say, but as I was fumbling over my response, she cursed to herself and began to retreat back into the room, closing the windows behind her.

"No, wait!" I shouted.

She stopped and leaned forward once more. "What do you want?"

"I want to help you. I can get you out of there. I'm *important*," I said with hopeless effort.

"Don't lie to me," she said. "I am betting you are just a private, just a green boy."

I blushed and lowered my head in defeat. She saw through my fabrication and straight into my pathetic attempts to win her over. I had always read that a woman would fall for the strongest, most powerful man. I just didn't know they were also keen spotters of the truth.

"You are right, I'm not much of a soldier. I hate being one. I'd rather be back home in western Germany with my mother and father. It isn't my choice, you know, being in the position I'm in."

"And what position is that?"

"I am conflicted in my heart. I want to serve my country, but I know that what they are doing in secret is wrong."

"Have you ever killed a man?"

I did not answer; instead I looked at my feet and rubbed my neck until it turned red.

"It was an accident, wasn't it?"

How did she know? I had never told anyone, not even my closest bunkmates. I had shot an innocent man when first arriving in Paris, but it was not my fault. I reminded myself once more, it was not my fault.

"No matter," she said, looking back into the room. "Is it true that you can help get me out of the city?"

I didn't hesitate to answer, "Yes, of course."

"Good," she said with a faint smile. "Come back tomorrow, and I will be ready."

She closed the window once more, and I backed away, my heart fluttering like a feather in the wind.

Claire

I closed the windows and drew the curtains tight so that the chilly draft would not sneak through during the night. Dousing the oil lantern next to the bed, I pulled the large brown comforter from beneath the bedcovers and slid in. I was in just my underwear, as my hosts had not prepared any nightclothes for me. I was chilled, but I did not complain. It was the nicest bed I had been in for a long time, and to be honest, it was soft. I tried to fight the drowsiness that weighed down on my eyelids, but before long I was fast asleep, dreaming of fantasies from my youth.

The morning came quicker than I had anticipated. I was not ready to wake up, but within a few moments of the sun breaking the horizon, the door to my bedroom opened and a young French maid walked in carrying a silver tray with biscuits, butter, jam, and a cup of freshly poured herbal tea.

"Get up, miss," she said in a crisp voice. It was not inviting, but I did not argue.

I slipped out of bed and pulled on my clothes from the night before. She stopped before leaving the room and looked me over. She seemed unimpressed by the sight and made it her prime intention to show her disapproval. I lowered my head and dressed myself completely before I looked up again.

The door was closed partway; I was alone again. I walked over to the tray and, with a timid hand, picked up the larger of the two biscuits. I broke off a piece and stuck it into my mouth. The flaky baked dough crumbled in my mouth as I swallowed. The next piece was still warm, and before I realized it, the first biscuit was completely gone.

Embarrassed by my gorging, I stuffed the second biscuit into my coat pocket for later. I took a sip of the tea and gagged. I had always hated tea, though my mother always told me to drink it, as it would keep me healthy. I never heeded her advice—a mistake I regret still.

I turned for the door, leaving the tea on the tray without a second sip. When I reached the threshold, a handsome soldier blocked my path. He gave me an odd look as he moved his eyes from my head to my toes. I was uneasy, but I kept my eye contact with him.

"*Guten Morgen, kleine Blume,*" he said with a wide smile. "*Hast du gut geschlafen?*"

I played the words in my mind until I pieced together his sentences, fragmented as they were.

"Yes," I said in German, "I did sleep well, thank you."

He gave a curt nod and then motioned for me to continue down the hallway to the stairs. I did not turn around as I walked, but I knew he watched me the entire way, fantasizing about me, about what he would do to me. I shuddered at the thought and descended the stairs.

We went only to the second landing, not all the way to the ground floor where we had entered the night before. On this level, every doorway had guards, and when I approached a particular door, they waved me away, muttering curses under their breath.

Finally, I found an open door. I entered and saw a long, rectangular table with high-backed chairs around it. Massive windows lined the far wall overlooking the city, waking still from the long evening. I walked around the table; it was bare except for a few scattered papers with the Third Reich seal stamped on the top of the ledgers. I paid no attention to them, fearing that I might get myself into trouble.

I reached the window and peered out into the lonely street below me. A few cars rumbled in front of the castle, but no one seemed to notice me staring out from my perch. I felt like a lone bird overlooking the city from her nest. I was completely alone up here, surrounded by a city of thousands.

I scanned the groups of people starting to emerge from their simple dwellings, heading for their designated destinations, each with their own agenda to complete.

"You are not supposed to be in here, you know," a voice said from behind me. I recognized it immediately as the soldier who had walked with me up the stairs the night before.

Turning, I smiled and said, "I am a guest. Is it not my choice to go where I please?"

He frowned. "Sadly, no. You are a guest in this establishment not out of good favor but instead as a demonstration of public pacification."

"What do you mean by that?"

"You are to be executed this evening, before dusk. You nearly killed Hitler, which would not be good publicity if it got out to the people. They would see him as weak and vulnerable—yet we all know he is strong and capable of great feats."

He bowed his head and continued in a soft voice. "I tried to reason with them, the generals and commanders, but they decided that this should be your fate. Pray to your god, whomever that might be, that you may be spared."

He left me alone, closing the door behind him. I began to cry and turned back to the window.

"Help me, Gabriel."

Eliza

I awoke in a field of flowers—white and yellow petals as far as the eye could see. In the distance was a large green hill with a small cottage atop it; a thin stream of smoke rose from the chimney, and out front I could see a woman hanging clothes on a line. She was radiant in the sunlight. She wore a blue summer dress, fitted to her eloquent curves, which complemented the straight blonde hair that fell across her shoulder.

A young man with a trimmed beard emerged from the cottage and embraced his wife. They shared a kiss. I smiled and began to walk toward them through the field of flowers. At first, my journey was quick and without resistance, but as I neared, the hill seemed to grow larger. With each step, the slope became steeper. My feet slipped on the grass, and my hands only grasped stems and white roots.

I began to cry. I was so close, but they rose into the distance until the hill was a mountain and I was stuck on the side slope, covered in dirt and sweat. I sank to my knees and began to weep.

I looked to the top of the mountain, where the small cottage was now just a smudge against the bright blue sky, and cried out at the top of my lungs, "Mother! Father! Help me!"

The only answer I received was the faint whisper of the wind as it blew across my sweaty face, chilling me to the point of shivering. The white clouds turned into enormous black thunderheads filling the entire sky. The cottage disappeared into the darkness above. A crack of lightning raced across the sky, followed by a bellowing rumble of thunder. I shrieked in terror as I ran back to the field of white and yellow flowers below.

When I reached the bottom, however, the flowers decayed into ash and the grass shriveled up, leaving behind a scorched expanse of cracked soil. Rain began falling in heavy sheets, and before I knew it, I was drenched.

I felt a sharp pain in my chest, and when I looked down, I saw a pool of crimson blood staining my white dress. I tried to stop the spread, but before I knew it, the stain had covered my chest and spread down to my stomach, growing until it dripped out of the bottom of my dress to the ground below me.

I felt a sudden tingling pain growing in my right cheek. It burned like a dull ember at first and then grew into a roaring fire. Another burst of pain erupted across my face and through my entire body, and I gasped for air as I opened my eyes in the dark apartment that had been my home for the past few months.

"She's back!"

"Quick, get her to the table. The bullet passed through, so it will be much easier to stop the bleeding."

"How much time do we have before the patrol comes back around?"

"Not enough, but we have to stop this bleeding before we worry about that."

I couldn't make out faces as I was lifted from the ground and placed on the kitchen table.

I groaned, but before I could say another word, my heavy eyelids sagged.

"We are losing her again!" the voice shouted. "Rosaline, apply pressure here! Eliza, hold on!"

My eyes closed.

I was dead.

Joshua

I slept through breakfast. When I woke up, the morning was already half-gone. I strained my eyes to read the clock hanging above my dresser across the room.

10:25.

I sighed and rolled out of bed. The crumpled letter from the French military office lay on the floor next to my feet. Stains from my tears soaked the letterhead, but I did not move to pick it up again. There was no point.

I dressed myself and made my way downstairs.

10:29.

Entering the kitchen, I went straight for the cabinet and grabbed a small chunk of the bread left over from supper the night before. It was hard to chew, but I forced it down with a couple of sips of tap water.

10:32.

I called out for my mother and Petyr, but no one answered me. I walked into the family room next to the kitchen. It was barren. The table had been cleared of everything, and the chairs were perfectly lined up, as if readied for a family meal.

10:40.

I lingered awhile longer before leaving. When I entered the foyer, I noticed that the front door was ajar. I approached slowly, so as to not startle an unknown animal. I crept on quiet feet until I reached the doorway.

10:42.

I reached out, grabbed the knob, and pulled the door back, exposing the front porch and street beyond.

10:44.

I saw a note hanging on the front of the door. It was written in German, a scribbled message too sloppy for me to decipher, until the last line, which was written in French.

Attention! Relocation will commence tomorrow morning at 8:00 a.m. Please be prepared with one piece of luggage per family. We expect your complete cooperation in this time.

Sincerely,

Pierre Laval

10:48.

"Joshua," I heard my mother say from behind me. "Did you call for me? I was in the basement, and . . ."

She raised her hand to cover her mouth. "What is that?" she asked as she took the note from me and read it herself.

10:50.

"We have to leave," she said. "Now."

Gabriel

I skipped lunch and went straight to my patrol post outside of the castle grounds. I was on duty until six, just before sundown. I walked the route slowly, trying to make the time pass, but it didn't seem to help. Every time I walked by her window, I looked up in hopes of seeing her, but every time I passed I was disappointed.

On my final pass, I kept walking. I had given up hope.

"You didn't stop," a man's voice said from a nearby bench. "Why?"

He spoke fluent German, but when I looked to see who he was, I could tell he was French. He was old—older than my own father. A war veteran, I guessed, from the way he sat and held his head high. He had a slight shake as he stared at me with his dull grey eyes.

"I am on patrol. If I stop, I'll get in trouble."

He scoffed. "Yet you looked at that window with every pass but this last time. Why?"

I frowned. The man was persistent, but I just gave some other excuse to cover my true intention.

"You are a terrible liar, son," he said. "I know why you keep stopping at this window. She's a fine girl."

"How did you know about her?" I whispered as I looked around to see if anyone was listening in on our conversation.

"I have my own sources, son. They also tell me that you chatted with her last night, something about getting her out of the palace. Am I mistaken?"

I blushed. "Well, I mentioned it . . ."

"Yet you have no plan for getting her out, do you?"

I frowned, embarrassed. "I was working on that plan. I have to wait for the cover of darkness to actually act on it."

He licked his lips and nodded. "After sundown would be a good idea—were the circumstances not so dire."

"What do you mean by that?"

A sharp whistle cut through the midafternoon air, piercing my ears. It was followed by the bellowing voice of my field commander.

"Gabe!" he shouted. "What the hell are you doing? You are on active patrol!"

I ignored him and pressed in toward the old man, asking him to repeat what he had said.

"You don't know?" he said with a slight frown.

"I don't know what?" I persisted.

My commander gave out another thunderous yell for me to get back to my patrol.

I ignored him yet again. "Tell me," I demanded.

"They plan on executing Claire at sundown as an example of how the French people should fear the new government and submit. There will be no mercy."

My throat went dry as the words replayed in my mind.

I straightened and saw my commanding officer stomping toward me, nostrils flared and face red as a ripe tomato.

What could I do to save Claire?

A voice in my head whispered, *It is your fault. You are a murderer.*

Joshua

"Petyr, did you use the bathroom yet?"

He looked up at me with ashamed eyes. "No," he mumbled.

I was annoyed, but I kept my voice calm so as not to scare him. "Well, go. Mother would give you a spanking if she were here right now. I'm not as mean." I rubbed his hair and winked as I motioned for him to hurry to the bathroom so he could get back down here.

He giggled and ran up the stairs.

The order called for only one bag per family; the rest was to be left behind. It made sense for traveling, but my heart sank when I had to leave all my things in my room, never to be touched again. Mother said we would be able to repurchase everything, but I knew she was just saying that to soothe Petyr's nerves.

"Keep a positive mind-set when we leave the house please, Joshua?" she had said to me as we were packing alone in her room. "Your brother does not know better, and I don't want to scare him."

"You can't protect him forever," I'd said.

She stopped packing and locked eyes with me. I could tell the comment cut her deep.

"I can't," she said, "but I can keep him safe for the time being. He does not need to know about the horrors that lie beyond that door. He is just a kid. He should be outside playing with his friends, not locked in the house, living in fear."

"One day he is going to have to face reality, and you can't stop that from happening."

"I can prevent it for now," she said. "You had to grow up too fast, Joshua. I don't want your brother to have to also."

"I didn't have a choice like he does," I said in a cold voice.

She frowned and walked around the bed until she stood in front of me with tear-filled eyes. "What she did, I cannot change," she said.

"And yet when you could do something, you chose to do *nothing*."

My mother's face was emotionless. "I did everything I could do. Do not think yourself the only victim, Joshua. We all suffered."

"Some more than others," I said as I turned and left the room. I knew the words hurt, and I meant them to: she deserved it after what she put me through for a few coins to get us our meals.

"Joshua," my mother said, snapping me out of my daze, "take our passes and put them into your pocket, please?"

I took them and stuffed them into my coat. I looked up at my mother. She was stressed, her hair frazzled and her face flustered. She was going through our bag once again to be sure we had everything we needed for the relocation.

"Mother," I said.

She looked up from the bag but didn't say anything.

"Mother, I am sorry for earlier. I just . . ."

She stood and embraced me. "I know, Joshua. I know you didn't mean what you said. I am sorry I put you through that; no boy should have to do that."

I felt the tears welling up as I held her close to me, but I pushed them back and forced myself not to cry.

Petyr rushed back downstairs to join us, not realizing the heaviness of the moment that my mother and I had just shared. She pulled away and wiped her now wet cheeks. Petyr inquired, but my mother ignored his question. I took his hand and led him outside to the sidewalk as Mother followed after.

"Where are we moving to?" Petyr said as he squinted down the street.

I didn't know how to answer that. Mother was not near, so I had an opportunity to tell him the truth. I knew where we were going; I had heard stories. I had this one chance to break my little brother from his fantasy realm and into reality.

"We are going to a lovely place in the countryside. Mother has it all arranged for us. Papa and Grandmother are going to be there too! Mother said she is tired of city life and needs to get some fresher air in the country."

He smiled up at me, and I smiled back. I had lied, but I knew it was the better option of the two. He was still too young to be exposed to reality.

I had always been told that lying was a bad thing, that you should never do it. I guess those people had never been in the middle of a war zone. At this point, lying was the only way to keep the mood positive. But at whose expense?

Eliza

I gasped for air as I shot upward from the table. Pain rushed through my left side where the bullet had traveled through. I screamed in agony. A hand whipped out from behind me and muffled my mouth, causing me to scream louder. Three more sets of hands grabbed my shoulders and arms and pulled me back to the table until I finally calmed down.

I couldn't see their faces in the dim light. I recognized where I was, however: I had not left my apartment yet. The memories flooded my mind, and I began to shake.

I was shot. They took my sister, left me to die. How am I alive? Who are these people?

"Eliza, you need to calm down," a woman's voice said as the grip on my left arm tightened. "Eliza, you will recover, but if you move too much you will rip out the stitches in your shoulder. Please, don't move more than you have to."

I did not know who was talking to me, but I obeyed after a few more attempts to break my physical restraints. I was exhausted, thirsty, and hungry. When I was completely relaxed, the hands of the mysterious people let go and let me lie in peace.

"What happened?" I said through chapped lips.

The woman who had spoken earlier moved closer, sounding as if she were right next to my ear. "You were shot. I heard it and came to your aid, along with my husband, son, and daughter. I don't think you know us; we do not leave our apartment often."

"Ms. Lis?"

"Yes, dear," she said as she placed a hand on my forehead. "My first name is Adelaide, but you may just call me Ada for short. It is Eliza, correct? Or is that your sister's name?"

"It's mine," I whispered. "My sister . . . where is she?"

Ada was quiet.

"My sister . . . *where is she?*" I asked again, this time through gritted teeth.

"We don't know," Ada said. "Victor, my husband, saw them taking her to a large convoy that was destined for the north side of the city, where they are rounding up people to live in ghettos."

"And why did you four get spared?"

"We hid," she said. "We have a secret compartment in our apartment. The Germans ransacked the place, but when they did not find us, they moved on. When I heard the gunshots from below, I told Victor that we needed to come up and help."

"Thank you," I mumbled as I held back the tears.

"Here, Ada," Victor said as he entered the room. "I made some soup for you and Eliza."

I had no strength to sit up, let alone eat anything, but I forced myself into a propped position on my elbow. I could see Ada and her husband next to me, their faces shrouded in the dim light cast from the nearby candles. I thanked them and then took a sip of the warm liquid.

It flowed down my throat and warmed my innards. Even though my mouth burned with each drink, I gulped down as much as I could before coming up for air.

I coughed and handed the bowl back to Ada. Rolling over, I closed my eyes and let myself relax until I was drifting off to my dreamscape once more. Tomorrow I would find my sister and save her.

For now, I needed rest.

Joshua

"Please continue to move forward!" a soldier shouted from behind us. "The checkpoint will be closing in approximately fifteen minutes!"

"Mother," Petyr whined, "we are not going to make it through."

My mother gave me a worrisome look and motioned for me to comfort my brother. I complied, even though I didn't really want to do it.

I knelt down to Petyr's eye level and whispered to him as I straightened his coat and hat again. "What does Mother always say when we are waiting for cookies to bake?"

"Remain patient and the good will come soon."

I smiled and nodded. "Exactly. We just have to be patient, even if we don't want to. If we wait, we will get through and find a safe place to stay. Then we can play a game tonight if you'd like."

"Do I get to choose what game we play?" he whispered back, trying not to draw attention to us.

I chuckled. "Absolutely. Do you want to get onto my shoulders for a bit so you can see around?"

He beamed and began climbing up my back before I was even able to set my feet. I stood and hoisted him onto my shoulder.

"Joshua," he said with a whimpering voice.

"Yeah?"

"They are beating that man," he said, pointing to the front of the crowd.

I stood a bit taller so that I could see over the people around me and scanned until I found the man. He was standing on his own, cradling his left wrist in the crook of his right arm. He was shouting at the guards in French, but they did not seem to understand. I couldn't hear what he was saying. A pair of SS soldiers began shouting at the man, pointing their fingers at him and then to the ground, but the Frenchman did not comply; perhaps he did not understand what they were trying to explain.

Another guard held a nightstick at the ready, and just as the civilian turned his back, the soldier attacked him without mercy, teeth gritted as the weapon cracked bone and flesh. I watched as blood splattered onto the soldier's face; when the Frenchman collapsed, the soldier stopped, wiped his brow, and then walked away as if nothing had just happened. The other two guards stood in shock, and the crowd of people fell silent around us.

Two more soldiers came from behind the checkpoint, gathered the man's bloody corpse, and dragged it behind the fence and into a nearby building with blacked-out windows. I put Petyr onto the ground next to me; tears streamed down his face, and he wouldn't look at me. I tried to console him, but even I, his own brother, could not seem to reach him.

"Petyr," I whispered. "Petyr, look at me. Everything is fine. That man, he was a criminal, a bad man. He was just being punished for his crime."

I looked up to Mother for some sort of support, but she was still staring, hand over her open mouth, eyes wide with terror. I looked back to Petyr, who was still crying, his blank stare fixed on the ground beyond me. I could not break him from his trance. I stood up and looked around the crowd just as the whistles began to blow, signaling that the checkpoint was about to shut down.

I swore under my breath, grabbed my brother's and mother's arms, one for each hand, and began to push my way through the throngs of people standing idly by, still staring at the place where the Jew had been beaten to a pulp. I reached the front after much resistance and called out to a soldier standing next to the checkpoint hut. His rifle was slung over his shoulder, his helmet a tad too large for his boyish face. He looked over at me when I called out to him, but he just waved for me to get back into the crowd. I yelled again, and this time he waved harder, gritting his teeth.

I screamed at him to come over to me. He looked for his superior, cursed, and then jogged over to me, mumbling German as he approached.

"What do you want?" he grumbled as he looked over his shoulder to see if anyone was coming to scold him for talking to a civilian. "I am supposed to guard that hut, the people are growing restless, and I can't just help anyone on a whim."

I looked to my left and saw the crowd beginning to surge forward against the guards and their barricade. I was at the far right side of the crowd, away from the main bulk of the agitated civilians.

"I need to get through," I pleaded as I pulled Petyr and my mother closer. "My brother, he is sick and needs a doctor. My mother is also running a fever. We are in need of shelter and food. Will you please help us?"

"I can't," he said, shaking his head. "I am not permitted to aid civilians past the checkpoint without proper authorization."

I shook my head and pointed at the crowd. "In a matter of minutes, that barricade is going to burst, and thousands of French civilians will demand passage beyond this checkpoint. Let us through, and that is three fewer people you have to keep track of."

He considered it for a moment and then shook his head. "No, I can't. It is far too risky."

"Please!" I begged, grabbing his arm and squeezing it while I looked him straight in the eye. "My brother is going to die if he doesn't get help."

The soldier frowned. "Fine! Hurry, this way, before anyone else sees."

He led us around to the side, beyond the view of the pressing crowd and stationed soldiers. He pushed us through a grate hidden by one of the barricades to the other side.

He barked, "Don't get caught, stay out of view, go to the storehouse on the northern side of the city. There are refugees that have put together a makeshift hospital. You will be able to get the medical attention that you need there."

I reached out my hand and shook his. "Thank you, sir," I said. "My name is Joshua."

"Gabriel. Now get out of here!"

I nodded, grabbed my brother and mother by their arms again, and ran to the nearest alleyway, out of view of the soldiers stationed by the checkpoint building.

Claire

It wasn't the first time I had been told I was about to die. When I was a child, I had fallen from a tree and cracked my head open. The doctors did not believe I would live through the night, but after multiple prayers and a few procedures, one doctor did the impossible and I lived.

The doctor was named Orson Reynolds, a war veteran from Le Mans who'd served as a combat medic. During the war, he had been hit by a piece of shrapnel, which punctured his neck. My grandfather, also a combat medic, was able to close the wound with a roll of fishing line that he kept in his shirt pocket. My grandfather and Doc Reynolds remained great friends until my grandfather's passing due to pneumonia in the middle of November 1936.

Since my grandfather's death, I had lived with Doc and his wife, Margret, in their country shack, which also served as their personal underground winery. I never knew my parents, but like my grandparents, Doc and Margret treated me as their own daughter.

"You look somber. Why?" Henning said as he sipped his tea across the table.

I glared at him and then turned my gaze to the window again.

"Being angry at me will not help you any. The real enemy is

just down the hallway, meeting with the leaders of France. I, for one, fancy you, Claire."

"Then why don't you get me out of here?" I mumbled.

He smiled and set his cup down. "Plans do not manifest from nothing. They need timing, precision, and proper execution to achieve the desired results. If you are too hasty, you will fail."

I did not answer and instead took my own cup of tea and sipped it. It was cold. I had been too stubborn to drink it when he initially offered it to me. I regretted my arrogance as I drank the cold liquid.

"The better question," he said, "is whether *you* have a plan to get yourself out of your sudden predicament."

"If I told you, then my plans would be thwarted and I would be executed even sooner."

He laughed. "You really think I am going to rat you out when I have already told you my eventual goal of disrupting our fearless leader's reign of terror? Please, you are the least to worry about having your plans found out and then disrupted. Odds are, you have not made even a single attempt to escape."

I blushed because he was right. I had thought of escaping but not seriously. I was a master of hiding, not a master of escaping from confinement. I had always been taught, "Don't get caught," but no one had ever taught me how to escape if I *was* caught.

"So, do you have a plan?"

"What?"

He rolled his eyes and repeated himself. "Do you have a plan to get out of here?"

"Well, no," I said. "I mean, I have thought about it, but the looming shadow of my death sentence has been on my mind instead."

He smiled and placed his pale hands on the table. "Well, it is a good thing I am here to help you, isn't it?"

"Oh, you have a plan to help me escape?" I said as I raised my eyebrow in suspicion. "Wouldn't you be endangering yourself if you helped me?"

"Bah, I am not that important anyway. Easily replaced, just like everyone else." He pulled a small, folded piece of paper from his pocket and slid it across the table.

"What's this?"

He smiled and motioned for me to read it. I hesitated but then picked it up and read it. I don't know what I was expecting—perhaps a profound message of hope or sound wisdom—but all the paper said was *Trust Me.*

I looked back at him, but before I could say anything, a shroud of black cloth covered my head and pulled tight against my face, restricting my breath. I tried to scream, but the dense fabric muffled it. My head became light as a feather as consciousness slipped, and before I knew it, I was on my feet, being dragged from the room against my will.

This is where I die . . . I thought. *Trust me . . . Trust me . . . Trust me* . . . I repeated the words in my mind until darkness consumed me.

Gabriel

After my post at the checkpoint, I was let go from active duty and granted leave. The checkpoint had been a nightmare: thousands of families separated from one another, most not even able to move into the ghettos on the northern side of the city. I sympathized with them but tried not to let it get to me as I made my way toward the palace, where they would be holding the public execution. I thought about the boy Joshua and his sick brother and mother as I walked with haste.

I saved the boy and his mother too. I was right in letting them pass so that they could get some medical attention. Did I risk the safety of the Fatherland? Did I jeopardize everything we fought to make secure? No, someone else would have done the same . . . right?

When I arrived, the crowds had already gathered outside the palace, where the soldiers had set up the makeshift gallows. General Staff Officer Henning raised his hands as he began his address to the citizens of Paris.

"Good evening," he said in German. A second voice echoed Henning, but this man spoke French so that the populace would be able to understand. I searched the crowd for the old man I'd spoken to earlier, but I couldn't find him among the throngs of people.

"I have called this meeting together to ensure that your cooperation remains just that: *cooperation*. I have been witness to rebellious attitudes recently; however, as you and I both know, this is unacceptable behavior."

Murmurs rippled through the crowd.

He turned to the side, where a small line of four people stood waiting with black hoods over their heads. My heart sank as I watched them walk up onto the platform. I could tell by their physiques that there were three males, but the last one was a woman.

"Claire," I whispered to myself.

I pushed people out of my path as I tried to make my way to the platform. I didn't care about Henning's droning; I was focused on Claire, hidden by black sackcloth. I grew desperate; the people would not let me pass but instead deliberately stepped in front of me to hinder my progress. I pleaded with them, but most spit in my face and said harsh words as they refused to move.

I didn't care what Henning was saying; my focus was getting to the platform to save Claire. I threw elbows, pushed civilians to the ground—I created such a commotion that some of the SS soldiers took notice and moved to intercept me.

I watched as nooses dropped around black-draped necks. Henning did not stop. He raised a hand. The executioner moved forward, hand on the lever to release the floor beneath the criminals.

I was so close, but I knew that I would not reach her in time. I reached into my jacket and pulled free my pistol, raised it into the air, and shot three times.

The lever was pulled, the criminals dropped, and the entire crowd fell into chaos.

I failed.

Eliza

I woke in my bed. I rolled over to wake my sister, but when I placed my hand where she slept, all I found was blankets. The memories flooded back into my mind. *She is gone.*

The door opened, and Ada strolled in, holding a white candle with a flickering flame. She did not speak until she sat next to me on the bed, eyes fixed on mine. She placed her hand on my forehead and then moved my hair from my face.

"How are you feeling?" she said.

"Better," I lied. "I feel like I am a new woman." The smile crept across my face while the truth ached in my heart. I was not better—I was far from it—but I had to remain strong.

"I hope I am not too much a burden for you and your family."

Ada chuckled. "You are far from that, Eliza." She pulled my shirt down shirt down exposing my shoulder and inspected the wound.

"It seems to be healing for the most part. Tomorrow, or the next day, I'll be able to remove the old stitches and replace them with new ones. How does that sound?"

I smiled. "Thank you. I would appreciate that."

"You are curious about what is going on outside, aren't you?"

The question caught me off guard, but she was right, I had been wondering what was happening outside the apartment.

How long had it been since they had taken my grandfather and sister from me—two, three, four days, perhaps a week? I had lost all track of time.

"The Germans have set up small communities across Warsaw called ghettos. They are rounding up everyone from around the city and placing people inside them. They split people up depending on race, gender, age, and religion—basically anything that can be considered different."

I frowned. "So my papi is still with my sister?"

"I am not certain about that, Eliza. We do not venture outside often, only to gather supplies, but even then, we are careful in our interactions. Anyone could be a spy for the Germans. We are careful to root out a Judas before making plans or trading offers with them."

My papi had been a Judas. Always willing to undermine someone if he gained prestige and profits in the end. When we came to live with him, my father had warned me of his father's scheming nature. I still believed it was my papi who caused my father to disappear, but I kept such thoughts to myself.

"What will we do then?" I said. "When I am fully healed, that is."

"Well," she said, looking at the door, "my husband and I thought it would be best for us to travel north to the port city of Gdańsk and find a ferry to take us to Denmark. Victor, my husband, has relatives who fled to Denmark just before the invasion took place. They have sent letters beckoning us to join them. They say the Danes are quite hospitable."

I nodded and even gave a faint smile, but in my heart, I knew that we would never make it to Denmark. It was impossible to get past the Germans. It was a lie fabricated for Victor and Ada's children, but I was too old to believe such lies. I played along, though.

"I think that is a fantastic plan, Ada," I said as I placed my hand on hers and squeezed lightly.

"I'd best be heading back to bed," she said as she stood once again. "It is good to see you improving. God must be watching over you, Eliza. Sleep well."

I nodded and waited for the door to close before I pulled the covers away and slipped on a pair of pants, an old shirt, and my old leather shoes. I couldn't stay here any longer while my sister was out there, alone and afraid.

I grabbed a piece of paper, dabbed my pen in some ink, and scribbled out a thank-you-and-good-bye note to the Lis family. When I finished, I laid the note on my desk, doused the candle Ada had left for me, and snuck out of the apartment into the cool summer night. I turned back to the building and thanked them in my head.

I was just another burden to them if I stayed; they had already done so much for me. However, it was time for me to leave. It was the least I could do.

Gabriel

The crowd was in an uproar. Soldiers shouted at them to calm down, but they were terrified and didn't seem to care. The massive tidal wave of fleeing civilians pushed me away from the platform.

Frustrated, I began throwing people out of my way again. As I approached the platform, a soldier put his hand on my shoulder, but I threw my shoulder into him and followed with a solid punch to his nose. I heard it crunch as he fell to the ground among the retreating civilians.

When I reached the platform, all the criminals were gone. I looked around in desperation, but I couldn't find them.

Were they so swift to clean up the bodies? Where would they have gone? I saw them fall through the floor, I saw the ropes tighten as their bodies caught, and I heard the screams . . .

I panicked. Soldiers with guns drawn were surrounding the area. I had to get out of the public square before I was caught. I turned to run but was met by the soldier I had punched in the nose just a few moments earlier. His nostrils were drenched in blood, and his nose was shifted to the left slightly. He bared his teeth and gave a hideous scream as he rushed me. I absorbed his impact and fell back onto the hard ground.

I coughed and gasped for air. He pinned my left arm and hit me across the face with a balled fist. I was dazed, but adrenaline kicked in, and I hit him in the gut as hard as I could, which caused him to double over and release my arm from underneath his knee. My body ached, but I did not let it overtake me. I stumbled away but was soon tackled by the soldier once more.

He dragged me to the ground, but this time I was ready. As I fell on top of him again, I guided my knife into his gut. The blade slid easily into his flesh as I pushed as hard as I could against him.

His eyes widened as I held myself mere inches from his face; sweat dripped from my forehead onto his, and blood began to bubble around the creases of his lips.

"I'm sorry for this," I said as I yanked the blade upward, opening his stomach further.

Blood spilled everywhere around us, but no one seemed to notice, the crowd still fleeing the gallows and the lone gunman.

I pulled my knife free and staggered on again. Blood stained my shirt and hands, and immense pain returned with a rush, driving me to one knee. I blinked hard, took a deep breath, and ran for my life. I didn't look back, didn't stop. All I knew was that I needed to get away from that place as quickly as possible.

Soldiers shouted at me in German and French, ordering me to stop, but I ignored their commands. They opened fire. I felt the burn of the bullet as it ripped through my left arm. I screamed, but didn't stop. Another tore through my calf, but still I limped on.

I turned the corner into an alley and made my way into a café entrance. Civilians were scattered throughout, waiting in silence for the chaos to subside, but when I entered, it turned into a madhouse.

I tried to calm them down, but the more I waved at them to stop, the louder and more violent they became. A coffee cup was chucked at my head, followed by a chair. I dodged both and made for the door. I knew that if I stayed a moment longer I would be a dead man. I dashed out the door once more and grabbed my calf to dull the pain.

Gasps erupted behind me as well as shouts for the police and SS to apprehend me. I got up and limped away as quickly as possible. I made it about halfway to the next block when a massive green truck with a covered back sped up behind me and swerved to block my path. I yelled and jumped to the curb.

Four men jumped out of the back, lifted me from the ground, threw a black sack over my head, and tossed me into the back of the truck. I shouted, but a powerful fist met my face, and I blacked out.

I thought I could play the hero, but it seemed that I would simply be the dead fool.

Eliza

My lungs burned as I ran. I was sore, but I did not stop until I reached the north side of town. I took a less direct route to avoid being detected, through alleys and abandoned buildings, and even across a few rooftops.

By the time I had reached the northern district, the moon was high in the sky. The night was frigid despite it being late summer. I finally stopped at the end of an alleyway. A lone rat scampered across the road to avoid me. I shuddered at the sight but didn't let myself become distracted.

I had heard rumor that the largest of the ghettos was in the northern district, but the information was not necessarily accurate. Nonetheless, I made my way across the street and into the next alleyway, moving as quickly as possible for fear of getting caught.

The alleyway was a dead end. I backtracked and continued northward again. The streets were dirty; it made my stomach churn. The city had fallen far, and hard. I scowled as I looked through the dirty windows into abandoned department stores and side markets.

I remember when the city was thriving and vibrant. Has it only been a few months since the invasion?

I rounded the corner and nearly ran into an elderly looking man. He had dark circles around his eyes; I could tell that he had not slept in a long time. He was babbling as he clutched a brown paper bag against his chest.

"What do you want?" he growled.

"I am just . . ."

"Are you trying to steal it from me?"

I backed away from the crazed man. "What are you even talking about?"

"Did you steal it? Did you take it from me? Where did you put it?" he repeated, louder this time.

I put my finger to my mouth and shushed him, but he grew louder still.

"Guards! Guards! Thief! Thief!"

I bolted across the street and didn't bother to look back. The man kept raving about the thief that had stolen something precious to him. A whistle pierced the night, and my heart sank. I heard a soldier shout at me, but I didn't stop. A bullet struck the building next to me. I screamed and ducked into the next alleyway.

Even more whistles erupted in the night, followed by dogs' barks and the shouts of men. Another dead end loomed before me. I punched the brick wall and whimpered as I searched for an escape route. The voices grew louder, and my hope shrank. I ran back toward the entrance of the alley and found an iron door leading into one of the stores.

I put my shoulder into it, but it didn't budge. Again, I threw my entire body weight against it, but again it did not move. I kicked at it a few times, gaining only a throb in my foot. I rammed the door one last time and fell into the darkness and down the stairwell into the basement. I hit the concrete wall at the bottom and gasped for air. My vision blurry, I struggled to get back up. I looked up at the doorway and saw the silhouette of a tall, lean soldier. He turned his head and shouted something in German.

While his attention was distracted, I scrambled farther into the basement, stumbling over shelves, old boxes, and stacks of crates. I wanted to puke, but I crawled deeper into the darkness until I found an overturned desk and hid underneath it, trying to catch my breath.

I heard footsteps descend the stairwell. Their voices were hushed, but I could make out a few words among them. A gun clicked, followed by a flashlight. I closed my eyes and put my hand over my mouth to keep from breathing so loud. My entire body ached. I heard them shuffling around, and then they seemed to stop altogether. My eyes darted back and forth, trying to pierce the darkness; without the flashlights shining in the room, I was completely blind again.

I lifted my head from behind the desk but could see nothing. I rose to a crouch and then stood as quietly as possible. I lifted my foot and set it down without a sound. I did it again. No sound, no whispers, no *breathing*. I stopped moving and waited.

I heard the click of the gun before I felt it against the back of my skull.

"Hello, dear," the soldier sneered.

Part 2—October 2, 1940

Gabriel

The door slammed behind me as I was thrown onto a concrete floor with a single drain hole in the center. It smelled of piss and sewage. The only source of light was a small slit in the wall about ten feet from the floor, through which a steady sunbeam shined, creating a single glowing line on the door behind me. I crawled into the corner opposite the light and watched in silence as it made its steady rise to the top of the door and then disappeared.

I sighed and pulled my knees up to my chin. I had not sat in such a way since I was a boy, hiding in my closet from my older cousins. Whenever they visited, they wanted to play hide-and-seek, but really it was an excuse for them to all hide from me until I found them, and then each slugged me in the arm or the gut and then ran off to hide again. On the off chance that I was given an opportunity to hide, they *all* searched for me. If they found me, they'd beat me up and sometimes even burn me with the iron poker from the fireplace. After the second time being burned, I made sure they'd never be able to find me, and they never did again. It was the worst part of my childhood.

The dark closet was always my safe place when I was a kid, and this cold, dank room reminded me of it. Perhaps if I just kept my mouth shut, my captors would forget about me and I'd just die alone.

After the light disappeared, I didn't know how much time passed before the guards came back to my cell. Perhaps a few hours. I lost all knowledge of time. Had it been a day, a week, perhaps a year?

Two large men walked in and shouted commands in German at me. I did what they said; I was far too weak to be defiant. The first one clubbed me across the face with his nightstick as I stood up. I fell back to the ground, moaning as I felt the blood run out of my mouth.

"Why?" I protested.

The stick fell again, this time across my ribs, driving all air from my lungs.

The two guards then picked me up, one underneath each elbow, and dragged me down the hallway into the next room. A large metal tank sat in the center, a large overhead lamp illuminating it but creating a shroud of darkness beyond its edges.

I knew what was about to happen. I screamed for the guards to stop, pulled my legs up and tried to stop their progress, but I was too weak. They dragged me on until I was hovering over the tub. It brimmed with water mixed with ice. I screamed as they hoisted me into the air and plunged me into the frigid water.

They held me under the water with their massive hands. I clawed at the sides, but my hands found no purchase, and my thrashing grew more intense. I couldn't breathe. The chill caused the oxygen in my lungs to deplete at an alarming rate, but just before I blacked out, they pulled me up from the water.

I coughed and gagged as I gasped for as much air as I could take in, but before I could make any sense of what was going on, they plunged me back into the ice water, this time pushing me to the bottom of the tank without hesitation. My vision went fuzzy, then shaded to black. Yet again, just before I passed out, they ripped me from my watery grave and gave me a second to breathe.

Five times total they dunked me. The last time, the guard who had hit me with the nightstick wrapped his hand around my neck and squeezed. My throat burned, and in that moment, I thought I was going to die. Instead, the guards pulled me out, threw me to the ground next to the tank, and walked away into the darkness. I could hear their laughter in the distance—or perhaps it was the constant ringing in my ears from the intense cold. Regardless, I was delusional. I was terrified. I felt the scars on my back where my cousins had branded me burn with intense heat. I tried to crawl to the edge of the light to get away from the tank. I wanted the disgusting cell that was mine; at least they couldn't take that from me.

I crawled a few feet and looked up. Above me stood a man and next to him a young woman. He smiled while she covered her mouth. I opened my mouth to speak, but the world receded instead into frigid blackness.

Eliza

I wanted to run away from the ghetto. Most nights I did not sleep, for fear of being attacked by a soldier demanding to lie with me. The first night I was there, I was passed around by ten German soldiers. They stripped me of my clothes and then each had their turn at trying to rape me. Each time, I waited for the last second and then fought back. Then they just hit me across the face until I was bloody and raped me anyway.

When I screamed in pain, the soldiers did not seem to care. I was just something they could use and cast aside until they needed to release their frustration the next day. A few were gentle with me; they caressed me and kissed my lips as if they actually loved me. Before they left the small barracks that I shared with about thirty other women, they would toss a few coins as a payment for my services.

I used the money to buy bread and small portions of meat. At first I had been ashamed of the men using my body, but I needed to eat, and eating required money. After a few weeks, I began to seek out willing customers. It was not hard to find soldiers with a few coins to spare. I was nervous the first few times, but soon I gained confidence and sold myself to four or five men a night, then slept all morning and ate in the afternoon, only to walk the streets again at night like the urchin I was considered.

None of the other Jewish women could bear to look at me. They whispered names at me as I passed, and the Jewish men threw stones and spit at my feet as I went into public to buy my daily bread. They shouted insults, and some hit me with canes or bags. But as soon as a soldier rounded the corner, the Jews sulked back into their hovels, out of sight and mind.

My only friend was a woman named Iva. She was only a few years older than I, but she appeared to be in her forties. She was a whore too. She was a Gypsy from the other side of the city, but we often shared food and kept each other safe at night. I did not trust her, to be honest, but then again, I had no one I could trust but her.

"You have to be commanding with your body. You have to let the soldiers know that they can't just have you when they want you, but instead that they have to deserve your time," she said one evening while we were lying in my bunk, facing each other. She often stayed with me instead of walking back to her own apartment across the city.

"Tell me, what do you do with a man when he buys your time for himself?"

I had never thought about the question before, so when I responded, it came out as a jumbled mix of words instead of an actual answer.

Iva rolled her eyes in annoyance. "That's the problem with you *Jews*," she said.

The words cut deeper than she knew, but I did not say anything. She used it as an insult, but I never let her see that it bothered me.

"I'm a Gypsy," she continued. "A free spirit, one with nature, body, and mind. If a man wants me, he has to deserve me. And if he does end up deserving me, I don't let him just lie with me how he pleases. It's sensual, rough, and soft, and above all, there is communication. I give him what he wants, he gives me what I want."

I leaned closer and whispered, "What do you want?"

Iva smiled and then kissed me with her cracked red lips. I had never kissed a woman before, but I liked it, so I kissed her back.

She pulled away and smiled again. "Information, dear. All I ever ask for is some piece of information. Forget the money: it's the secrets the soldiers carry that are the most valuable."

Claire

I hated watching, knowing I couldn't do anything. My gut clenched as the soldiers drowned the man. I knew it was necessary. He was a traitor, they told me. This was a way to break deserters, to leach from them any information they might have against the Reich. Yet as I watched, I bit my nails, knowing that *I* was a traitor also. I was a resistance fighter, brought up in wine cellars and dank catacombs, sworn to secrecy about the thousands of hidden cellars across the country, my own home being one of the largest.

Dmitri told me that fighting against the Nazis was important, that it would be worth the sacrifice and toil. I watched as they dunked the soldier again and again, and I wondered if this is what Dmitri had meant. If this was the life of a traitor, I did not want to fight anymore. I just wanted to hide again.

"Why are you doing this to him? Isn't he a German soldier?" I whispered.

Henning glanced right, giving me only half of his attention. "He is a traitor, and traitors need to be taught punishment."

"But you are a traitor, I am a traitor. What gives you the right to torture this man?"

He frowned and turned to face me, his attention undivided now. The gurgles of the soldier echoed in the large concrete room.

"You and I, we are similar. We know of our crimes and cope with them. I know that I am a traitor because I plan to kill my fearless leader. You know you are a traitor because you have been hiding and smuggling precious cargo away from the SS soldiers. This man, he is unaware of what he disrupted. The planning, the cost of bribes, the months of patience all thrown to the wind due to his rash thinking. He is lucky, though: if caught by anyone else, he would have been shot in the streets. Yet I know who he is and will use him for my plans instead."

I wanted to curse at him. He was just a puppet master, pulling the strings of his underlings to do his bidding.

"Who is he?"

"A private in the SS, the soldier who tried to disrupt your execution. The chaos he created did make it easier to make you disappear."

Gabriel, I thought.

"What are you planning to do with him?"

He smiled and patted my shoulder. "Now, now, Claire, why ruin the fun by spoiling the plans?"

"Tell me straight, then," I said, fists clenched. "Do you plan to kill him?"

Henning's smile faded as he studied my face with more intent. "You care for this man," he said. "You know him, but from where?"

"He visited me the night before my scheduled execution. His name is Gabriel. He is a good man, Henning."

He sneered and faced the tub again. Gabriel hung on to the two soldiers with what little strength he had left. His hair was matted to his forehead, and his skin was pink and raw from the extreme cold. His entire body shook from the treatment.

Henning motioned for them to dunk him again. Gabriel screamed as he was submerged; large air bubbles ruptured at the top of the ice water.

This round was longer than before. His arms began to thrash, and I grew anxious. Seconds ticked by like hours, but Henning was like a stone statue, arms crossed and eyes fixed on the struggling soldier.

I jumped forward, seizing his arm as I screamed, "*Let him live!*"

"And why should I?"

I looked at Henning and then to Gabriel in desperation, trying to figure out a reason.

"If you free him, I'll do whatever you want. I'll be your personal assistant, bodyguard, *whore*—whatever you want! Just let him live!"

Henning narrowed his gaze and then, with a flick of his wrist, motioned for the torture to cease. The two soldiers hoisted Gabriel out of the metal tub and let him fall to the floor with a loud thud. He began coughing as his entire body shuddered.

Henning stepped forward to inspect Gabriel, smiled at his prize, turned back to me, and said, "Be in my quarters at nine twenty tonight. You will be most welcome."

I covered my mouth and held back tears as I stared at Gabriel, my savior and champion, lying on his stomach and gasping for those precious breaths to keep from passing out.

I could not stand the sight anymore, so I walked back to my room to prepare myself for my first night with Henning. I was nervous, but I had no choice. I had bargained with the devil to save this man's life, but at what cost?

Joshua

"When do we get to go home, Mother?" Petyr asked as we sat around the small fire in the center of our abandoned shack.

"Soon, dear," she said, holding him close to her as she kissed his forehead. "The fighting is going to stop soon, and then we can go home and sleep in our own beds."

"And eat our own food?"

She laughed. "Yes, and eat our own food."

"But I won't have to do my chores anymore, would I, Mother?" he said with a wily smile.

I laughed and said, "If you don't have to do your chores, then you can do mine instead."

He looked up at Mother with eyes as large as saucers. "Is that true, Mother? Would I have to do Joshua's chores too? Please, I will do my chores, I promise!"

Mother smiled. "Well," she said in the sternest tone she could without breaking out into laughter, "if you don't do your chores, I will have you do all the neighbors' chores as well! I hear Mrs. Harrington is looking for a new gardener during the summer. I'd put you to work for her."

He buried his face in my mother's chest and begged her not to make him work for Mrs. Harrington. She was a wicked old woman who hated children, and Petyr was no exception.

Mother and I laughed as Petyr pleaded with her to change her mind.

The shack trembled with a furious rumble, and the laughter stopped. Mother's expression turned grave, and I jumped to my feet and ran to the dirt-covered window. Peering through the cloudy glass, I searched for the bombers, but I couldn't see any in the sky.

"I will be right back," I said as I ran for the front door against my mother's protests.

I flung open the door and stepped out into the afternoon humidity. The temperature was warm for October, but not uncommon. I covered my eyes with my hand and peered at the sky through squinted eyes. I could make out about fifteen bomber planes flying high above. Bombs were dropping near the city, but not within. We were about three miles from the outskirts, but even at this distance the frequent explosions felt like earthquakes.

I watched as the planes flew in a V pattern above the city. The antiaircraft guns below fired large rounds into the air, and after a few seconds, five planes plummeted to the ground. My belief that the Allies were here to help us sank like a ship in the sea. I watched the German fighter planes climb into the sky to battle the bombers and their escorts, and before long, the Allied air raid had disbanded and disappeared into the distance.

I sat down on the porch of the shack and watched as black smoke rose in increasing intensity across the cityscape. *What can I do to stop this nightmare from happening?* I thought. *Lord, when will this all end?*

I heard the cart before I saw it. I stood and walked to the end of the porch, where I peered down the road to my right. The cart came over the small hill, and I caught glimpse of a young girl in a wide-brimmed sun hat. She directed the cart off the road and up to our shack, where she pulled the reins and stopped her horse next to me.

"Afternoon," she said in French.

I greeted her with a slight wave and asked, "What are you looking for?"

She looked down at me, her face hidden by the wide brim of the hat. "To be honest? Something to eat. I'm quite famished. Do you have something to trade, perhaps?"

I dug into my pockets hoping to find at least *something*, but I had nothing to offer.

"I don't know what you are looking for exactly, but we don't have much of anything since we relocated from the city."

She raised her head, the brim covering her face except for her mouth.

"There are more than just you?"

"My mother and brother are inside," I said, scratching my head. "What are you doing out here, anyway?"

She mumbled something to herself underneath the brim.

"Excuse me?" I said a little louder than before.

She stopped talking to herself and then removed the hat. Her blonde hair fell down against her back. Her icy blue eyes met mine, and when she smiled, I felt my heart skip a beat.

"I'm sorry, love," she said in a chipper tone. "Sometimes I forget there is someone here with me."

I was so confused that all I could do was laugh. She was gorgeous, but I could not just tell her that—it would be unconventional.

"Joshua," my mother said as she arrived at the door. "Joshua, what is going on? Are you all right?"

"I'm fine, Mum," I said, turning red as the pretty young woman giggled to herself. "I was just talking to . . . uh . . ." I turned back to the girl on the cart. "I never asked you your name."

She smiled and pushed back her bangs from her forehead. "I am Violet. I live just up the road here with my grandfather and grandmother. He's a doctor from the Great War."

Mother pushed past me, her hands clasping her elbows and her eyebrow furrowed. "A doctor?" she echoed.

"Yes, ma'am," she said. "He has been living in the same house for near twenty years."

"My son, Petyr, has a high fever, and he can't seem to break it. Would your grandfather be able to look him over, perhaps? I have nowhere else to go, and each day he grows worse."

Violet frowned. "I'm sure it will be fine. Hop onto my cart. I'll bring you there. It is just up the road a bit."

We gathered our small bag of clothes and the lone heel of bread we had been rationing for the past few days and climbed up onto Violet's empty cart. She snapped the reins, and we rolled down the dusty road.

"Are we going home?" Petyr said in a drowsy voice.

"No, Petyr, not yet," Mother said as she held him close to her chest. "Soon, but not today."

Eliza

"You do miraculous work, you know," Nikolas told me as he pulled on his pants. "I have decided that I will pay you double for tonight. You are not like the other girl . . . Iva, is that her name? I fear I might be falling in love with you." He laughed and pulled his shirt over his shaggy blond hair.

He was a beautiful man. He was in his mid-twenties, he had told me, and came from Berlin, raised on a farm where his father and mother managed crops and a few sheep. He was my most loyal customer, and each time we finished, he would cradle me and sing beautiful songs in German till he left.

"Why do you say that you are falling in love with me?" I asked from the bed, letting the sheet fall away to expose my left breast. I didn't care about being naked anymore and just let it be as it was.

He buttoned up his SS collar and combed his hair to the side before he walked back over to the bed and sat down on the edge. He smiled and moved the sheet over my breast.

"Well," he said, tracing my jaw with his steady fingers, "you are a forbidden fruit."

"What does that make you, then?"

He smiled. "Adam."

We both laughed until I reached up and pulled him down into my arms, kissing him and unbuttoning his clothes again.

Each time he tried to pull away, I pulled him closer to me, digging my nails into his uniform in hopes of keeping him with me for just a little longer.

"Eliza," he said through a fit of laughter, "I need to get back to my post before I'm caught. Franz is not one for waiting of late. I was barely able to get him to let me sneak out tonight to see you."

"When will I get to see you again?" I said in a whisper between kisses. "Tomorrow?"

He pulled away once more. "I am not able to tomorrow; maybe Wednesday, though. The patrols are becoming more frequent, breaks not as long, and some of the soldiers are becoming frustrated with men like me running off with pretty Polish girls at night."

I stopped kissing him. "But you will come back to just me, won't you?"

He rubbed his neck. "I will try to come back as soon as possible, Eliza, but I can't promise you anything."

I lay back down and then rolled onto my side, facing the wall away from him. He sighed and tried to roll me back toward him, but I did not budge.

"Just leave the money on the stand there. I'll get it when I leave for the day."

"Eliza," he said, trying to roll me over again, "I am sorry. I want to make this up to you, but I don't know what I can do."

"You know what I want."

He sighed. "You know that is against my orders. I can't just go into the records office and steal whatever information I would like, even if it were concerning your sister's whereabouts."

"Then leave me," I said.

He whispered something to himself in German and then whispered, "I only have a name."

"Who is it?" I said turning around to face him.

"Adam Czerniaków. He is the Ältester of this ghetto. He will be the one with your answers." Nikolas frowned. "That is all I can share."

I got up from the bed, kissed him on the cheek, and whispered, "Thank you."

The next time Nikolas visited me, I pushed for more information on Czerniaków. "And how does someone set up an interview with him?" I said as I undressed myself to just my nightgown.

He rolled his eyes and unbuttoned his shirt. "You are really killing the mood, you know, by asking about the head Jewish official of Warsaw."

"I just need a meeting with the man; five minutes is all, and then I'll be out."

Nikolas stood, arms crossed over his muscular chest. I bit my lip in anticipation and crossed my legs in a seductive way as I pulled down on my white gown, letting the tops of my breasts peek out from the fabric.

"Five minutes," he said pointing a finger at me, his face stern, but he could not hold back his playful smile. "I can't believe I am doing this. It could get me killed, you know."

I squealed for joy, bounded forward, and jumped into his arms. I kissed him and then nuzzled my head against his neck. I was overjoyed, and I was sure to make that night the best he had ever had.

Joshua

We clattered up a rocky driveway to an old, almost colorless shack with clouded windows and drooping shutters. It looked like the shell of some former, glorious self that was now just taking up space. A young man with a pipe in his mouth leaned against the doorframe, watching us as we came to a stop next to the porch.

"I thought Doc told you not to bring back any strangers," the man said, squinting at us.

I felt uncomfortable, unwelcome, but Violet smiled and reassured us, "Ignore him. You are most welcome."

"Don't tell them what is not true, Vi," he said sternly, removing his pipe from his mouth. He was taller than I by a few inches. He had a crooked nose and sandy-blond hair, and his biceps were nearly twice as large as my thighs. His scruffy semblance of a beard had been shaved within the last day. He looked like a soldier, one who had seen years of battle.

Petyr began to whimper as the large man's anger grew and his tone became harsher.

"Dmitri," Violet uttered, "quit it. These are our *guests*; they need medical attention, and I told them that Doc would be willing to help. Don't let your ego get in the way of their needs."

"My ego?" he huffed as he clenched his fists and began walking toward our cart. "I'll show you my ego!"

"Dmitri," another voice said from around the corner of the house. The man's voice was calm and smooth, filled with age and charisma.

Dmitri stopped, unclenched his fists, and returned to his pipe in quick succession.

"Violet," the older man continued, "are you going to introduce me to our guests or just sit up there on your cart?"

"Oh, right!" she said as she scooted off her wooden bench and hit the ground with a loud crunch. "Doc Reynolds, these are my new friends that I met on the way back from town."

She pointed to my mother and brother first. "This is Cecilia and Petyr. Petyr loves playing outside and enjoys looking at bugs." She made a funny face and tickled Petyr until he began to giggle, chasing his tears away with joyful bursts of laughter.

"Ah, a young scientist, I see," Doc said with a faded smile. "I have always been fascinated by nature—bugs are included in that as well." He winked at Petyr, who covered his eyes and hid his face in my mother's chest.

Mother laughed and held Petyr tight against her. It was the first time I had seen her genuinely smile in months. I had not realized how much I had missed her smile.

"Petyr is shy at first, but after a bit, he warms up to people rather quickly," she said apologetically.

Doc raised his hand and smiled. "That is quite all right. I am sure I can find a few books about bugs and nature lying around in our basement for him to read as you stay with us."

Mother smiled again and thanked the man for his hospitality.

"And this," Violet said, turning to me as if I were being pre-sented as a brand-new art piece, "is Joshua."

Doc reached out his hand and met mine with a tight grip. He smiled. "You have a strong handshake," he said. "Not many boys your age know what a good handshake can say about a person. You are confident, brave, and a romantic."

I blushed but didn't say anything. I heard Violet giggle behind me, which made me blush even more.

He laughed and clapped me on the shoulder. "Nothing to be ashamed of, my friend. I too am quite the romantic!" He winked at me and turned to Dmitri. "Will you help them to the basement? Be sure that they have a place to stay—I am thinking the eastern quarters. I believe that Leo cleaned that section up sometime last week."

Dmitri frowned, put out his pipe, and walked into the house, leaving the door wide open.

Doc scratched his head and turned back to us. "Please forgive Dmitri," he said. "He lost his sister a few months back. It has weighed upon him since."

"What happened to her?" I asked.

"Joshua," my mother barked from behind me.

"No, it's quite all right," Doc said. "Claire was her name. She was captured by a group of Nazis on the south road from Paris while delivering cargo to some of our friends in the Orléans area. They accused her of smuggling unmarked goods and arrested her. To make an example of her, they sentenced her to a public execution."

"Oh," Mother said, "I am so sorry to hear that."

"It is the way of life in times of war," he said as he looked up to the blue afternoon sky. "Let's continue this conversation inside, shall we? No sense in standing in the blistering sun. May I offer you some water or lemonade?"

"Water will be fine," Mother said.

Doc nodded and smiled. "Very well. Follow me, and mind your step going down."

He led the way, Mother and Petyr close behind, and I followed them as well, but I turned in the doorway to catch a last glimpse of Violet as she mounted her horse-drawn cart. She glanced my way, smiled, and then gave a quick wave as the horse jerked her cart forward and around the side of the house.

I stood in the doorway for a few seconds longer, hoping she'd come back, but then Mother called after me, and I ran down the stairwell to the basement to get my glass of water. I hadn't realized how thirsty I was.

Claire

I knocked on the door and waited in silence. The stone hallway was cold. Living in a bunker was a lot gloomier than I had hoped, but at least we were safe. The sound of water dripping echoed from a far-off room behind me. The door latch clicked. The knob turned. My heart beat faster against the inside my chest. The door opened to a bright room with Henning standing in the doorway, dressed in grey slacks and a plain white shirt. He was wearing his glasses, and his usually slicked hair was ruffled from confusion and stress. When he saw me on the other side of the threshold, he frowned and motioned me in.

"You are late," he mumbled as he shut the door and walked barefoot back to his desk on the far side of the room. Behind it, a double-shelved bookcase stretched across a majority of the wall. An iron furnace in the far corner hummed, radiating a bright orange hue that made the room shimmer with light as well as heat.

"Take a seat, please," he said, motioning to an open chair opposite his own. He sat down in his own leather chair and adjusted his glasses as he read and compared two letters on the desk.

The room, although underground, gave off a sense of security; in the oddest fashion, it reminded me of home. As I had been exploring the bunker's tunnels, I thought often of the cellars on our farm back in Paris. The wine storages there were some of the grandest in the area, my father would tell me as I helped him count the bottles. How I longed to go back and walk the vineyards with Dmitri, Leo, and Violet.

"We will need to smuggle you back into the city somehow, but we are still trying to—" Henning was saying. I focused on him, and a look of annoyance crept across his face.

"Have you been listening to anything I just said?" he growled as he put the letters down.

"I'm sorry," I mumbled. I lowered my gaze and flattened my dress across my thighs. "It's just that I miss home."

He sighed and leaned back into his chair as he folded his hands across his chest. "You miss Paris that much?"

I nodded.

"And your parents and siblings?"

Again, I nodded, but I said nothing to correct his assumptions about my personal life.

"I know that you lived on a winery south of town. I also know of your involvement in smuggling wine to and from Orléans and beyond. I believe, if I'm not mistaken, that when you were arrested, that you were actually transporting a shipment of wine bottles to La Rochelle, to be shipped out from the port there?"

"Yes," I said. "It was my mission to get to the port in three days, then take another shipment back to Orléans to pick up the full payment."

"And what would you have gotten if you would have received your full payment?"

"About three thousand pounds."

Henning's eyebrows rose in surprise. "Three thousand?"

I nodded.

"That's quite a lot for a few bottles of wine."

I snorted. "These aren't just a *few bottles of wine*. These were special bottles of Burgundy wine that have been aging for near fifty years. They were bottled long before my parents even thought of me; forty-three bottles of Burgundy, twelve Champagne, and twenty-two of La Loire. These are not just your typical bottles: these are the best of what France has to offer."

He nodded. "I see. And where are these provisions now?"

"I figured you would know better than I. After all, you were the ones who arrested me."

He chuckled and leaned forward in his chair.

"I cannot lie: I do not know where the bottles are either. I wish I did, but I'm sorry to say that they are missing." He pursed his lips. "Yet I am sure there are more bottles in storage, no?"

I squirmed in my seat. I knew the answer, but if I told him, the entire operation that my family had built up in secret over the past five years would be foiled within a few days.

"I know of only one location: a small farm on the east side of Paris. It is not much, just a small farmhouse."

It was only half a lie. The farm east of the city *used* to be a storage location, but it was not within our primary network. The larger network was actually in the southern countryside near the river, in the basement of my grandfather's old farm cellar. The area used to be lush with vineyards and plant life, but due to the war, the foliage had wilted away and the farm looked barren and unappealing—the perfect hideaway for a vast underground wine headquarters that was attached to hundreds of miles of intertwining tunnels.

"I'm sending you back to your family, Claire," Henning said in his usual dry, bored tone. "It is more helpful to our cause for you to continue your previous work. Since we have a common goal—thwarting the advancement of the German empire to the point of complete collapse—my personal council and I have decided to release you from your imprisonment here, to instead be a viable ally on the outside, cutting off the main source of income being supplied to the Germans. Your involvement with smugglers has given Hitler's plan a lot of roadblocks to overcome. As you are probably aware, the majority of our war effort has come from your country's vast production of wine, which we then sell at an inflated price as an export to fund our overall war effort. Your family's involvement has caused a larger dent in the trading process than you might think. With the majority of the expensive wines already being seized and sold, the less desirable bottles we are coming across now do not command the same profit that the initial bottles did."

I raised my eyebrows in confusion. "You . . . are letting me go home?" I almost whispered. I had a hard time hearing it myself, so I repeated the question.

"Yes," Henning said in a calm but firm tone. "Your mission is to go back to your underground compound and continue your smuggling way of life. The rebellion must continue if Hitler is to be disposed of."

"What is the catch?"

He smiled and leaned forward, resting his elbows on the desk and his chin on his folded hands.

"You are always looking for the hidden message where there is none, Claire. All I ask in return is a mutual agreement of secrecy. If we succeed in our plot to eliminate the tyrant whom we call our leader, and *you* restrict the flow of the commerce throughout Germany, perhaps when this war is finished, we can strike an accord that equally benefits both parties."

"And if I refuse?"

He flashed a smile and opened the drawer on his right. Fishing inside, he removed a revolver and laid it down on the desk between us. He looked back at me, grinning.

"You won't."

Eliza

I made my way through the streets from my apartment in the Polish side of the ghetto to the Jewish side, avoiding anyone I could. I was a Jew, but Iva had gotten a fake baptism note for me that allowed me to live in the Polish district. I was living a lie—a traitor to my family—and I knew it, but I needed safety more than a deity.

When I arrived at Czerniaków's office building, I found the sidewalk busy with crowds of Jewish men. Some of their beards had been cut off by German soldiers as a form of mockery. I stopped and covered my mouth as the men entered the tall, white building. I knew the severity of the situation, but the German soldiers did not care about Jewish tradition.

What would they have done to me if they found out who I really was?

A pair of Jewish men entered, carrying a large recording device. I had seen its like only once before in my life. When the door closed behind them, I looked to see if anyone was watching and snuck into the building on silent feet.

The entrance hall was dim and smelled of fresh-brewed green tea. I pulled my notebook closer to my chest and made my way to the front desk. A tall man with thin black hair slicked back by a comb stood behind the desk, reading a newspaper clipping through thin, wire-framed glasses. When I approached, he looked up with a faint, tired smile.

"*Dzien dobry*," he said.

I smiled and returned the formal greeting.

"How may I help you this morning, miss?"

"I have a meeting with Mr. Czerniaków, sir. He is expecting me. My name is Talia Chmiel."

"Just a moment, please," he said as he pulled out a large, leather-bound ledger. He opened it, exposing thousands of individual names in cramped cursive, categorized in alphabetical order. I was astonished, yet suddenly nervous.

What if Nikolas had not called in an appointment? Would the SS arrest me?

"I have to make a call, miss," he said. He turned and dialed the black phone on the back desk. He spoke just quietly enough that I couldn't hear him. I strained to hear, but all I could pick up were muffled phrases. He hung up the phone, turned back to me, and motioned to a white door to my right, which bore a nameplate reading, *Private*.

"Mr. Czerniaków will see you now. Please proceed through the door and up the stairs to the fourth floor. His office will be marked."

I nodded and then made my way through the door, into a small corridor, and up a metal spiral staircase to the fourth-floor landing. There, a small gold rectangle emblazoned with *Adam Czerniaków* hung on the wall. I turned the knob and stepped into an ornate office.

It was much larger than I had expected. To my left was a pair of white doors that I assumed led to a meeting room; a violet rug with a gold hem covered the barren area between the double doors and Czerniaków's large wooden desk at the far end of the room. A small fire glowed in the hearth near the desk, giving the room a welcoming mood, accented by the scent of cinnamon rising from a steaming pot of tea on the nearby table. Light music played in the corner on a stationary phonograph.

When the doors opened, I heard a voice say, "Farewell," and then almost immediately a chipper "Hello" was directed toward me.

I curtsied for the man, let him take my hand and kiss it, and then followed him to the seat in front of his desk.

"Ms. Chmiel, it is a pleasure to have you here today. I know that our business will be most beneficial for the future of our great city."

His round face accented the redness in his cheeks and neck. I could tell he had been sweating, and the odor that filled my nostrils was quite unpleasant compared to that of the tea.

I smiled and crossed my legs as I leaned in. "And what sort of business would that be, Mr. Czerniaków?"

"Well, the orphans, of course!" he said, sounding bewildered. "Mr. Ulmbech told me that you were hoping to open a new school for the orphans, if the Germans were to lift the ban on public schooling. When he offered a chance to meet with you, I knew that I would be a literal fool if I passed up such an opportunity."

Nikolas, the sly fox, I thought. *Orphans needing an education— he's smarter than he looks.*

I coughed into my gloved hand. "Apologies, sir," I said as I covered my mouth. "I trust Mr. Ulmbech informed you of my needs?"

"Oh, yes, and I am a strong supporter of your next steps for a proper education. It hurts to say that many of these children have lost their families due to the Nazi occupation." He paused and rubbed his large chin in deep thought. "I have been fighting for the safety of the children since the occupation started nearly a year ago, you know. When I was put in charge of the Jewish community, I pleaded for a proper education and the safety of all the orphans, but little progress has been made. I fear that we are fighting a losing battle for the future of our city and its people."

I could hear the sincerity in the man's voice. He did care for these children, but it appeared that for all his efforts, they were just words tossed to the wind. I cleared my throat and removed a photo of Isabella.

"Mr. Czerniaków," I said as I handed over the photo, "I was hoping you might be able to tell me if this girl was perhaps in your records. Her name is Isabella Gorecki. She is a cousin of mine, and I wish to find her. I fear that she was taken from her mother and has no one to call family, except me."

He studied the photo and then shook his head in disgust. "No, no, I do not want to meddle in a search party for a missing girl. She is somewhere; you will find her."

I stood and placed my ungloved hand on his and squeezed. He looked up and gazed into my eyes. I did not even have to act, as the emotions began to run out over the brim.

"Please, sir," I said in a choked voice. "I need to find her."

Claire

After our meeting, Henning escorted me to my room to pack my belongings, few as they were, for my journey home. When I was initially arrested, the guards took most of my things, save for the clothes I was wearing at the time. If Henning had not stepped in to stop them, I am certain they would have stripped me naked and taken the clothes as well. I wouldn't have been surprised if they had shot me in the head while they were at it.

I decided to stop at Gabriel's barracks before Henning saw me off at the western door. The metal door was ajar when I arrived, and I saw light coming from within, so without hesitation, I knocked. I heard the rustling of papers being cleaned up, and then a chair scraped across the concrete floor and fell over with an echoing clamor. The door opened, and there stood my German soldier, wearing a pair of black trousers and a grey button-down shirt, the swastika embroidered onto his right arm. His hair was messy, as if he had just gotten out of bed, and his eyes were red—probably from lack of sleep.

"Oh, it's you," he said in a surprised voice.

I smiled. "Were you expecting someone else? I can go if you'd like."

"Oh." He ruffled his hair with his free hand. "No, come in, please." He ushered me in and righted the chair so that I could sit.

He seemed to have been in the process of getting dressed. He slid a gold watch onto his left wrist and inserted a pair of silver-and-onyx cufflinks. He grabbed a comb and slicked his hair to the side, smiling when he was satisfied.

I chuckled to myself as I watched him finish up. It felt odd to watch a *man* take this much time to dress appropriately, while I, a woman, was usually ready within five minutes of waking up in the morning. This, in my mind, was a bit excessive.

"Are you going on a date this morning, Gabriel? It's near three in the morning," I teased as I crossed my legs and leaned forward on the arm of my chair. "Is she pretty?"

He was straightening his tie as he glanced over at me with slight annoyance.

"I am to be your escort," he said, looking back at the mirror.

I laughed. He stopped and turned his full attention on me, frowning.

"Why are you laughing? This is not something that we should be joking about. You were almost killed; I was almost killed. If we are going to work together, we cannot just think this will be an easy transition for the both of us. I am German, and you are . . . French. Those two things go together as well as oil and water."

"You are going to be my escort back to my home, you know," I quipped.

"Your point being?"

I pointed at him and smiled. "You expect to be trusted by my family wearing that uniform? They will shoot you before you even get five hundred yards from the property."

He frowned and looked down at his near-perfect outfit. No doubt the idea of taking it all off again was unbearable.

"I have one rule," I said, leaning back into the chair and crossing my arms to look tough. "You listen to what I say and do what I tell you."

He straightened and glared at me. "I am the one in charge, though," he said. "I am the soldier, the trained veteran who is to *escort* you and observe your dealings with these peasant smugglers and rebel fighters."

My good humor vanished, my eyes narrowed, and my tone grew colder than a January night. "Listen," I declared, not breaking eye contact for a second, "you may be the soldier with a lot of training and weapons experience, but remember that these *peasants* are my family, and when I say they will kill you before you even *see* our property, you had best believe that my brother would not hesitate to put a bullet between your eyes. You seem to think you are entitled to everything you see. Remember that it was *me* who asked to keep you alive. You did nothing to save me; it was Henning who orchestrated everything, not you. I owe you nothing."

I spit on the floor, stood up, and stormed back to the door, swinging it open with fury. I turned around one last time and said in a low voice, "Take off the uniform, *Boche*, else you won't need to change when they stuff you in that wooden box and stick you underground."

I slammed the door and walked back to my room to get some last-minute sleep before breakfast.

Eliza

"Did he give you any useful information?" Nikolas said as he traced my arm with his steady finger.

"He told me that she might be in an orphanage, but nothing beyond that, really. He said he was going to keep his eye out for her, but I am concerned that it won't go anywhere. Warsaw is a large city; Bella is an eight-year-old girl on her own."

The horror of that statement made my stomach clench and knot. I wanted to throw up, but I kept it down as I tried to relax next to my lover. He had the ability to keep me calm, even in the worst situations. I pressed into him, buried my face against his bare chest, and began to weep. He didn't say anything; what could he say? He just held me against himself and hummed a tune, kissing my head every few minutes.

I don't remember falling asleep, but when I woke up, Nikolas was standing at the window, gazing out into the night sky. The moonlight flooded the room with an eerie white glow, accenting the shadows of each piece of furniture caught in the light.

"Nikolas," I said, "what are you looking at?"

He did not respond but instead motioned for me to join him at the window. I was nervous, but I got out of the bed and walked over to him.

"Do you see it?"

I looked out the window but saw nothing except the faint lights spread out across the city. I had never looked out my window at night—never realized that I could see most of the city from my window.

"I am not sure what I am supposed to be looking at," I said as I scanned the cityscape.

"That is what I mean," he said. "It all just looks the same. I can't tell the difference between the Jews and Gypsies, the Poles and Germans. From here it all looks the same, but down there, among the people, everything becomes so muddled and confusing. I wish I could change things."

"Why can't you change things?"

He shook his head. "It's not that simple. One man's vision for the future can't change the world."

"What about Hitler's vision?"

"What do you mean?"

I was nervous. We had never talked about our ideals. What if he found out who I actually was?

"Isn't that what he has already done? He had a vision, and the world has changed. As *just one man*, he gathered together an *entire* country to share the same vision for a future that he believes would be better for everyone."

Nikolas pulled away from me. "But it is the best for the world's future. One ruling body over the entire world would bring unification, freedom, and *order*. It was the best for the Poles that we came here and *saved* them from the Jewish scum that plagued this country for far too long."

He took out a cigarette and lit it with the lighter from his pocket.

"Then again, that's what they are already doing in the western parts of Poland. Camps, near a dozen of them, are now being formed to house the Jews, Gypsies, and other bastards that are not worthy to live in this world with us. Himmler gave the command to just kill them all. I was never a big fan of him before that address. Now I kind of admire the man. He had the guts to follow through with his plan to eradicate all these worthless people you call friends."

He looked at me and puffed on his cigarette. "I wouldn't be surprised if you were on the next shipment to the west. No one knows about them yet. Not anyone important, that is. We tell the passengers they are just going to a new place, a better one. I love watching their spirits lift as they hear the possibility of a new life. You could be on one of those trains. I'd like to see your face when they push you into that cattle car, naked, with hundreds of other worthless people knowing you were about to die." He withdrew his cigarette and let out a cloud of smoke. "I could put in a word to keep you here for a time until I grow bored of you. Then I'll just find a new slut. That's the best thing about you whores: there are enough of you to go around, and if I don't want you anymore, I can just kill you without a penalty. Else, I'll just say you were a Jew and ship you to one of the mobile gas trucks instead."

He took another drag and laughed. He grabbed my hip and pulled me close to him.

"But I don't want to lose you yet. You are my very own *whore*. To do with you what I please. You've been the easiest so far; so willing, so desperate, such a dumb girl. I could tell you anything and you'd just stand there with a blank stare!" He laughed and smacked my rear with an open palm. "Stupid bitch."

The words cut deep. I wanted to hurt him. My stomach clenched again; I was terrified of this man, but I could not seem weak. Not here. Not in front of *him*.

I cleared my throat and crossed my arms as I looked out the window again.

"You said it all looks the same out here," I said, trying to hold back the tears. "What did you mean when you said you wanted to change things? What would you do to *change* things?"

"If I were in charge," he boasted, "I would kill them all and burn this city to the ground."

"And what about me?" The tears began to well up in my eyes.

"I would not kill you. I could never bring myself to that point, not personally."

I wanted to sigh in relief.

"Instead, I would make you watch as I destroyed this place and everyone in it."

Joshua

As I reached the basement, my eyes adjusted to the dimness. A sliver of light showed around the edge of a large, cracked door on the far side of the room. When I opened it, I found Dmitri, holding a lantern in front of him, his face downcast and his brow furrowed.

"Do not get too comfortable here," he growled. "It won't be long before you are on your way again. This is a secret place, not a hostel for runaway refugees."

I scratched my head. He was so much larger than I; how could I even act tough around him? "I have to get back to my mother," I said as I tried to inch past him against the wall on my left.

He put out a trunk of an arm and blocked my way. I looked up but remained silent.

"And stay away from Violet," he said. "I have seen the way you look at her. She doesn't need to get herself into any trouble with the likes of you."

I nodded in agreement and waited for him to remove his arm. When he finally did so, I slipped by and around the corner, passing open rooms in which stacks of cots were stored along with empty wine bottles. I followed the path as it sloped downward until I entered an even larger room at the end of the hall.

A wine cellar? I thought as I stepped farther into the large storeroom—more like a storehouse. Along the walls stretched shelves that stood about seven feet high, bearing thousands of wine bottles all nestled in their individual alcoves. Each bottle bore a small gold plate just below the bottle's cork. I scanned the bottles and their labels. They were so well organized, clean, and *old*.

I began to read them aloud to myself as I passed by the row at eye level. "Cabernet Franc, Cabernet Sauvignon, Caramenre, Gros Verdot, Malbec, Merlot, Petit Verdot, Muscadelle, St. Macaire, Sauvignon Blanc . . ." A few I had never even heard of.

"See any that you like?" I heard from behind me. I straightened up and moved away from the shelves as quick as I could before turning around.

Doc stood there with his hands clasped behind his back and a wide grin on his face. His eyes were warm and vibrant, and his posture was like that of a younger man.

"I was just looking," I said, my voice cracking a bit as I spoke.

His smile never wavered as he nodded. "It's not a crime to look, Joshua," he said. "A man's greatest chance of growth comes from curiosity. I can tell that you are a young man who loves to *learn*."

I turned red and rubbed the back of my neck. "I guess so," I said.

"No need to be anxious with me. I am just an old man with a few interests, which I love sharing with others. Wine," he said, taking one of the bottles from the shelf, "is one of my greatest interests. Has been since I was a boy. My father used to own a winery in the southern part of France. He was a master at telling when the grapes were just right to harvest. Quite remarkable, when you think about it."

"Are you like your father?" I said.

Doc stared at the bottle for a few moments longer and then replaced it on the shelf before turning his attention back to me. "No," he said, folding his hands in front of him. "He was a mean old man without any friends. When my mother passed at a young age, my father shut himself in his cellar, only to come out once in the morning and once in the evening to walk the vineyards alone. Else, he locked himself downstairs with his wines, documenting, buying, selling, and perfecting his craft till he died of tuberculosis just before the Great War began. My brother, Kristof, and I enlisted, leaving my father's treasures behind with our sister, Lily, who at the time was married to a nice young man named Asher, who also enlisted and was put on the front lines. The war was harsh to my family. Kristof and Asher both died in the trenches.

"When I returned home with the news of their deaths, it was too much for my sister. She left me with what remained of my father's great fortune: a single bottle of Pinot Noir, which was the first bottle he had ever received. It was handed down through his family for over a century. It dates back to 1794, just before Napoleon's rise to power in 1799, making it one of the most expensive bottles to ever be sold. It was his most prized possession, which he had passed to me, his eldest son, and I to my sister while I was away. When she moved to America to find work in 1919, she left the bottle behind for me to keep, as it was mine by right. I have not heard from her since." His face was strained, as if filled with guilt and regret.

"What happened after she left? Obviously, you acquired more than just that one bottle."

He chuckled. "I suppose I have," he said, and the strain disappeared from his face within an instant. "After my sister left, I was lost and, to be frank, alone. I moved to this farmstead, where

I soon met Margret. We tried to have children, but soon came to find out that she was infertile. A friend of mine from the war came here in the late 1920s with his four children, seeking medical aid, but he soon passed from tuberculosis. His children stayed with my wife and me—we were in our mid-forties at the time—and soon we adopted them as our own."

"Dmitri, Claire, Violet, and . . ." I said, trying to recall the last name.

"Leo," he chirped. "You have a strong memory and a sharp mind. A deadly pair if used properly."

I smiled. "So what about the rest of this wine and this cellar? How did you create such a large underground bunker?"

"A lot of time, effort, and hard work," he said as he retrieved two wooden chairs from the far corner of the room. He handed one to me as he sat in his own across from me. "Yes, the kids really helped make this dream of mine come true. I always feared that we would fall into another Great War after the first one. We were a limping country, even if we were on the winning side of it. I knew that if I wanted to survive, I would have to think bigger than a mere store that sold a few bottles of wine here and there. So a few of my close counterparts and I made a vow to keep our French traditions alive, even in the face of the greatest tragedies that might affect us, such as another Great War."

"There is more than just this one storehouse, then?"

Doc laughed. "Oh heavens, yes! These large wine shelves conceal tunnels, my dear boy. They lead east and west to caches in the countryside. Few people know of their existence—allows for easier smuggling."

"Smuggling? You are *pirates?*"

"Not quite pirates; *freedom activists* is a better term for our way of life. We trade wine and other goods with families in similar situations throughout the country and neighboring borders to keep the *French* wine in the hands of *French* civilians."

"Do you fight against the Germans?"

"Well," he said, scratching his head as he spoke, "we do not care to fight them. They are a bother to meddle with. We tend to keep our operations out of their knowledge. It works better that way, we have found. Though, recently, our operation has slowed down dramatically, causing a lot of stress on trade due to fear of being discovered, arrested, and potentially executed for treason."

I pondered the idea for a moment, eyeing the old doctor to see if I could somehow read his real intentions, but my gut made me trust him for some reason.

"How can I help?" I finally said, leaning forward in my chair.

"By staying out of our way," Dmitri said as he entered the room carrying a large wooden crate filled with bottles. Leo followed close behind, a look of sympathy carved on his face as he locked eyes with me.

I turned back to Doc and waited for a response, but the answer I longed for did not come.

"I think it is best you go back to your mother and brother for now," he said, patting me on the shoulder. "I have told you far too grand a tale for today, filling your head with whimsical dreams."

"I am not a child," I said as jumped to my feet, nostrils flared and fists clenched. I could feel the exhaustion bearing down on my shoulders, but I remained strong before the old man. "I want to help you. I want to do *something*."

Doc leaned back in his chair and grinned. "Such a fierce spirit. You are a rare kind, Joshua, one whose flame should not be suffocated by fear and comfort. Meet me in the east study after dinner tonight; I will speak with you about how you can help with our operation."

With that, the doctor took his leave and retreated down the hallway to my right and disappeared into a room. I felt like a hero, a warrior, having stood up for myself for the first time in my life. I was alive in that moment.

Meet me in the east study after dinner . . . I repeated in my head.

I walked back to our room with a spring in my step. Even though I wanted to share my excitement, I had to be sure that my mother suspected nothing. If she found out, she would definitely disapprove.

Eliza

My heart stopped.

I did not turn to face him, but I knew he was watching me. I could feel the hatred he had toward me now. I was unsure of what I had done, what I had said to make him feel this way. Only a few hours before, he had been so sweet, so accepting, as if he *loved* me, and yet now he looked at me as if I were a mangy dog.

He moved in and grabbed my neck from behind, yanked me closer to him so that his mouth was almost touching my right ear. I stood as still as I could, but my legs began to shake. I could hear my heart pounding in my chest, and my breath came short.

"I know what you are," he whispered. "You thought you could lie to me, use me to get what you wanted. You thought you would be clever by falsifying your baptismal papers to make you not a Jew. It was clever, I will give you that, but there are two things that I hate the most in this world. Do you want to know what they are?"

I did not answer. Tears cascaded down my face as if two waterfalls poured from my eyes. I was hyperventilating.

He's going to kill me. He's going to kill me . . .

"Not answering," he sneered. "I'll tell you anyway."

He turned me around and slammed me against the window as he pulled out a long combat knife and placed it against my throat. I tried to lift my head higher, but he pressed the blade firm against my skin, which broke. I felt the drip of dark red blood and imagined it seeping onto the glistening blade.

"I hate liars." He pushed his forearm into my chest, and I gasped as the blade dug deeper into my neck. "And I especially hate Jews. Turns out you are both."

I closed my eyes, certain I was about to die—and then I heard a loud crash and felt the knife removed from my neck. I opened my eyes in terror as Nikolas slumped to the floor, the knife clattering across the floorboards just beyond his reach. Standing in front of me was Iva, who held a broken blue-and-yellow-painted vase; blood drenched her hands where the pottery had cut her palms.

She was shaking, eyes wild and breathing uneven and rapid. Her black dress slumped down her left bicep, exposing a fresh cigarette burn just below her clavicle. Large chunks of hair had been pulled from the left side of her head, and blood seeped from an ugly wound near her left eye.

"I didn't mean to kill him," she said, putting her bloody hands over her mouth. "I didn't mean to kill him."

I pulled her tight to me as she shuddered with shock. "Shhh, you did not kill him," I reassured her. "He is just knocked out, which means we need to get out of here, now."

She nodded, grabbed my wrist, and led me down the stairs and into the foyer. It was empty. Even the furniture had been removed from the building—to be burned in some refugee's small fire, I guessed. We stumbled out the back and into the alleyway between the tall buildings. Trash littered the dark path, and the smell of urine mixed with sweat filled my nostrils. I wanted to puke, but I pushed through until we reached the street.

"You need to get out of the city," Iva whispered as we crept between the pale yellow circles cast by the streetlamps. "You are a wanted woman: they know who you are now."

"What about my sister? I have to still find her," I pleaded.

She frowned. "She is gone."

My heart sank. "No, how do you know that? Did you find her?"

Her eyes shifted.

"Tell me! What do you know?"

"There have been rumors."

"What sort of rumors? What have you heard?" I insisted.

"I cannot be sure, but there have been whispers that your sister was smuggled out of the city just three days ago, headed north-west toward the coast with a man named Rudolph. He is a good man; she is safe with him."

I wanted to scream, in anger that she was fleeing north without me, but also with delight to know my sister was still alive. If Iva trusted this *Rudolph*, so would I—until I found her myself. A mix of emotions clouded my head, and suddenly dizzy, I sat down against the wall.

"We cannot delay any longer, Eliza," she said, tugging my wrist. "You have to leave *now*."

I grabbed her wrist, my head clearing for a short moment. "I am not leaving you behind. You are coming with me to the coast. We will find my sister and then get onto a boat headed for the west, toward safety."

She smiled and patted my hand. "Don't worry about me, child. They cannot take anything from me that they already haven't. I am dead inside, but you are still young and vibrant. You will live on beyond this war: long life awaits you. I have seen this to be true."

"What are you talking about?"

"You are pregnant, dear," she said, pointing to my stomach.

"No, that can't be possible!" I looked down at my stomach with desperation, my head becoming cloudy again. "I can't be pregnant. I can't birth a child into this horrible world."

Iva got close, so close I could feel her breath on my lips. "You will live through this, and your child also. You will grow well into your years, and your child shall love you for everything you provide for her. This will come to pass, but first you must leave this city. Go west. Go as far west as you can."

"And my sister?"

"Pray to your God that He will guide you, for I can only do so much in the short time given."

I placed my hands on my stomach again and wept. *I am not ready to be a mother, am I?*

"Hurry now. The guards are about to switch."

Joshua

After my mother and brother had fallen asleep, I snuck out of my cot and down the hall to the eastern study where Doc would be waiting. I felt like a spy, creeping through the dim hallways at night, against my mother's wishes. The risk of getting caught fueled my excitement as I padded across the slick concrete floors. As I slipped through the halls, my mind clear and focused, my heart pounded with excitement. I felt like Sherlock Holmes on a case to find the dreaded mastermind Professor Moriarty before he could follow through with his evil plans.

I rounded the corner without stopping and ran straight into an unsuspecting Violet, my forehead bouncing off hers. The books she carried flew into the air and scattered on the floor around us with a tremendous clatter. We both fell down, and I felt a throbbing in my head that intensified with each passing moment. I clasped my forehead and discovered a goose egg beginning to develop just above my right eyebrow.

When I looked up, she was mirroring me with her left hand above her left eye.

"That is going to be a big bruise in the morning," she mumbled as she blinked hard.

My stomach churned nervously. "I am so sorry," I apologized. "I did not mean to run into you."

She waved away the apology. "It's nothing," she said as she staggered back to her feet. "It's not the first time it has happened, nor will it be the last, I am guessing. Leo and I have bonked heads far more often than any other siblings in the history of the world—well, maybe. Regardless, it was an accident."

I rubbed my neck and bent down to grab a book—just as she reached for it. We collided again, this time on our crowns.

We both howled in pain and rubbed our heads with furious effort to make the stinging pain subside.

"All right," she said through gritted teeth, "I'll grab these on the right, and you grab the ones on the left."

"I'm grabbing the ones on the left?"

"No, I'm grabbing these on the right."

"But you told me to take those, right?"

"Right. Wait, no."

"Is it your right or my right?"

"Just grab the books closest to you!" she declared, exasperated, as she bent down and began collecting books.

I laid a hand on the last book just as she did, and we picked it up together, rising to stand face-to-face over its worn cover. I could feel her breath on my lips, and my heart raced even faster. The pain disappeared from my head, and it was as if all other worries melted away with it.

I leaned closer, my lips brushing hers, and then I closed my eyes and pressed my mouth to hers, without a clue about what I was doing. She didn't return the kiss, and for a moment I felt like an idiot. Then her hand released the book that separated us and wrapped around my neck, pulling me into her, as her other hand dropped the pile of books onto the ground and found my waist.

I don't remember dropping the books, but somehow in the mix of things, my hands found her hips and I pulled her into me, my back pressed against the wall. Time was suspended in that moment. I forgot about my mother, Petyr, the Germans, Dmitri, everything. I was with Violet; I was *kissing* Violet, and nothing else mattered.

When she pulled away from me, our lips seemed to hang on in desperation for just a few more seconds of bliss; I caught the glimpse of her shy, quirky smile.

Then she scooped up the spilled books, smiled at me again, and rushed down the hall, looking back at me just before she rounded the corner.

I leaned against the wall for a few more seconds, replaying in my head what had just happened, the taste of her lips on mine, my heart beating so fast that it seemed likely to burst from my chest at any second, a rush that I had never felt before in my life.

I have never felt this way before. What is this feeling? What just happened? I scratched my head and thought about her, about our kiss, and concluded, *I think this is what being in love feels like.*

Gabriel

I approached the large door that read *Henning* across the center beam, the small note summoning me clenched in my hand. I stood in the doorway for a moment, waiting for Henning to make some rude or witty comment insulting my intelligence.

"Come in and shut the door, please," Henning said without looking up.

I walked into the room and took a seat across from him. For being in a bunker, Henning's office was quite beautiful; I wondered how he'd gotten all this *stuff* down here without being caught. I marveled at the multitude of paintings, books, and medals on the wall to my right.

"Are you a reader, Gabriel?" he asked, still focused on the letter he was writing.

I cleared my throat before answering. "My mother was a constant reader, but I was more like my father and did not read as much as I should have, to be honest. I was never fast when it came to reading literature, nor did I catch all the hidden and deeper meanings that my teachers always asked us to identify."

He looked up. "It is a shame, really, for a man of your intelligence and aptitude to not be a reader. I believe that a man who reads separates himself from the rest of the society by raising himself to another level of intelligence. The man who does not read limits his worth and will never know even the possibility of being great."

"And what if a man is better with his hands and speaks with a masterful tongue, so much that he can call an entire army to do his bidding?"

"Where does such a man learn these skills? From watching? 'Whoso loveth instruction loveth knowledge: but he that hateth reproof is brutish. For a man shall be commended according to his wisdom: but he that is of perverse heart shall be despised.'" Henning leaned back in his chair and squinted at me. I tried to envision how he must see the young soldier sitting opposite him.

"Do you believe in God, Gabriel?"

"What does that have to do with anything?"

"It's just a question. Do you believe in God?"

I shifted in my seat. I had always claimed that I was a man of faith, but I had never lived it out. I hedged with fact. "My mother was quite earnest, reading the Bible and speaking about God to our family. My father was also quite religious, though he never talked about it outside of our house."

Henning frowned. "That's not what I asked you, Gabriel. I asked if *you* were a man of faith."

"I would not align myself with being a religious man, no," I said in a voice like a mouse's squeak. I felt so ashamed of my answer, although I could not understand why I felt so sorry for myself. "Why is it important, anyway?"

Henning stood up and walked to his bookshelf, from which he procured a tattered leather book, its pages edged in gold leaf, bearing the title *The Holy King James Bible* in golden German script.

"I said once that a man who reads sets himself apart from others, much like a wise man sets himself apart from a fool."

"What do you mean?"

"Think of it in this way, Gabriel. Is it better to lead a group by yourself or to lead a group while being advised by others?"

I pondered the idea for a moment. I feared there was some hidden meaning to the question, but I took the bait. "The second," I said with confidence.

"I agree," he said as he hauled the book back to his desk and took his seat with a slight sigh, "but why is it better than the first option?"

I had no answer. I felt so incompetent for not being able to match this man with his wit and jabs.

"I will tell you, Gabriel. Please remember this always. It is better to lead hundreds with *trusted* advisors, for their knowledge combined will create a far superior number of recommendations accompanied by a multitude of perspectives, compared to the single lens the one leader can bring to the table. As it is written in Proverbs, chapter 11, verse 14," he said as he cracked open the old Bible, "'Where no counsel is, the people fall: but in the multitude of counselors there is safety.' Yet still there are snakes in the grass to undermine leaders of promise and power."

"And which are you, then?" I said, leaning closer as well, trying to imitate the officer. "Are you a snake or a saint?"

"Why don't you answer that for yourself instead?" Henning said.

I paused, then said, "All right, I believe you are a—"

"But," he said, raising a slender finger in objection, "before you do so, let us reflect on the facts of the situation."

I sighed and accepted the proposition with a lazy wave of my hand.

"Very well," he said airily. "I am a religious man, and thus I am more a saint than a sinner. Yet I have killed men and enjoyed such. That makes me eviler than most, I would conclude. On the contrary, I am part of—actually, I am the head of a classified task force that is planning to undermine and take out the head of the snake that has slithered into leadership of our country. In doing so, I risk not only my life but also the lives of countless others in order to save millions in not only Germany but the entire world.

"Now, let me ask you again, just because I am a German Nazi who is part of the Reich, who sits on the council of Hitler himself, who has a wife and children and my own home back in Germany, with passions, dreams, loves, and losses, does that make me an *evil* man? Yes, I have killed men, and I liked it at the time, but I was young and naive—a fool with a gun who thought the only way to bring honor to his family was by killing as many enemies as possible, only to be left with an empty void in my heart that was filled even years later with the nightmarish screams of the wounded and dying. Now tell me, am I an *evil man* for seeking justice? Not for my past sins but for the future of our world."

I had so many questions, but the longer I sat staring at him, the more uncomfortable I became. Finally, I shook my head. He frowned.

"There is a reason I kept you alive, Gabriel," he said. "Claire, she played a part, or so I want her to think, but I let you live because I know you are capable of great things. However, I need to be able to trust you with valuable secrets. Can I trust you?"

I figured I had no other answer but yes, so I agreed and scooted closer to the desk.

"I need you to take care of someone for me. Not now, but perhaps in the near future. A certain Jew who has been asking too many . . . *questions.*"

"Why not send one of your errand boys to do it?"

He sighed. "They cannot be trusted anymore. Their loyalties have always been questionable, and thus I have never told them about the entire operation. They know only fragments of information too miniscule and indirect to make any sense of the whole."

"Yet you have told two strangers? I am not sure that makes much sense to me," I said. "Wouldn't that add even more risk to what you are planning?"

Henning smiled. "I have only told you what you need to know. Yet you might be thinking, *If he is telling the truth, I could go and tell someone.* Imagine if you were to tell a superior officer that *I* was making wild accusations of murder and treason. It would be your word versus mine, and I will tell you this: I would win that argument."

I frowned. I hated being used as a pawn, but I had no choice, it seemed. "What do you want me to do?"

"When the time comes, I may need you to eliminate someone for me," he said, sounding quite chipper. "I already said that. Do you have a hard time listening? Perhaps some tea would clear your mind?"

"I am fine," I said, holding back my annoyance as best I could. "Whom do you want me to kill?"

He smiled, pulled a manila envelope from a drawer, and slid it across the desk to me.

I opened it and read the file.

"Does Claire know?"

"She does not, nor should she ever find out," he said. "For now, accompany her back to her family. Earn their trust, but do not allow yourself to be led away from your duty as a soldier. This"—Henning pointed at the file in my hands—"is your second chance. When I send for you, there must be no hesitation. Is that understood?"

"What about me being a wanted man?"

Henning smiled and rolled his eyes as he sipped his drink. "Bah!" he said, waving a free hand at me. "I have already blotted it from the record. There is no written document of you being a deserter, wanted felon, or anything of the like. I rewrote your assignment to be an active soldier under *my personal watch*, and since your officer is below me, he had no choice but to accept my request for immediate transfer. So I suppose this should be a celebration for you, Gabriel! Though, if you choose to divert from my direction, I can submit a new document calling for your immediate arrest and execution."

"What am I to tell Claire?"

"Nothing," he said. "Act as if you are hearing everything for the first time, just like her. Make her believe that you are just as much a victim as she is in this situation. It's the only way she will truly trust you."

I gripped the file in my hand as I reread the name and description over and over in my mind. The small photo in the top right-hand corner made me sick, knowing that I would one day have to meet that person face-to-face.

I looked up and frowned. I hated this imposter who had just preached about being a good man, defending his case, and yet was now sending me to do this evil duty without batting an eye. I wanted to kill him. I felt the weight of my pistol hanging on my right hip. How easy it would be to shoot this man here and now . . . but I didn't.

He eyed me with those fox-like eyes. "Do you understand what is expected from you, Gabriel, if and when I send for you?"

"I understand," I said in a stern tone. "It shall be done."

Claire

I dug my teeth into the soft red skin of the apple, letting the juice rush into my mouth. It was delicious—sweeter than I had anticipated. It reminded me of summers on the farm with Dmitri, Leo, and Violet as we would sit on the riverbank, fishing and nibbling on apple slices before tossing the cores to the fish.

When I opened my eyes, Gabriel's menacing gaze met mine. He sat across from me, eating stale toast with a thin layer of butter spread over it. He had taken my advice. Instead of the prestigious military attire, he wore simple clothing like a civilian from France. He had cut his hair shorter, and atop his head was the flat cap common among the teens of the area. He had also shaved, and he wore a pair of round black glasses.

Had I not known better, I would have mistaken him for a local boy, one I might have considered pursuing. Yet I knew what he really was: a Kraut in disguise.

"Good morning, you two!" Henning called as he walked into the dining area, sounding quite cheerful.

I glanced at him as he circled the table like a vulture searching for prey.

"Why are you so chipper this morning?"

He stopped and smiled as he put his hands behind his back. "Because, Claire, today Operation Valkyrie is to be put into effect."

"Operation Valkyrie?"

He grabbed an orange and sat at the head of the table, facing Gabriel and me. "Yes, Claire." He paused, cut the skin away, and then dug his crooked teeth into the juicy orange. "Operation Valkyrie is our plan to overthrow our fearless ruler!" He paused and turned his attention to Gabriel. "However," he said, pursing his lips, "some of us here are not very trustable at the moment."

Gabriel dropped his spoon and frowned. "Look, I was the one who was trying to save Claire from being executed. Then your goons arrested me and almost killed me!"

"You couldn't be trusted," Henning said, cutting the orange into smaller pieces.

"I can't be trusted? You are the one planning to overthrow Hitler himself! How am *I* the threat in this situation?"

"You, Gabriel, are a loose end that needs to be singed. You know valuable information about our operation here; hence, we are sending you with Claire instead of keeping you here."

"Wouldn't it put your entire operation into more danger if I were to go and tell a commanding officer what you have been planning all this time?"

Henning laughed as he set the rest of his orange on the table.

"Think of it this way, Gabriel. *You* are a wanted man at the moment. There is a hefty price on your head. You are a deserter, a traitor, and a lover of the defeated French. What do you think will happen if you turn yourself in to a commanding officer and paint him an elaborate picture of a mysterious operation that involves some of the most prominent men in the Nazi party attempting to overthrow their leader? Tell me, how will that play out for you?"

Gabriel frowned and then cursed under his breath.

Satisfied, Henning picked up the other half of his orange and nibbled on the fragrant contents.

"And what about me?" Claire asked.

Henning snickered. "What about you? You are just a French bitch without direction. Odds are, if you turned yourself in telling wild stories about a government conspiracy, they'd shoot you—or rape you and then shoot you. I'd hope for the first option, if I were you."

I glanced up at Gabriel, who was sullen, but when he looked at me I saw concern in his eyes. It made me uncomfortable knowing that a soldier was just as scared as I was.

I was full, even though I hadn't even eaten much of anything. "When do we leave?" I said, pushing away from the table.

"Within the hour," Henning said. He sucked on the remaining juice from his orange. "I will be sure that Klaus gets your things together for the journey back to your family. I trust you have your papers in order?"

I rummaged through my pockets until I found the yellow slip of paper that had been falsified to hide my true identity.

He nodded in satisfaction and then turned to Gabriel. "And you?"

Gabriel pulled the yellow slip from his breast pocket without looking up from his bowl. Henning frowned but said nothing about Gabriel's attitude. He rose from his chair and wiped his nose with his handkerchief. "We will depart before dawn. Be sure you have everything you need before you come to the back entrance at the top of the eastern stairwell."

After he left us alone once again, I tried to eat something else, but I was not hungry. I looked at Gabriel, but he did not notice me staring—he didn't seem to care that I was there.

"You can't trust him, you know," he said without looking up.

I shot a glance at the door that Henning had just closed behind him. "What do you mean, I can't trust him?" I shot back.

"He saved my life. I owe him so much. I don't like him, but I respect him for what he has done."

"He's a snake," Gabriel said. "He is using you, and when he is done, he will throw you to the wolves. You are valuable to him. Why, I have no idea, but you can't trust a German. Especially one with such a rank."

I squirmed in my chair. "So why should I trust you?"

He looked up from his bowl and frowned. "I am someone who can't be trusted either," he said, "but I also won't lie to you."

"How can I know that you won't lie to me?"

"Because you are in love with me, and I don't lie to girls who are in love with me." He flashed a smile, gathered his dishes, and left me sitting alone in the dining hall with cheeks as red as roses in late spring. I was embarrassed, but I couldn't argue against the fact that I had feelings for him. I pushed the thoughts out of my mind. It was time to be focused, determined, and not distracted. It was time to go home.

Joshua

As I made my way to the eastern study where I was supposed to have met Doc almost thirty minutes prior, it felt as if I were floating on air, my feet suspended above the ground like an angel's. The sensation was short lived, however, as I came across Dmitri leaving the study with a rifle slung on his shoulder, leading three other men I had never seen before who also carried guns.

They were dressed in camouflage, deep green mixed with black and brown. Dmitri ordered the men to continue on without him and waited until they were out of earshot before he turned his attention to me. He was frowning.

"I don't like you much," he said in a low voice.

Comforting, I thought as I waited for him to continue.

"I also don't trust you."

A great start, it seems . . . two for two.

"But I feel I have not given you a chance to prove yourself," he said, letting his stern expression fade into a look of sympathy and regret. "I don't know why I am telling you this, of all people, but ever since I lost my sister Claire, I have been more protective of Violet and Leo. It's nothing personal; I just care for them, you know? They are all the family I have left. You are a brother, right?"

I nodded.

"Think of it as if your mother was not around and your brother was all you had left: the stress, the guilt, the worry that would weigh upon your heart and mind every day as you took care of him. Now think of losing him, knowing that you'd had a chance to intervene, but didn't, and because of that he would be gone forever."

I was shocked. Here I had thought this boulder of a man hated my guts because I was coming into his territory, interrupting *his way of life*, but in reality, he was taking the role of a father far too young. I felt sympathy for the man.

He reached into his pocket and removed a gold watch on a chain. "When I come back," he said, "I expect you to return this. But for now, I want to leave it with you as a token of respect and goodwill, to prove that my apology is sincere and that my heart is right with God."

I took the watch and ran my fingers across the neat engravings that decorated the outside casing.

"Dmitri," I said, "I appreciate your generosity, but this belongs with you and your family."

He frowned. "Joshua," he murmured. It was the first time he had called me by name without yelling or cursing at me. "I don't know if I am going to make it back."

The words hung on the air like dense fog.

"What do you mean, you don't know if you are going to make it back? You are not going far, right?"

"Doc just found out that one of our nearby transport lines was discovered and rummaged by a German patrol earlier this morning. If that is the case, it's only a matter of time before they find us here too. We're going to scout the area and gather any information we can about the German patrols."

"You are going behind enemy lines with a few rifles and three men?" I said. "You are mad."

"Mad, or desperate to keep my family safe?"

I looked him straight in the eye and said, "I'm coming with you."

"No, you are not," he retorted. "You are not trained. You'll get yourself killed."

"What about being desperate to keep my family safe?" I scolded. "Take me with you. I can help you out there."

He shook his head. "No, it is too dangerous. If you follow," he said as he turned to walk away, "I'll shoot you myself. Don't make me do that, Joshua. I am just starting to like you."

Gabriel

Henning was there to see us off from the compound, along with about fifteen other soldiers dressed in civilian clothing, all pointing their rifles at us as we walked away. They blindfolded us before we left the compound and walked us about two miles through dense forest before telling us we could remove the restrictions. They pointed us north, and that was the last I saw of Henning and his ragtag band of civil soldiers.

I hated him for keeping us in secrecy for so long, yet admired the man for attempting something so noble at the price of his own life. I hated Hitler just as much, perhaps even more than the next man, but I was a coward in the face of real adversity. I was all for killing the dictator in theory, but if I had a gun in my hand and the chance to shoot the Nazi in the head, I feared that I would not be able to follow through with the execution.

We traversed the French countryside for a few hours before resting next to a small stream that cut through the center of the forest. The water was crisp and cool on my face as I splashed my sweaty forehead.

"You sound like a pig when you slurp that water, you know," Claire said as she massaged her reddened feet. A few scabs had begun to form around her toes, and I could tell she was in pain.

"You should get better socks," I said as I sat back on my haunches, wiping my forehead dry. "If you don't take care of your socks, your feet will blister and then get infected."

She winced as she moved her fingertips over the tender skin.

I got up and made my way over to her.

"Don't!" she protested as she pulled her foot away from my reaching hand. "I don't need your help. I'm fine."

I dug into my satchel and found a salve that had come in my medical pack.

"Here," I said, handing the ointment to her. "It will help the pain." I dug deeper into my bag and retrieved a fresh pair of tube socks. "Take these as well. I have an extra pair in my pack besides these."

She took them and then thanked me. It was more a mumble than actual gratitude, and yet I knew it was a step in the right direction.

"So how long do we have till we get back to your property?" I asked as I walked back to the creek to fill my canteen.

"Do you think just because you gave me some ointment and socks that we are now *best friends*?"

"I did not mean to offend," I said.

"Well, I don't want your friendship, *Kraut*. Do not think that I am a naive girl who you can just control at your will. I promise that I would put a knife in your neck if I had a chance—"

A twig snapped behind us, and as I turned, drawing my gun, I saw three rifles pointed back at me just a few feet away.

Claire

I heard the twig snap.

I turned to see who was there.

Gabriel faced three men with hidden faces, all with guns drawn. I could tell by their clothing that the intruders were not Germans, but I feared for Gabriel. I tried not to care, but he was a good man regardless of his side.

"Wait," I said without thinking, "please, don't shoot." *Idiot. Why would they listen? We'd be better off dead: two fewer witnesses to worry about.*

"Claire, shut up. I'll take care of these three," Gabriel said through gritted teeth. "*Was wollen sie?*" Gabriel said to the three men.

They looked at one another, their eyes narrow and full of hatred.

He said it again, this time with more emphasis. The masked men tightened their grips on their rifles and advanced as they shouted back at him in muffled French.

"*Il est Allemand,*" one said to another. "*Faut-il le tuer?*"

The one on the far left said no; a sudden sigh of relief flooded over me. They were not going to kill the German.

"*A propos d'elle?*" the one on the right said, gesturing at me.

I stood up and raised my hands in defense. "I am French," I said with as much confidence as I could gather in the moment.

"This is my friend Gabriel; he is from Kehl. He speaks two languages; he is my guide. We do not mean harm."

The three French soldiers looked at one another and then motioned to Gabriel. "Tell him to drop his gun, then, if you are so peaceful," the middle one said.

I looked to Gabriel and then back at the apparent leader of the trio and said, "Only if you do so also. We do not want bloodshed from either side."

Gabriel lowered his pistol, and the three lowered their rifles as well. The tension was still present in the fragile truce, and yet I breathed easier.

"Who are you?" I asked as I moved to Gabriel's side.

The middle man pulled the lower part of his mask down as he approached, revealing a chin covered in stubble and grime. His expression was grim and defeated; this man had seen battle, I could tell.

"I am Marcus Fredrickson, member of the Freedom Fighters of France. On my left is Nicolas Reed and on my right Yorwick Hann. Now, who are you and what are you doing in this part of the countryside, if you are in fact *peaceful people*?"

"This is Gabriel, and I am Claire Decroix. My grandfather, Orson Reynolds—"

"Orson Reynolds," Marcus said in a hushed voice. "You are the granddaughter of Doc Reynolds?"

"Well, not technically," I said, rubbing my burning neck. I was so nervous, how could I explain myself so that they'd believe me?

Just then, another man broke through the brush, a rifle slung over his shoulder and a hunting knife in his left hand. He wore a camouflage outfit that made him hard to see even as he stood before us.

"Marcus," he said, breathless, "German patrols are moving into this sector. We have to move—"

He stopped and looked at me as if he had just seen a ghost. Pulling off the mask, he stepped forward with careful steps as if not to startle me.

"Claire?" he said. "Is it really you? Claire, we all thought you were dead."

Tears filled my eyes, and I wrapped my arms around him as tight as I could. I did not care if I broke all his ribs: I did not want to let go. I buried my face in his chest and sobbed. He enveloped me in his large arms and squeezed tight in return. Kissing my head, he muttered things that I could not understand, but I did not care. I was safe again. Dmitri was here, and I was safe.

In the distance, an engine roared. My brother pulled away despite my efforts to keep him close.

"They are coming this way," he said as he looked back through the dense thicket. Turning to Marcus, he pointed to Gabriel and me and said, "Get these two back to the tunnel. I will take Nicolas and Yorwick with me and lead the Germans off course."

"No, Dmitri, I won't let you leave. I just got you back. Don't leave me, *please*!" I pleaded as I clawed as his shirt.

He grabbed my arms and held me tight as he shook me out of my hysteria. "Listen to me! Listen to me, Claire! Listen! The Germans will be on us within a matter of minutes. Get back to the tunnel. I will be right behind you. Trust Marcus: he knows the way."

"No, I won't leave you again," I said.

"There is no time to argue. *Go!*" he cried as he pointed away from the approaching army.

Marcus grabbed my hand and shouted for Gabriel to cross the winding creek and climb the hill beyond it. As we dashed away, I looked over my shoulder to see my brother and the two soldiers disappear into the thick brush.

As we reached the base of the hill, rapid gunfire echoed across the woods.

"Quick! Up the hill!" Marcus shouted, shoving me up with his free hand. We scrambled for the top, and after the initial fifty feet, the remainder of the grassy knoll was quite easy to climb. Gabriel reached the summit first, then Marcus, and then me. They had already started back down the other side when I turned back to see if I could spot my brother among the trees. I scanned the woods and clearings but could not find him.

A sudden movement in the tree line caught my eye; after a few seconds, Dmitri plunged out of the woods in a dead sprint toward the hill. Behind him, I could see the trees shaking, hear the shouts of a hundred Krauts chasing him with bloodlust, the roar of the tank engines as they plowed through the trees like a predator chasing prey.

"Run, Dmitri!" I screamed. I started to slide back down the hill toward him. "Run!"

He was almost there. I could meet him halfway down the hill and then help him up. *He is so close, just a few feet farther.*

"Run! Dmitri, you are almost here! Hurry!"

Bang!

Dmitri stumbled, but he kept running, clutching his left arm.

Bang!

This time it was a clean hit. He staggered and then dropped to his knees. I did not hear the final shot. I did not hear anything. I just *saw*. Saw how my brother fell forward in the grass. Saw the bloody shirt on his back. Saw my brother in the grass, dead.

My brother, my hero, had fallen.

Gabriel

I looked back to find Claire. She was gone. I stopped, then ran back up to the crest and found Claire sliding down the grassy slope toward the bottom.

"Claire!" I shouted as I took off down the hill after her. She was already halfway down the hill, but I caught up with her with ease. I grabbed her elbow and shook her.

"Claire! Get up!" I yelled. The grass around us erupted as gunfire rained down.

Before I could yell for her to move, she was already sprinting toward the summit. Marcus was standing on the top of the hill, firing his rifle down on the approaching Germans.

I glanced over my shoulder and saw a grey mass moving through the trees, followed by the gigantic armored division roaring like a pack of lions as they tore the trees up by the roots. I pumped my legs harder as I pursued Claire up the hill. Marcus was out of bullets and was now throwing stones.

We pushed over the crest and ran down the opposite side as fast as our legs could go. Claire stumbled and fell head over heels the remainder of the way down. I ran faster to help her up, but when I reached her, she pushed me away, tears strewn across her face, her face red with anger. She sped into the brush, but I did not follow.

Marcus threw me with a confused look, but he did not stop. Instead he ran after Claire, and before I knew it, they were both gone from sight.

What's the point? I thought as I stood staring at the bramble and thick trees before me. *She hates me for who I am. I'll never be accepted where she is going. Better that I surrender and accept my fate as a traitor.*

I pulled out my pistol and checked the chamber. Six bullets. Six bullets versus an entire platoon; I was about to seal my fate with these metal casings. I pulled back the hammer, wiped my brow with the back of my shaking hand, and stood ready.

The first German soldier crested the summit, and I fired without hesitation. He dropped like a sack of bricks and slid halfway down the hill face-first. I stepped to the right, behind a tall oak tree.

The second was a bit more careful and actually had his rifle ready, but he did not know where I was. He drew up his rifle and searched the base of the hill for me before making his way toward his comrade, who lay in the bloodstained grass just below him. He bent down, and I fired the second shot. A clean kill through the head.

Two more came over the hill. Two shots, two kills; I ran for another tree as two more soldiers appeared. I fired and hit one of them, and then I fired again, but as sure as my aim had been for the first five, this last shot just grazed the target's shoulder. I was out of bullets, out of time, out of hope.

He yelled for me to surrender, and I walked out from behind the tree with hands raised high. He galloped down the hill with his rifle pushed hard against his shoulder, ready to fire without hesitation.

"Down on your knees!" he screamed in German. "Down on your knees!"

I complied, my hands still raised high above my head.

A shot rang out, and the soldier dropped without another word. I whipped my head around and saw Claire standing there with a smoking gun.

"That's two, Kraut. Grab that rifle and let's go!" she yelled as she took off into the brush once again.

I didn't think twice. It was as if I had just woken from a dream that I had been trapped in. *What was I thinking, trying to take on an entire platoon with only six bullets?*

I ran to the dead German, grabbed his rifle, and took off into the woods after Marcus and Claire. Within a few minutes I found them, and without saying a word we ran until our feet were swollen and the sun had disappeared.

After what seemed to be an eternity of traveling, we finally arrived at a large, jagged rock shelf that jutted into the air about fifty feet. The moon was our only source of light, but Marcus strode confidently to the cliff wall. I was certain it was a dead end, but Marcus pulled aside a large section of green moss and opened a grey-painted door. I gagged at the musty smell that wafted out from the passage beyond.

"Where does this go?" I said, trying to keep from throwing up. "It smells like a sewer."

"It leads to safety," Marcus said as he grabbed a lantern hanging just inside the door. He lit it and let the orange flame grow in intensity.

"How can we trust you?" I said.

Claire was already making her way into the tunnel as if she knew where she was going. Marcus watched her disappear into the darkness, then turned back to me and frowned.

"Either stay here and get shot by your brothers, or follow us and maybe be spared. It's up to you. I would prefer to put a bullet in your head here and now to end the troubles that are bound to come with you, but I can't deny that you brought Claire back. For that, I'll give you a chance."

He spit at my feet, then turned and walked into the darkness, the lantern bobbing up and down. I sighed, looked back to make sure no one was following us, and closed the door behind me before I chased after the fading light.

Eliza

We stayed in the shadows across from the building that Iva claimed was my gateway to freedom. It was an old barbershop, its windows boarded up and the door replaced by a large woolen blanket. I readied myself to move across the street, but Iva grabbed my wrist and pulled me back into the shadow of the building.

"No, not yet!" she whispered as she pointed down the street.

Rounding the corner were three leashed dogs, followed by a pack of five soldiers in SS uniforms, rifles slung over their left shoulders. They were laughing and pointing at one of the men in the group, who was making a funny face. I guessed he was making jokes about a Jew that he had seen earlier. It made my stomach turn; I hated them, all of them. I wanted to kill them all. I balled my hands into fists and clenched them until my knuckles turned white.

They passed us without so much as a glance. We scuttled across the road as quietly as we could and pulled back the blanket. The space behind it smelled like a rotting corpse, so I covered my mouth, holding back my vomit. Iva passed me and continued to the far side of the room.

I followed with hesitation. Iva led me behind a counter and pulled a panel from the wall, revealing an even darker space. "Go," she ordered. I ducked and squeezed through the small space into the hidden room. It was pitch black, like a forest on a moonless night. As my eyes adjusted, I made out shadowy objects leaning against the wall and piled on top of each other.

I turned around to face Iva, who stood silhouetted in the doorframe. I could not see her face, but I knew she was frowning, perhaps even crying.

"Come with me," I said as I reached out my hand.

"I can't," she said. "I have to stay here with my family. I have to help others like you escape from this persecution."

"No," I whispered. "No, you can't stay here. You have a chance to get out. Come with me, Iva. I can't do this alone. I don't know the way."

"You will find the way. Warsaw has been your home, but now your destiny lies in the west. Go north; find a ship, then sail to Britain. It is your only chance, Eliza. For you and your baby."

I placed my hand over my stomach. I was still in disbelief that I was actually pregnant. I had denied the signs, but something was telling me that I had only a short time to find safety for my child before I was engulfed by danger.

"Find me after the war, yes?" I said.

Iva put her hand over her mouth and let out a quiet whimper. "Yes, I will," she said through the tears. "Here, take this." She handed me a small slip of thick paper. "Be reminded of me until we meet again."

I knew the photograph—an image of her standing in a summer dress on the bank of a river. I had once asked her for a copy.

"This is your favorite photo," I said as I held it with trembling hands.

"And now you will have it to remember what I look like," she replied.

"I will see you soon," My voice cracked between quick gasps and a waterfall of tears.

Iva nodded, even though we were both aware that it was a lie.

I said one final good-bye, watched Iva set the panel into the wall once again, and then made my way to the back of the room, where I found another door. I opened it with caution, uncertain of what awaited me on the other side.

I stepped into the darkness, closed the door behind me, and waited. It was so silent that my ears ached. I reached out in front of me, but I could not feel the wall. I reached to my sides but still felt only air. Behind me, concrete walls stretched off into the darkness in either direction.

I waited for what seemed an eternity, and then I heard it: a faint noise somewhere in the distance. I stood still, clutching my stomach with my left hand and the photo with my right. My heart beat loud as thunder; my breath was short, and sweat flowed like a river from my pores. Tears clouded my vision as I peered through the darkness.

Below me a faint light appeared, growing in intensity with each passing moment. *Below me,* I thought. *How is the light below me?*

"Hello?" I said.

There was no response to my meek query, but the light continued to grow.

"Hello?" I said again, this time a bit louder, as I reached for the doorknob behind me.

Again no response from the coming light. My worry grew.

The light was only a few meters away now, revealing the bottom of a wooden staircase. As the light grew, it illuminated the stairs all the way up to where I was standing. The light passed into view then, and I shielded my eyes.

"You are the one that Iva was talking about, I assume?" an old man grunted from the bottom of the stairwell.

"You . . . you knew I was coming?" I squeaked.

He grunted again. "Are you looking to get out of the city or not?"

"Yes. Can you help?"

He said nothing else, but turned and headed back down the corridor at the bottom of the stairs, the lantern swinging from side to side. The stairs began to disappear once again into the darkness.

I watched for another moment as the light retreated, and then I ran after him, trying to hold back my tears as I left behind the only home I had ever known. *Farewell, people of Warsaw. May God have mercy on your souls.*

Joshua

Doc was waiting in his study for me, reading, as I had expected, and sipping on a glass of red wine. The bottle sat on his desk, uncorked and half-empty from what I could tell by the shadow reflecting through the glass. I closed the study door behind me as quietly as I could, keeping hold of the pocket watch in my free hand.

"I was starting to think you were not coming," Doc said without looking up from his book.

"I apologize. I was held up a bit."

He waved his hand as he closed his book and placed it in a gap on the third shelf that matched the shape and density of the book he'd been reading. He grabbed the glass of red liquid, took another long drink, and filled it again until it was near running over the edge.

"Come, sit with me by the fire," he said as he motioned for me to take the medium-sized yellow chair across from his faded golden one. Mine smelled of musk and had a small tear in the left arm, exposing the white and brown innards that made up the old recliner.

The fireplace was nothing grand. The hearth was blackened all around its mouth, unlike the brick facing on either side of the mantel. As I scrutinized the wall with squinted eyes, I realized the red brick and white mortar were painted on.

"Yes," Doc said, scratching his head as he took his seat across from me. "The wall is only a painting, nothing more."

I smiled and said, "It looks real."

Doc laughed and sipped his wine once again. "Looks and reality are perceptions of the eye. The eyes lie to the brain, and so the brain falls victim to fantasies and dreams that will never amount to anything tangible."

"And what about having a dream that you work hard to make a reality? Is that not what Hitler did with his country?"

Doc frowned. "It is a different type of dream, Joshua. Hitler's 'dream,' as you call it, was a plot to revenge the mockery of his pride, both personally and to his country. Yet at the same time, you are correct in saying that he has a dream for a better future for Germany. However, does a man's dream always benefit everyone who is in turn affected, or does it benefit only the one who aspires to make change?"

"It depends on the dream, I suppose," I said, shifting to rest my elbows on my knees and lean closer to him. "What if I saved the French people from German rule? I would be a hero in the eyes of so many. It would be *my* dream to free this country from tyranny."

"Consider your position first," Doc said, pointing with a slender finger. "To the French and their allies, yes, you would be the savior we have all dreamed of in these long months of oppression. You would be esteemed as the one who brought your own people out of oppression, much as Moses did for the Israelites in the desert. Do you know the story?"

"I remember only bits and pieces, but I'd be willing to listen to it again."

"Moses freed the Israelites from Egypt and Pharaoh's oppressive rule. Yet when they were wandering in the desert, seeking the Promised Land that God had promised them all, the Israelites grew restless and blamed Moses for their misfortune. Do you know what they wanted instead of Moses?"

I shook my head.

"They told Moses to let them go back into the hands of their oppressors, the Egyptians, for they knew their lives would be better in captivity and bondage than wandering in a barren wasteland."

"What is your point?"

Doc sighed and leaned back in his chair. "My point, Joshua, is that your dream, although honest and well intentioned, would work for a time. The French people cry out for a savior from the Germans, as they should, but after that, when they are saved and have the *freedom* that they have so longed for, they have no direction. I am not saying that our current situation is ideal, and I would much rather be free than under an oppressor's hand, but think of those who live comfortably now that someone forceful has taken the role of leader. Yes, it is uncomfortable at first, but when is it not uncomfortable to take a stand for a change from the normal? We cry for peace and freedom, but in our hearts we desire a leader, and I am afraid that, in our case, a tyrant will suffice."

"And what will happen when the tyrant falls from his throne?"

Doc frowned and swirled his wine in the glass.

"Chaos."

Eliza

The old man was quicker than I had expected, and my stomach roiled as I chased after him. I was stressed, hungry, and tired, but my only hope was to keep following this strange man with the lantern. As we moved farther into the tunnel, the walls seemed to close in around me. The stale air was hard to breathe, and before long, my coughing reverberated throughout the tunnel.

"How much farther?" I said between coughs.

The man grunted and then spit on the ground. "Not far. Keep moving, else you will get lost."

Fearing that I might lose track of the old man, I shoved off the pain in my stomach and sped up. We walked for what seemed to be hours, the path twisting left and right, rising and falling, making me stumble on the uneven ground. I heard a door close in the distance to my left—or perhaps it was behind me, or in front? It was hard to discern direction in the darkness. The only point on which I could fix my eyes was the bobbing light that the old man held high before himself. Without it, I fear I would have been lost forever.

Again a door opened and closed in the distance; this time it was louder, and I could discern that it came from in front of us. The old man stopped and turned to face me. I almost ran into him, but stopped just before I smacked into his hot lantern.

"This is it," he grumbled. "Don't talk to no one. Just follow close, and you will be safe. Well, I think you will."

My stomach was uneasy again. I swallowed the urge to puke and stepped up behind the old, ragged man. He grabbed the bronze knob on the door and blew out his lantern light. He pushed open the door with a grunt and waited in the dim passage for a moment before stepping forward, motioning for me to follow him. I stepped up and into a dusty hallway with an old chandelier hanging from the ceiling. The electricity hummed as it produced a faint glow in the six fake candles.

There were five doors on each side of the hallway, each with a number and place card nailed to its center. I examined the closest door and read to myself, *Number 1—Train Depot Route.*

The man closed the door behind me, and on it I glimpsed the label, *Number 11—Warsaw Tunnel: Proceed with caution! Warning: Tunnels should not be traveled without a guide!*

I sighed, relieved to be out of the maze of darkness. Without the old man's help, I would certainly have gotten lost and died among the dark, twisting paths, and for a moment I was happy he was there to guide me to safety . . . or so I hoped.

The old man hung up the lantern on a hook next to the eleventh door, combed back his wiry white hair, and limped to the farthest door on the left. He knocked in a coded pattern that was too rapid for me to follow. A slit in the middle of the door slid open, revealing a pair of brown eyes and bushy eyebrows. The eyes squinted at me, but the old man waved his hand and grunted something in a strange language.

The eyes shot me another look, the slit slid closed, and the latches on the other side of the door started to click and snap out of their locked positions. The door sighed open, drawn by a very short man with a cane and small hat with a crooked bill. His brown eyes studied me again as the two men exchanged greetings and what seemed to be unpleasant words. This agitated midget of a man kept pointing at me with knobby fingers. The old man protested—or at least I hoped he was arguing my case—while I stood there like an idiot, unwelcome and unknowing of the fate of my baby and myself.

The old man looked at me and frowned. "Iva sent you here?"

I nodded, a sudden sadness washing over me at the thought of her.

The old man turned back to the midget and said some more things that I could not understand. The midget then looked at me and frowned. He said in broken Polish, "Iva, I always love her company when she comes by. It has been a long time since she visited me, though. I miss her."

"I'm sorry," I said in a soft voice. I had said sorry so often in my life that it just was a natural response to sadness. Oftentimes I didn't even mean it, but for some reason, I felt the pain of this man's heart for Iva. *She was a prostitute, though; perhaps this man was one of her frequent customers?* I thought. Yet at the same time, I remembered Nikolas, how he had made me feel while I was with him. Perhaps this was no different from what I felt for him.

The midget wiped his eyes with his free hand and said something to the old man before he disappeared into the room beyond the door.

"You are lucky," the old man said. "If it were not for Iva, I don't think you would have been permitted in. Her friendship just saved your life."

"Not just her friendship," I said. "She risked everything to save me."

Claire

I could barely walk upright as we made our way through the tunnel. I knew the way, had traveled it multiple times, but still I tripped and stumbled into the wall. Gabriel tried to help me, but I thrashed out of his arms many times before I finally vomited and then fell to my knees, sobbing uncontrollably. Marcus pointed at me and told Gabriel to carry me the rest of the way. At first I fought him, but soon I just gave in and let him pick me up, knowing that it was useless to resist his help. I just kept crying.

"He's gone, Gabriel," I sobbed, clutching his shirt tight in my hands. "My brother, he is gone."

"I know he is, but you have to be strong. Your family needs you right now."

"I can't, not without Dmitri." I pressed my face into his chest. I remember wanting it to just end right there, to die and join my brother, but I knew that was not how it would happen.

When we got back to the compound, Lily was the first to meet us. The look of horror on her face when I told her about our brother—I will never forget how she looked as she dropped to her knees next to me. She held me in her arms and mourned with me. Doc was there; he said nothing when he heard my brother's fate. I don't think he even shed a tear. I didn't blame him for that, though. How could I? He was like a father to all of us siblings.

There were new people at the compound also. I didn't know them, didn't know if I could trust them, but for the time being I didn't care. All I wanted was my brother back. All I wanted was for things to be the way they used to be. I blamed God for what had happened. Doc told me it was not God's fault, but I knew it was. And I was going to put Him on trial for my brother's death.

Part 3—May 1944

Gabriel

Almost four years had passed since my first encounter with Claire on that dusty road outside of Paris. I could not believe the amount of hardship we had endured to get to where we were today. When we first arrived at the underground compound in October of 1940, I was unsure if I would be welcomed, much less trusted by Doc and his family. They put me on trial after the shock of Dmitri's death had passed. I was kept in a small cell when I first arrived, for nearly a week, until they figured out what to do with me. I did not fight them; I was just grateful to rest in a bed again for a time.

Marcus did not trust me, as I had expected, but I still fought to gain their trust, individually and together. It took weeks, months for them to trust that I was not a dirty German soldier looking to expose them; it took longer for them to accept me as one of their own. Doc, at least, saw me not as a threat but rather as someone who could lift heavy crates for him.

For the first few months, I was set to helping Joshua, the seventeen-year-old French boy, to map out our trade routes, since he had the best penmanship and I could translate German for him. Even he hesitated to work with me at first, but soon we developed a good friendship, one built on trust and respect for one another's talents.

Claire did not leave the compound for close to a year and a half. The thought of going on a trading expedition made her uneasy. She claimed it was due to the constant thoughts of Dmitri, but I knew it was because she just did not care about the wine anymore. She did not care about anything, it seemed. She was heartbroken in a way that nothing could mend. When I asked her what I could do to help, she would get angry and then begin crying. I stopped asking and just learned to accept our relationship for what it was. I never brought up her brother. But I waited, always willing to be there for her when she needed me.

Lily and Leo took over the trade routes. Doc did not think they were ready, but Marcus insisted that they were the only ones that could do it at this point. It was a heavy responsibility for them, but as time went on, they not only continued the trade routes but also expanded them, moving even more cases of wine across greater distances.

As the war in the east pulled more German troops out of France, Doc saw an opportunity to reestablish a foothold in the south and east. It was a risky move, but it was the best for our operation.

The Freedom Fighters of France were becoming bolder as well. The United States had entered the war after the bombing of Pearl Harbor in Hawaii, and the Allied forces were beginning to see a faint glimmer of hope on the horizon. When I took Joshua into the city, we often heard whispers about insurgent forces taking out key trade lines and small German outposts, each small act of resistance compounding the overall effect on the occupation of France. It made me optimistic for the end of the war, for a return to normal, or perhaps a new world with a chance for hope.

There was a change on the wind; I could feel it. As Joshua and I walked back to the compound, I turned to him and smiled. It was a rare thing to smile in such days, but I mustered one anyway.

"That is a rare sight," he said, smirking. "What are you smiling about?"

I shook my head and thought about Claire, and my smile widened.

"Are you going to just keep smiling, or are you going to tell me why you are smiling all of a sudden?"

"There is a change on the horizon, my friend," I said in a bright tone.

Eliza

I woke to the sound of my baby girl crying in the crib on the other side of the room. I jumped out of bed and walked over to find her lying on her side, holding her left ear. Emilia had just turned three and had also developed a slight ear infection. I grabbed a thin cloth from the end table next to the bed, soaked it in warm water, and rubbed it in gentle circles over her ear until she stopped crying. She whimpered as I picked her up and cradled her in my arms, rubbing her back and whispering a Polish lullaby into her ear. It was her favorite—the only thing that lulled her to sleep again—and thus I sang it to her often as she was struggling to sleep.

I took her with me upstairs to the attic, where large glass windows stretched across the roof. The moon was bright and full, and the stars were shining with such brilliance that I sighed with delight as I looked up into the vast night sky.

It had been a long while since I escaped Warsaw, but even in those years of hiding and running, I only made it a small way up the Vistula River. The old man, who I later found out was named Klaus, took good care of me during my early months of pregnancy. The night when the midget let us through the door was the night I found out about the underground Polish army. Klaus was a strong believer in freeing Poland, as were many of the other men and women I encountered while staying in that bunker just three miles from the Polish capital.

The pregnancy was terrible but swift. Emilia was healthy when she was born, recovering so fast that my midwife called her a miracle from God. I, however, took almost three weeks to recover enough to get out of bed. Klaus let me stay with the group as long as I wished, but when I was ready to move on, he made sure that a trusted convoy of freedom fighters brought me up the river.

Three men escorted Emilia and me to the nearby town of Płock, where I was introduced to an old Jewish woman by the name of Camille. She owned a building with an antique storefront on the ground floor and kept a boardinghouse on the upper floor. I was one of nine Jewish refugees in her care.

I found an old rocking chair in the corner of the attic and pulled it out into the moonlight, wiping dust from the seat with my free hand. Emilia was pointing and babbling as I took my seat in the chair and began to rock her back to sleep. I was so tired. It had been a long winter, and most of the refugees were too weak to help Camille with her store. She was nearing eighty years of age, and her once vigorous productivity dwindled with each passing day. I had tried my best to help where I could, but with Emilia, my time was quite preoccupied.

I turned to the stairs as I heard Camille's soft footsteps ascending to the attic. She stopped just inside the door and smiled at Emilia and me rocking in the chair. My daughter's arm dangled from my left shoulder as she nodded in and out of consciousness.

"She is growing up so fast," Camille said in a hoarse whisper.

I smiled and rubbed my daughter's back with a gentle hand. "She has an ear infection, but I know she is going to come out of it soon. She is stronger than she looks; she has always been a fighter."

Camille grabbed an identical rocking chair and sat across from me, smiling. "She learned that trait from her mother," she said, pointing at me. "It takes a strong woman to live a life as you have. Always hiding, always on the run, all while raising a child without a father. That takes courage—something that you are full of, it seems."

I laughed and shook my head. I was now twenty-five, still young and naive, but after Emilia, I felt I had grown into womanhood almost overnight. I thought of my mother often, how she cared for Isabella and me when we were younger. She was so gentle with her touch and even gentler with her words. She was a God-fearing woman who had enough faith and courage to move a mountain. I longed to be half the woman she was.

"My mother was strong," I said. "She always was willing to sacrifice something that she cared for in return for our happiness and comfort."

"She sounds like a great woman," Camille said with a bright smile. "I know that you will walk in her shoes one day. Emilia will know what you had to sacrifice for the sake of her safety. It may take her a long while, but one day she will know what you did for her."

"I don't want her to know what I had to do for the sake of her safety. No one should ever have to know what sort of hell our country, our people, have experienced during this time. It should never be told; it should be forgotten."

Camille rubbed her tanned and wrinkled chin with small, stubby fingers crooked from her arthritis. "Let me ask you something, Eliza," she said, her gentle tone much like the one my mother used when teaching me something. "What good does it do someone to hide the past if they are trying to improve the future?"

I thought for a moment and then replied, "It is not beneficial at all."

"Right you are. Without written documents from our past, would we not fall back into our old ways of pain and misery, with no hope for a brighter future?"

"I suppose so," I said.

"Then tell me why your story should not be told to your daughter and to everyone else who is willing to listen?"

I swallowed and then said, "Because I don't want my daughter to know what terrible things I did in my past."

She sighed. "Eliza," Her voice was sweet, but stern. "You want your daughter to grow up to love and respect you, yes?"

I nodded in agreement.

"Then you must tell her the *truth*. It may be dark and full of misery and pain, but tell her the real story of what you overcame to save and to *provide* for her."

"I can't tell her the story. Not while she is still a child. She would not understand."

Camille reached out and grabbed my hand, tightening her grip as she stared into my eyes. "Then write it down for her to read when the time is right. Write it down so that she will remember what you did for her, for your family. Tell her the truth so that she will always remember—so that you will always remember."

Claire

I spent most days underground, hiding in my room, coming out only to eat and to use the bathroom when I could not avoid it. For the better half of three years, I didn't see the light of day. Call it pain, call it guilt: I dreaded the outside because I knew what horrors it held. At first it was hard to even get out of my bed, let alone leave my room, but after months that trickled by like sand in an hourglass, I began to regain my sense of humanity.

Gabriel was always there to check up on me. I often told him I was just fine, when in reality I was so broken on the inside that I just wanted to cry into his arms and scream. *I am stronger than that*, I told myself. He never asked about that day, never mentioned it, and I appreciated that aspect of his character. He was just there when I needed him to be, whether to talk or to sit in silence—he was always there.

I don't remember the first time I felt the butterflies in my stomach, but of late they came with such frequency that it felt unnatural when I *didn't* feel them. Whenever we were in the same room, I wanted to be near him. I wanted to touch his face and to pull him close to me, but I never acted on it.

"Do you want to play cards?" Gabriel said as he poked his head through my doorway. He stood sideways to peer over the threshold, his wiry smile and his shaggy hair filling my stomach with those familiar butterflies again.

I sat up in my bed and set the book I had been reading aside on the coverlet.

I pushed my hair back behind my ear and nodded. He smiled and practically skipped through the doorway to pull up a chair opposite my bed. He sat and crossed one leg over the other as he fished in his bag for a pack of playing cards. He pulled them out and popped the top off.

"What would you like to play today?" he said as he pulled the cards free of their cardboard prison and shuffled them in his hands with quick precision, sure not to lose a single one to the concrete floor below.

"I don't care," I mumbled. "Any game will do, really."

He laughed and leaned forward with a wide smile. "Now, that is not the Claire I have come to know these past few years! You are usually so decisive with your requests, I know that you are holding back." He leaned in and whispered, "What do you really want to play?"

To be honest, I didn't want to play a card game; instead I just wanted to be close to him, to feel his arms around me, to experience what it would be like to be held by such strong hands as his.

I bit my lip and said, "Hearts."

He laughed and nodded. "That's more like it."

He dealt the cards between us, his quick hands careful not to drop any. He finished and motioned for me to take the first turn. I did not care about the game—in fact, I could not remember how to play it—but I faked it as best I could.

He raised an eyebrow as I placed my first card but did not say anything. We played a few rounds back and forth, but eventually he placed his hand on mine and gave me a concerned look.

"Are you all right? You don't ever lose at hearts. What is going on?"

I pulled my hand away and shuffled my cards instead. "Nothing. I'm just distracted."

"Would you like me to leave?"

"No!" I said as I grasped his forearm, clamping hard. Realizing that the gesture was unnatural, I let go and retracted my arm.

He caught my hand and held it there for a moment, and a slight smirk crept onto his face.

"I just would . . . like you to stay awhile," I mumbled, averting my eyes.

He nodded, stood up, shut the door until it latched closed, and then made his way back to the bed. I didn't know what I wanted from him, except to know that he was there with me, keeping me safe. I scooted over on the bed, kicking the cards to the floor with a noiseless flutter. He climbed in next to me and pulled me close to him. I held his hand in mine and felt his warm breath on the back of my neck. I shuddered but pulled his hand into mine, pressing it against my stomach.

He kissed my neck once, then twice, then moved to my cheek. I gripped his hand and closed my eyes. *This is a dream*, I thought as he kissed me. *I will wake up and be alone in my bed, only wishing this were reality.*

I rolled over to face him. My nose touched his chin. I could feel the steady heartbeat coming from his chest. I placed my hands over it and lay there next to him. Then I moved my hands down his chest to his stomach, under his shirt, and pushed it upward until it was over his head and arms. He was muscular, but in a lean way. I kissed his chest and felt his body shudder under the path of my wandering lips.

Soon we found ourselves naked under the blankets. A single candle on my nightstand cast the only light. I had never felt so exposed, and yet I was not ashamed with him. If ever there was a night of passion and blossoming love, it was that night with Gabriel in my cellar bedroom. As war raged above, our love, despite our differences, rose from the ashes of the world and began to bloom into the beauty it was destined to become.

Joshua

Violet and I saw each other with increasing frequency in the years after our first kiss. Oftentimes I caught myself daydreaming about her while I stacked crates or wrote letters for Doc. I was a hopeless romantic, but, man, was I in love with her. We kept our relationship secret from the others so as to not raise any suspicion or concerns. She and Leo were in charge of the trade routes, moving the wine to and fro with the other conspirators across the countryside. Our interactions as we went about our tasks at the compound were short, but when we were given a chance to see each other, we made sure to use every ounce of time we could.

When she returned from a journey, whether a one-day or a three-week trip, I was always there to greet her at the barn. I claimed I was tending the horses, but instead I stole as many kisses from her as I could. Mother was suspicious, I could tell, but Petyr was oblivious—he was eleven now, but had no cares for my love life.

Since our arrival, Petyr's health had improved, but my mother's health had recently begun to decline at a rapid rate. Doc was unsure of the cause and had recommended that my mother be confined to her bed back in February. In the three months since, she had obeyed, rising only to wash or to use the bathroom, and with each passing day her symptoms seemed to get worse.

"This sickness will pass, I'm sure," she said to me one afternoon as I fed her chicken broth from a wooden bowl. "Don't worry about me. I'm stronger than you'd ever expect."

My mother always had a hardy spirit, but each time I visited her, I could tell that her strength was dissipating at an alarming rate. Petyr noticed as well, and his already worried state of mind intensified as he watched our mother weaken.

"Is Mother going to improve soon, Joshua?" Petyr asked as we sorted bottles from their crates into a larger box marked as fruit.

I wanted to tell him the truth: our mother was bound to die sooner rather than later, but I swallowed the truth and spat out a lie instead.

"Sure she will," I said without looking at him. "She is a strong woman; you know that about her. She's a fighter, and what do fighters do?"

"Fighters always win!"

I smiled and patted his shoulder. "That's right. Mother is going to win this battle, and afterward, she will be stronger than ever."

I knew it was a lie, but still I kept on smiling. It would come soon, I knew, and with it a tidal wave of brokenness and pain. I tried to prepare for it as best I could, but even as I did, I feared that I would never be ready for that final blow.

Gabriel

I left Claire's room as quietly as I could the next morning. I had guard duty at five, and I did not want to be late, for fear of Marcus's wrath. Even after nearly four years of knowing the man, he still did not trust me, even though I had proven myself time and time again.

I made my way to the upper level and snuck out into the muggy May air. When I breathed, it felt as if a wet blanket had been draped over my mouth. Within the first few minutes of being outside, I was wiping my brow with a sweaty forearm. I swung the rifle over my shoulder and walked down the dirt road to the southern checkpoint where the patrol started.

I had made the trek countless times before; I knew the thickets and winding trails so well that I could make the trip with my eyes closed. I walked slowly due to the humidity, or perhaps because I was tired from the night before. I longed to be back in bed with Claire, but I knew that patrolling benefited the whole compound, including her, and thus the trip was somewhat bearable.

I walked for about twenty minutes until I reached a small clearing with a shallow pond at its center. Usually, the pond hosted some of the hundreds of wild animals in the area, ranging from deer to foxes, but on this particular morning it was abandoned except for me. A thin fog hovered over the water like a ghost lingering over a grave. Grey clouds shaded the moon above and made it hard to see even the other side of the clearing.

"I was wondering when you'd finally make your way here, Gabriel," a voice called from the other side of the pond. "You are slower than Marcus. Perhaps it is the humidity. For that, I would not blame your sloth-like pace."

I held my rifle firm in my hand but released it when I recognized the voice hidden by the fog.

"What are you doing here, Henning?"

The tall and slender man strolled along the pond until he was only a few feet away. He wore civilian clothing in case anyone happened to stumble upon this unusual meeting. He removed his cap and rubbed his pointed chin. He looked *older*, due not to age but rather extreme stress.

"It is good to see you too, Gabriel," he quipped. "I didn't know if our paths would ever cross again after I had heard you'd been roped into helping those French civilians with their treasonous plans. I knew that Claire would scamper back to her hovel, but I did not expect that you would fall so far also. It is a shame, really; you could have been one of the greats, remembered for ages to come as a marvelous war hero among your countrymen. Instead you have fallen for a whore of a French girl."

I whipped my rifle around and pointed it at the German officer's head.

"Don't think I won't do it, you bastard," I growled through gritted teeth.

He did not even flinch. Instead he waved his hand as if to dismiss my threats without a second thought. "I believe you have every capability of shooting me where I stand, but you would be gunned down just as fast."

I heard seven pistols cock around the clearing's edge. *Stupid*, I thought. *I should have known he would not come alone.*

"Now," he said, clapping his hands together as he smiled, "are we going to talk as civilized men, without these *guns?*"

I lowered my rifle and slung it back over my shoulder. "What do you want?"

"It's time for you to follow up with your end of our bargain."

Eliza

A crisp knock at my door diverted my attention from my game of hide-and-seek with Emilia. She had grown to love the game, and I loved playing it with her, even when I was far too tired to muster any real enthusiasm. I handed her a wooden block that I had found in the house, a worn letter *J* marked on one side and an apple on the opposite side written in Polish. It was her favorite toy—the only real toy that she had to call her own.

I told her to play and went to the door, opening it only a crack. Camille stood on the other side of the door, a letter clutched in her hand.

"Eliza," she said, "this letter has just arrived for you."

I opened the door farther and took the envelope. "It's unmarked," I said as I examined it from multiple angles. "Do you know who brought it?"

"I did not recognize the boy, but he said he was sent by a woman. Her name escapes my mind at the moment . . . Eve . . . Evelynn . . ."

My eyes grew wide as I shouted, "Iva!"

Camille smiled. "Yes, that was it. Iva. It seems you know her?"

I ignored the question and turned back into my room, ripping the envelope open with furious fingers, trying to get to the note that was enclosed inside.

I read it without taking time to blink.

Dearest Eliza,

I hope this letter finds you well, as I am putting myself into a lot of danger for contacting you. I am in hiding. The Nazis are becoming ruthless with their search and seizures. Since you left four years ago, the guards have doubled and the city has become a cesspool of crime, corruption, and random killings—by both civilians and soldiers. Yet despite that, I have not forgotten you, nor have I ceased my efforts to help you track down your beloved sister, Isabella.

Although I have not been able to find her myself, I have heard word that she is in fact alive! My sources in the Home Army of Warsaw told me that your sister never made it to northern Poland with the small group of orphans on their first attempt and were in fact abducted, seeming to disappear for three years until she resurfaced again about three months ago in the outskirts of Warsaw, near death and quite malnourished.

Irek, the Home Army commander, ordered that she be cared for and nursed back to health. She made a full recovery and is now acting as an informant for the Home Army, passing on vital information across Poland.

I did not want to contact you sooner in fear of being caught myself, but as soon as I have more information about your sister's whereabouts, I will be sure to pass it along to you.

She is alive, Eliza! Have faith restored once more. Soon you and your daughter will be with your sister and able to leave this accursed country once and for all!

Your friend and ally always,

Iva

I folded the note and covered my mouth as tears fell from my eyes. Camille rushed to the bed and embraced me in a hug.

"What is it, dear? What did the letter say?"

"My sister," I choked between the tears. "My sister is alive."

Gabriel

"Bargain? We never made any bargain," I protested.

He smiled and snapped his fingers. A short soldier hustled from the tree line clutching a manila envelope in his hand.

"So easy to forget. I figured it would happen to you. For a man with an agenda such as yours, these lesser responsibilities seem to slip through the cracks unless you focus on them with all your effort. Not to worry, I brought an extra, *updated* copy for you."

The soldier handed me the envelope. I opened it and withdrew a file with a photo attached to the top right-hand corner.

"No," I said without hesitation as I slipped the file back into the envelope and handed it to Henning.

He frowned. "That is not the right answer, Gabriel."

"I don't really care about what you think is the right answer; I am not going to do your dirty work. I am happy and established. If I were to run off on your wild-goose chase, I would lose everything I have here."

"That is exactly why I came to you now," he said. "You are too comfortable, Gabriel. You are a German soldier; you do not just stay complacent for almost four years when deep inside you have a longing to *serve*."

"I can't do it," I said, clutching the envelope. "I'm not a killer anymore."

Henning stepped closer, until we were mere inches apart.

"This is to ensure the future of our country, Gabriel. Claire will understand that you had no choice but to serve. Hitler's time is coming to an end, sooner than you realize, but if you do not take care of this problem in the east, I fear that taking him out will be futile. This girl knows too much and must be neutralized before she is able to communicate to the Allied forces what is *actually* happening in the eastern territories. Our best-kept secret, our *final solution*, is at the risk of exposure if we do not dispose of these . . . mongrels that have stuck their noses into business that does not concern them."

"Why now?"

"When I first approached you about the problem, I knew only a few things about her, and to be honest, I figured that this *situation* would blow over. Yet as the years passed, she continued to ask questions, and she now works hand in hand with the Home Army of Poland, gathering information about our assets in the east."

"And why didn't you just take care of her then, when you knew that she was poking around where she didn't need to be?"

He sighed. "I will admit it, I was arrogant in my thinking that she would not stumble upon any useful information. After all, she is just a child, but my first mistake was in discounting her ability due to her age. I sent to have her arrested, but she caught wind of it and hid before my agents could find her. No one saw her for months after that, and I figured she had given up on her patriotic efforts. But I was proven wrong when she surfaced yet again in northern Poland after the surrender of Stalingrad."

"Why did she come back, then? The Russians are far too occupied to be of any importance to this . . . child."

"Not to her, Gabriel . . . to the Home Army."

"What do you mean? Are they planning to attack with the Russians? They don't have the men to pull off such an attack."

"That is what I thought at first, but then it dawned upon me: perhaps the Poles want to fight not on Russian soil but instead on their home front. The Poles are a patient lot, and I believe that they mean to strike us where we are most vulnerable in the east."

"Warsaw," I said.

"Precisely," he replied, his lips curling into a snarl. "We have been so preoccupied with the Russians that we failed to see the Polish conspiracy forming in our occupied territory. I predict that this girl's resurfacing was not coincidence but instead a plan timed to rally loyal Poles to the cause of the secret rebellion that will soon engulf Warsaw and the surrounding cities."

"Do you believe they will attack soon?"

"Not likely," he replied. "The Poles don't have the men, as you said, and will count on the Russians to aid in retaking the capital. Sources have informed me that this girl is one of the best spies the Home Army has because she is so young that no one suspects her."

I read the profile again, scanning over the small notes made throughout.

"She is only twelve?"

"Age is only a number, Gabriel," Henning said as he lit a cigarette. He took a long drag. "She may be young, but she is a spy nonetheless. She must be taken care of properly."

"Why not have one of your pony boys do it for you?" I sneered.

Henning frowned. "Because the Poles know my men. They have been in Poland since 1939. They can spot a soldier from a mile away. But you," he said, pointing, "given the right clothing and accent, you could pull off being a Pole." He looked at me with a cocked head and bit his lip. "Well, maybe a Dane. Regardless, you are the man for the job, and you will do it well."

I frowned and put the file under my arm. "Where is she?"

"Poland," he said, and he chuckled at his own joke. "Gdańsk, to be exact. Two weeks ago, she made contact with a Polish informant working undercover for the Reich. The Allies approached him first, but we have a larger price to offer."

He snapped his fingers again, and the short soldier sprang from the trees carrying a large cargo bag on his shoulder. He dropped it next to Henning's feet and then scampered back to the tree line.

Henning bent down, inspected the contents, and then turned back to me.

"These are your personal belongings now. Nothing representing German descent; you are now known as Benedykt Nadolski from Białystok, fleeing to the port city of Gdańsk in fear of the invading Russians. Do you know Polish?"

"A few phrases," I said as I tried to process everything that was happening.

"I'd suggest you learn more than a few phrases," he said, handing a translation book to me. "Now"—he pulled out a map—"you need to head to the Port of Calais. From there, you will travel by boat through the North Sea to Bremerhaven. I will meet you there and bring you to Berlin, where you will board a train to Włocławek and then on to Gdańsk." He handed over a small slip of paper with an address on it. "Go here, and my informant in Gdańsk will help you from there."

"What about all the tickets and boarding passes for the trains and ship? Won't they be suspicious why a Polish civilian is in France, trying to get back into Poland?"

"Don't worry about the checkpoints; I have already taken care of you, Gabriel." He smiled as he placed a hand on my shoulder and squeezed. "Now, lose the rifle and get on your way. The ship departs in two days, and it is a three-day trip from here."

"What about Claire?" I said, my heart sinking into my stomach like an anchor in the ocean.

"What about her?"

"I have to go back and tell her what I am doing. I can't just leave without telling her where I am going."

Henning folded his arms behind his back and frowned. "She has become a distraction to you, I can see. You told me that night that she meant nothing to you, but here you want to explain yourself before you leave. You slept with her, didn't you?"

I blushed but didn't say anything.

He nodded. "You leave me with no choice, then." He removed his pistol from the belt loop under his shirt. "I will make her death quick and painless." Turning to the short soldier, he waved his hand and said, "Kill him, and be sure to burn the body."

The soldier nodded and then smiled as he raised his own pistol and took aim at me.

"I'll go!" I shouted.

Henning stopped and turned around as he loaded his gun.

"I'll go," I repeated, desperation in my voice. "Just . . . just don't hurt Claire. Don't hurt any of them. They are good people, and . . . if keeping them safe means that I have to leave . . . then I'll leave."

Henning stared at me with his cold gaze, but he eventually nodded and said, "Your ship leaves in two days. I suggest you leave now."

Claire

I woke to an empty space next to me. His impression was still molded in the mattress, and the blanket where he had been just hours before. Naked, exposed, just like me right now. I clutched the blanket tight against me as I scanned the room to see if he had left any keepsakes for me. I knew that he had a patrol this morning, but when I looked at my clock, I grew concerned.

9:24. He should be back by now. I bet he is in the cellar room having breakfast. A smart man would not just come waltzing into my room without a reason other than to see me again. No reason to make the others grow suspicious, especially after last night.

I crawled out of bed and put on a fresh pair of clothing; baggy pants and a loose grey shirt, nothing extravagant. I put my hair up as I did most mornings and made my way to the cellar, where the others were already enjoying a bountiful breakfast. They greeted me as I entered, and I smiled and returned a friendly hello and good morning. He was not there.

I took my seat next to Leo on the end of the table. Grabbing an apple, I began to cut it into slices since I did not feel ambitious enough to rip chunks from it with my teeth. As I ate, I listened into the conversation that was already in play around the table.

"I have heard that with the defeat at Stalingrad that the Germans are pulling back into eastern Poland—by the thousands!"

Violet said from the other end of the table. She was next to Joshua, closer than usual, I noticed, but I kept the observation to myself. "I think that the Russians are going to try an offensive push into Poland in hopes of weakening the eastern front."

Doc grunted as he slurped his porridge; his glasses slid down his nose each time he took a spoonful to his mouth.

"What was the grunt for, Doc?" Violet asked, almost offended.

He cleared his throat and pointed his spoon at my sister, his eyes narrowed and his brows scrunched toward his nose, making them look like furry caterpillars.

"The Russians may have won Stalingrad, but they cannot marshal a concerted attack on the German front. The Germans are dug in too deep, and they will fight until their last breath to prevent the Russians from taking that ground."

"What about the Allies to the west?" Joshua said. "When will the United States join the war in Europe?"

"They have already," Leo interrupted. "They have sent pilots and a few troops to help with the supplies, but their focus is not here in the European theater. They have their own problems with the Japanese after Pearl Harbor. I predict they will never even set foot in Europe. Their president is far too indecisive to make an educated decision. By the time they get here, the war will be over."

"At least they are supplying the British," Violet retorted. "What are we, the French people, doing? We are all cowards for hiding underground in cellars and caves while the real fight is out there. Are we so juvenile that we have to have someone else fight our battles for us?"

The room went silent, all eyes on Violet. She stammered for some support from Leo, then me, and then finally turned to Joshua and raised her eyebrows, expecting him to say something.

"You are right to be frustrated, Violet," Doc said with compassion, "but to say that we, the French people, have done nothing in the war effort would be ludicrous and insulting. Look around you. Even before the war started, we were concealing thousands of gallons of wine in hopes of preserving them from the impending threat. We have done much with so little."

"But we need to do *more*," she pleaded. "This is a golden opportunity to assemble something against the Germans. With their focus in the east, we are in a prime spot to pave the way for the Allies to gain a foothold in France."

"What are you saying?" Marcus said.

"The Allies are growing in number each day. The Russians in the east, the British and French on the west, and the United States, the formidable beast that woke from its slumber to take back the Pacific from the Japanese. The Germans are tired. They have been at it for nearly five years, and they are starting to slide backward instead of making strides forward. This is the calm before the storm. There are groups already formed in the city and across the country—"

"No, no, no!" Doc shouted, attempting to silence Violet before she could finish.

"—to rise up against the German occupiers. If we *join them*—"

Doc slammed his fist on the table and stood in such a fury it seemed steam was about to spout from his ears.

"If we join them, this entire operation will be for naught, and in the end, we will all be dead!"

He stormed off, and Leo chased after him. Margret gave Violet a scowl and then shuffled after her husband and adopted grandson. Violet took off in the opposite direction, Joshua chasing her with a quiet look of concern.

Petyr, Marcus, and I were the only three left at the table. We looked at one another and then resumed eating in silence. I lingered to clean the table after we finished, in the hope that Gabriel would come in, but still he did not arrive. I made my way back to my room, closed the door, and went back to bed. He would return when I woke up. Perhaps he'd even join me again tonight. I smiled as I closed my eyes and drifted off once again.

Joshua

"Violet, come on, slow down!" I shouted as I chased her down the hall and up the stairs.

She let the door crash against the house as she sprinted out into the rows of budding grapevines. I kept shouting, kept chasing, until I finally caught up to her and grabbed her wrist.

"Violet," I pleaded as I turned her around and tried to hold her steady.

She was trembling. Her eyes were wet, and strands of tear-soaked hair straggled across her face. I tried to pull her into a hug, but she resisted until I drew her tight against me and shushed her, kissing her forehead. We sank to the field until I was sitting and she rested against my chest, staining my shirt with her many tears.

"It's not fair!" she sobbed. "It's not fair to let them fight for us. Dmitri fought for us. He was so brave. He would be ashamed if he were to see us like this. We are moles, Joshua, living underground in fear of the monster that has just exposed his underbelly to us. We need to strike it *now!*"

I rubbed her back and murmured empty words to console her back into reality. "Look," I said when her breathing had calmed, pulling her away from me so that I could look at her directly. "I know what Doc said was not what you wanted to hear—"

"You are starting to sound just like him," she said through gritted teeth.

"But listen," I said, grabbing her hands, "you can't let him stop you from doing what you need to do. I can't stop you either, but you are gone so often already. We all care for your safety. I would not know what to do if you were killed while on one of your trips. I would not have a reason to live on. We have to fight a different war, a *secret* war. It is just as important as if it were with guns and grenades. Ours is an economic war to keep our country from being completely sunk after this nightmare is over."

"Joshua!" Petyr screamed from the doorway of the house. "Joshua! Come quick!"

I could tell he was quite upset. He was waving to me with such desperation that I jumped to my feet and ran. I knew what was happening. I did not need an explanation; I just needed to run faster.

Gabriel

The trip north was grueling, to say the least. I slept no more than three hours the first day of the trek, yet despite my progress, I was still far from Calais by the time I finally took a rest outside Arras. I stayed away from the city and instead stuck to the forest road that I was forging by myself.

I thought of Claire in every moment I could spare from the constant pain in my feet and legs from the rough terrain. I hated myself for leaving without letting her know the reason for my absence, but Henning had left me little choice. After I had a few hours' rest, I continued northward but made it only a few miles more before I collapsed, exhausted, under an oak tree just off the dirt road.

I woke to the rumbling of a truck followed by the raw holler of a man who needed to cut down on his smoke intake.

"Hello!" he rasped. "What are you doing under this oak tree, good sir? Are you traveling somewhere?"

I stood and rubbed my eyes free of the drowsiness. "*Oui*. I'm headed northward to Calais to board a ferry to Denmark, yet I fear I won't make it in time. I am still a day's walk away, and the ship leaves in the morning."

The old man's jowls shook as he laughed. "Aye, you need a ride! So happens I am on my way to Dunkirk! Just a few miles out of the way to go to Calais! Come, hop in the truck with me! I will get you to your ship on time!"

I smiled and thanked the man as I climbed up into the passenger seat of his large truck. It smelled like strong vodka. As I looked around the cabin, I glimpsed an open bottle wedged between the door and the man's seat, covered to the lip of the bottle with a brown paper bag. I sighed and slammed the door. I could now smell the alcohol on the man's breath, but I had no choice but to trust him at this point.

"Headed north to get onto a ferry boat, eh? I've been on a ferry once; crossed the channel with my first wife."

I was too exhausted for small talk, but I humored him. "And did you enjoy the ferry?"

"Bah!" he shouted, lifting his hands from the wheel and waving them in a furious manner. "I hated the trip! Hated the ferry. I got seasick and puked all over the railing. My wife left me after that trip."

"I . . . I'm sorry to hear that."

"Ha! She was only my wife by word of mouth. I never *actually* married her, just slept with her and told people we were married."

"She was a mistress?"

He shrugged and then took a swig from the bottle in the brown bag. "*Mistress*," he slurred, "is such a strong word to use for such cases. I would just say . . . a *fancy* woman."

"I'm going to just try to sleep a bit."

"Fit to it what you will. Don't worry, I won't touch you or nothing," he said with a wink and a quiet giggle.

I rolled my eyes and readjusted in my seat so that my head rested against the door. My eyes closed, but the humming of the man as he drove mixed with the roar of the engine as we made our way down the road, kept me from falling asleep. Over the next two hours I obtained no more than ten minutes of solid sleep at a time before the noisy truck or the burping Frenchman woke me up again.

"How much farther till we reach Calais?" I muttered, half-drowsy. My eyelids were heavy, and I could barely make out what was in front of us just beyond the headlights of the old truck.

"Another . . . forty kilometerssss. But don't worry, I'll gett usss there safffe," he slurred. I watched his head bob and his eyelids droop.

Before I knew it, the man had passed out and leaned left, taking the wheel in a full turn with him. I lunged for the wheel, but before I could correct the drunkard's error, we were careening down the steep ditch and into the river below.

The right wheel snagged a boulder, flipping the truck a quarter turn to the left and throwing me against the roof and then the window, cracking it with my right arm. The truck slid on its left side and then flipped onto the roof just as we hit the water. The unconscious drunk fell from his seat onto the dashboard, the windshield opening a gigantic gash along his forehead. He groaned, but his eyes remained closed.

I was wide awake now, adrenaline stirring in my body like a wild flame fueled with gasoline. The truck sank into the murky water inch by inch. The cracks in my window and the windshield began to leak ice-cold water into the cabin. I gasped as the water splashed my bare skin. It poured in now, around the sides of the door and through the rusted undercarriage, and I could not force the door open against the weight of the water outside. I took one last gasp of air before the cabin filled completely.

The truck hit bottom. Suspended in the murky, frigid water, I kicked at the cracked window; nothing happened. I tried the windshield; again, nothing. The glass was too thick for my water-slowed kicks to break.

I dug with frantic hands through my pack until I found my knife and set its point at the corner of the window. With one swift smack on the end of my knife, the glass of the passenger window dissipated into the water like sea foam.

I grabbed my pack and pushed myself out of the truck to the surface of the river. I kicked hard and opened my mouth as I broke the surface. I shuddered as I treaded water, my breath short, my frozen body aching. I coughed and blinked hard, trying to regain both my vision and my breath before I went back for the driver. I tossed my bag at the shoreline, where it barely snagged the bank.

I sucked in a stabbing-cold breath and dove, kicking with such ferocity that I reached the broken window with three kicks. I found the man inside, floating against the seat, his bottle of vodka floating just below him. His eyes were wide open, bloodshot and horror stricken. His mouth was open also, and I could tell he had tried to take in air and inhaled water. I seized his arm and pulled him out of the wrecked truck, hauling him up and out of the water on the far bank next to my bag.

He was not breathing and already blue in the face. I felt ashamed that I had grabbed my pack instead of his arm when I made my escape. I sat on the riverbank, shivering, the dead man beside me, his eyes wide and mouth gaping, imitating his final moments of life.

Before I left, I closed the man's eyes and mouth, covered his body with a spare blanket I had in my bag, and prayed that his soul might be granted peace by God, even though I did not believe the prayer myself. I walked for the remainder of the night and into the next morning, not stopping until I reached the Port of Calais.

Joshua

I burst through the door of our room and ran to my mother's bedside, dropping to my knees and groping for her right hand.

Petyr ran in behind me, out of breath and knowing full well what was happening. He watched from a distance.

"Petyr," I whispered, "go find Doc."

"But—"

"Go," I commanded, not breaking my gaze away from my mother.

He scampered out of the room. I gripped Mother's hand tight in my own, squeezing it until her eyelids opened, exposing her old, tired eyes.

She searched the ceiling for a second and then realized I was at her side. Her gaze met mine, and she smiled as best she could.

"Joshua," she whispered.

"Yes, Mum," I said, gripping her hand again, my eyes watering and tears eventually falling down my cheeks. "I'm here. I am here; just hold on a few more minutes. Petyr went to go get Doc."

I heard Petyr's yell in the distance as he searched for Doc. A return call signaled that he had heard my brother. *Only a few minutes now*, I thought. *Just a few more minutes, and then it will be all right.*

"Joshua," my mother said again, her voice strained.

"Don't speak, Mum. Save your strength," I said. I turned to the door and yelled, "Doc! Hurry! My mum needs your help!"

"Joshua." My mother squeezed my hand. It caught me by surprise that she had enough energy to say my name so sharply. I examined her, waiting for her to say something.

"I am going home, Joshua, to be with your father."

I shook my head. "No, no, you are going to be all right, Mum. Just wait and see. *Doc! Hurry!*"

"Joshua, I am dying. There is nothing you can do for me now. It is too late. Don't let our last few moments be us trying to talk over one another."

I took her other hand in mine and kissed both.

"Take care of your brother. He will be scared."

"I am scared," I said.

"I know you are, but if you live in fear your whole life, you will never become great. I have lived in fear for so long that I forgot what it was like to actually live. Don't be like me, Joshua."

I nodded and then forced a smile. "I am in love, Mum. Can you believe it?"

She smiled and let out a quiet laugh. Blood bubbled from her lips even though they still formed a smile.

"You were in love from the day you saw her," she whispered. "Marry her, love her, and lead her."

"I will."

The footsteps and shouts grew in intensity. I could hear Doc shouting for me to keep her talking, but I knew it was too late. My mother was not going to make it this time.

"I love you, Joshua," she said as she caressed my face.

"I love you too, Mum."

She smiled again, closed her eyes, and let her hand fall from mine. I leaned in and kissed her forehead and then slumped against the cabinet next to her bedside. The ticking of the clock kept rhythm above me, but it seemed that time had halted.

I folded my hands.

Bowed my head.

And began to pray.

Gabriel

The journey was long across the sea. I slept for most of it but went to the deck to get some fresh air when I became nauseated. There were not many passengers on the ferry, maybe a hundred at best. The living space was small but comfortable, and I didn't have to share it with anyone. I made the most of the privacy, writing notes and letters to Claire—none of which I could send. I wanted to go back to her, but my terrible mission stood between us. I could only pray that she thought I had been taken, rather than thinking that I had abandoned her after our night together.

It took a day to reach northern Germany. When we reached port, I made my way down the wooden walkway into the bustling crowds boarding and exiting their respective ships in the massive dockyard. It was a mess, to say the least. The German guards on duty were doing their best to control the civilians, but even their jurisdiction was limited when tested against angry mothers with infants and small children.

I removed myself from the massive crowd and made my way to an alleyway that led to another street. It was as if I had passed into an entirely new city: this street was quiet and clean. There were a few German boys playing marbles in the lot nearest to me, but when I walked by, they paid no attention to me. I wanted to have the same mind-set as those boys, a sense of peace and a playful manner. Even in a war-plagued world, they still found time to play a simple game of marbles. I envied them.

I circled back to the port and found Henning at the top of a hill, just up the road from where my ferry had docked. He waited beside his black car, the Nazi flags fluttering from the front bumper, wearing a black coat and matching hat as he puffed on a cigarette and overlooked the park next to him. I approached but did not say anything. A pair of pince-nez sunglasses rested upon his straight nose as he observed children playing soccer.

"I was beginning to think you were not coming," he said without looking at me.

"I had some . . . complications come up on the way to Calais," I replied. The drunkard's face flashed into my mind but dissipated just as fast as it had appeared.

He nodded. "So I had heard. A shame for the man. He was a good source of information when we needed it. A bloody fool, as we found out, but a good man nonetheless."

"You knew of this man?"

Henning turned to me and smiled that cruel, twisted grin that I had grown to hate. "Did you think the man just stumbled upon you by accident?" he said with a laugh. "Come now, Gabriel. I do not let things happen by mere chance. Yes, he was sent by me to get you to Calais on time. However, these things do happen, and I am glad you made it safe back to your homeland."

"Why didn't you just take me with you instead of going through the hassle of the driver and the ferry?"

"Precautions," he said. "Best to not be seen together traveling cross country. Someone might recognize you from your earlier life.

He clapped his hands together and said, "Shall we, then? We have much to discuss, and the road to Berlin is long. I am happy to travel with you now, however, as we are back in Germany. I have grown fond of you Gabriel. I never know what to expect, and that makes me quite excited, to say the least!"

"Bruno!" Henning shouted as he opened his door on the rear passenger side. The portly soldier I had seen just a few days earlier emerged from the lead car and ran down the street, his face reddened by the sudden change in pace. "Bruno, bring us some whiskey for the trip. I am sure that my friend Gabriel here will need a good drink to make it through."

The soldier nodded and ran back to the lead car, disappearing into the back seat.

"Come now, Gabriel. You are to ride with me. Hansel will take your bag for you and place it in the car behind us."

I gave my bag to the young man in uniform and climbed in next to Henning. I closed the door and sighed. I looked out the window as we crept down the barren street, longing for the solitude of my cabin on the ferry. I closed my eyes and thought of Claire, whispering to myself, *Be strong: it will all be over soon.*

Eliza

The next letter arrived a few days later. The same style of envelope lay in front of my door. Camille had knocked and yelled through the door that I had received a letter, but with Emilia nearly asleep in my arms, I just kept rocking.

It seemed like hours before I could open the door and grab the envelope, tearing it open before I was even back in the room. I could hear light chatter in the family room downstairs, but I did not want to join them just yet.

> *Eliza,*
>
> *I received your letter. I am happy to hear that you are all right; it has been hard to keep it secret from you that I am still alive. I have changed my alias twice since you left, but I believe I am safe for the time being. I appreciate your concern for my safety, but my time in Warsaw is not yet finished. Irek plans to be in communication with Russian generals about the inevitable invasion of Poland. To be honest, I am unsure what will come of this. Irek is hopeful, but I do not think the Russians intend to leave our country in the hands of us Poles.*

Pray to your God that an oppressive leader does not again enslave us.

As for your questions about your sister, I have new information as of yesterday. It appears she contacted an informant in Gdańsk a few days ago regarding sensitive details of the German Relocation Plan in eastern Germany and through-out Poland. I am unsure what this means for your sister, but I am afraid for her safety. There have been rumors that your sister is now the target of a dangerous German assassin. I pray that she will be safe; however, the situation has turned quite grim as of late. I am happy to have found her, but I fear that it was better she remained hidden.

Keep safe, my friend.

Love,

Iva

My heart sank as I read the letter a second time. *An assassin sent to kill my poor little sister? What information does she have that drives the Germans to send an assassin after her?* These thoughts and more rushed through my head as I sat against the wall with a heavy heart and swimming mind. I had to do something, but what good could I do here? Gdańsk was where my sister was; that was where I needed to go also. I packed my bag and prepared to leave that evening. My sister was in dire need of help, and I planned to do the best I could for her.

Gabriel

A light tap on my shoulder stirred me from my slumber. I sat up in a hurry, my vision dizzy from the sudden jerk of my head.

"Easy, sir," a young solder said as he set his hand on my shoulder. "We have arrived in Berlin."

I rubbed my eyes and looked out at the dark street around the parked car. The streetlamps were bright but cast an eerie glow on the buildings beyond. It had been years since I'd last visited Berlin—near twelve, I figured. The city was strange to me: it did not feel like the Germany I had known growing up, the one I had loved since I was a boy. This Germany was a dark entity without a single ounce of goodness to its name.

I stepped out of the car and rubbed my neck as I scanned the area. We were at the train station. A lone train sat at the depot, its large fog lamp illuminating the tracks, making it appear like a silver ghost ready to pierce into the darkness and beyond.

I recognized the man who awakened me: it was Hansel. I studied him; he was merely a boy, young and scared—I could tell by his posture. He did not look me in the eye, but instead gazed around the depot landing, watching for unwanted figures to step into the light.

"Henning decided not to see me off, I presume?"

Hansel straightened and put his shoulders back as he snapped his head toward me, fixing his eyes upon mine.

"No, sir," he said in a cracked voice. "He had other matters to attend to, more urgent than your send-off to the east."

I rolled my eyes and removed a cigarette from my jacket, lit it with one of my matches, and began to enjoy the nicotine with every long drag. I felt the grogginess fall away from me as I breathed in the smoke and then blew it out again.

"Do you have your ticket stub, sir?"

I closed my eyes and put my head back as I let out a puff of smoke into the air.

"It is in my bag," I said. I glanced back and spotted it on the ground next to the car. "Fish it out for me, please?"

The soldier dug through my bag until he came up with the brown ticket written in German. He handed it to me, and I thanked him.

"Are you from Berlin, Hansel?"

"Well, yes," he said with hesitation.

I turned my gaze toward him again. "Why are you nervous? I'm not a threat."

"It is not you I am nervous about, sir," he said, rubbing his arm. "My mother and father were taken from their home a week ago, before I was assigned to be Henning's personal attendant. I . . . I am a Jew, sir."

I removed the cigarette and stared at the boy. "And why are you in Henning's personal service, exactly?"

The boy wiped a tear from his left eye. "Henning said—" He paused for a brief moment. "Henning said that since I was still fit to serve that I would serve him for anything he wished of me. I am not a real soldier, sir; he just gave me this uniform so that I would not be questioned about my past. He told me that if I served him like a loyal servant, my parents would not be harmed. I had no choice but to comply with his order."

"Where are you parents now, Hansel?"

The train whistle blew a thunderous decree that the train would be departing in a few minutes. The passengers began their silent exodus from the train depot, making their somber march toward the silver train without a single noise except for the scuffing of shoes on the wooden panels and the dragging of suitcases too heavy for a single person to carry.

"I . . . I do not know where they are. The last time I saw them, they were boarding a train headed to the east. Henning said they were being relocated to a shelter somewhere in eastern Germany, although he did not say where. I just want to see my parents again; I am an only child."

I pitied the boy, for Henning had told me of a relocation process that was being issued for Jews in the east, both in Germany and Poland. He had not told me much, other than that it was "the best for the people."

"You will see your parents again. In time," I assured him. "The war is on the cusp of ending, and we are to be the sure victors, it seems. When you have served your time, Henning will keep his word. He always does."

The promise was full of hot air. I did not believe anything that came from my mouth, but still I pushed it as if I were confident in Henning's plans. The man was a maniac. A genius, true, but a maniac nonetheless. The boy's parents were already dead, I figured, and I would be a devil to tell him—yet I felt that it needed to be shared.

"I just wanted someone else to say it too," he said, wiping away the tears. "I had almost given up hope and wanted to discontinue my service, but thank you, Gabriel. I will serve until the war is done."

"And a mighty fine job you will do at it, friend," I said as I shook his hand with a firm grip. "Now, I'd best be going." I grabbed my bag and turned toward the train.

I took a few steps before Hansel called out to me, "Mr. Gabriel! Your ticket, sir!"

I smiled as he handed it to me. "You are a good lad, Hansel. I will see you soon, and when I do, I'll be sure to buy you a drink for my thanks."

I thanked him once more, boarded the train, and took my seat next to the window. I gazed out at the platform and found Hansel in the sea of silent people. We exchanged a wave and a final farewell.

I never saw the boy after that day. I came to find out after the war that he died soon after our farewell in the death camp of Treblinka in central Poland. Henning's personal request.

Joshua

The funeral was not elaborate. Mother was a simple woman, and she would have thought an extravagant funeral to be tacky and unnecessary. We had no wood to make a coffin, so instead we wrapped her in a white sheet and laid wildflowers on her chest. She was buried under an old oak tree on the top of the hill about a mile away from the house and vineyard. It was the only tree in the area, and it overlooked a spectacular view of the neighboring vineyards.

Petyr took it the hardest, as I expected he might. He was always closest to Mum, even though he told me many times that he was afraid of her when she grew angry. I always laughed and told him that Mum was all bark and no bite, which was true; yet I always respected her words, even if I didn't want to hear them.

Doc did the ceremony. He read a few passages from the Bible and said a prayer over our mum, and then Marcus, Leo, and I lowered her body into the grave amid the tangled roots of the old tree. It was hard to keep the tears back. I had hoped somehow that she would come back to us, but still she remained in the grave.

"Joshua," Doc said in a calm, warm voice, "would you like to say anything over your mother?"

I gulped. There was so much I wanted to say, but I did not want to keep everyone outside for the entire afternoon. The sun blazed down on us, and the possibility of a German patrol always loomed.

Clearing my throat, I said, "My mum was always a strong woman. Up till the moment she died, she was always fighting for something. Most of the time it was not even for herself but instead for Petyr and me. What I will miss most about our mum was her willingness to be second, not in a defeated sort of way but rather in a sacrificial sense. She was always the last to eat, last to bathe, last to go to sleep, and last to have anything, making sure that Petyr and I were satisfied before she took anything for herself. Looking back, I never understood her reasoning, but now I know that it was not because she thought herself better than us but instead that she wanted to make sure we were taken care of, as we were her glorious children.

"When my father died, I knew I was not ready to take on the responsibility of being the man of the family. My mum also knew this and never forced it upon me. For that, I am thankful. Yet as we stand here today, as I stand before you all as a young man, I regret never accepting that responsibility that was mine to take. Instead, I hid behind my mum's skirts, as they say, and let her lead us, as I was unfit to lead."

I walked to Violet and took her hand in mine. "Some of you may have become aware of my love for Violet these past few years. I never told my mum, but she somehow still knew." I laughed. Everyone else laughed as well. I felt my eyes beginning to well up as I continued. "When Mum was here with us, I ran from responsibility. I ran from being a man of God and, to be frank, I have hated God since the war started. I blamed Him for my father's death; I blamed Him for everything until I was there at my mum's bedside. Then, I had a moment of clarity about my life. I forgave God, I forgave my mum, and I forgave myself for my selfishness."

I took Violet's other hand in mine and smiled. "I promised my mum that I would always love and care for you, and that is what I plan to do." I pulled from my pocket a ring made from a piece of twine with a small flower secured in the knot. Bending to one knee, I said, "Violet, will you marry me?"

Claire

The question was no surprise to any of us, and of course, she said yes. In my opinion, it was an odd time to propose, but I suppose God works in mysterious ways. It was a joyous time for everyone. I knew that Joshua's mother had always said she wanted her death to be something that was revered as a happy engagement; perhaps she meant it literally, but who is to say?

Violet and I had talked about Joshua quite often. She was mad for the boy—had been since the day she first met him, she claimed—much like I was for Gabriel, though I had always denied my love for the German soldier.

Before the evening meal, I took Leo with me to pick wildflowers for a centerpiece for the table. He was reluctant at first, but I convinced him that he could keep me safe from harm instead of stacking boxes before supper. Anything that got him out of the cellar was okay with my brother.

"What do you think of the engagement?" he said as he waded through the prairie grass on the edge of the thick forest. "It was a bit odd to propose on his mother's grave, don't you think?"

I laughed. "I guess it was just the right timing."

He chuckled in response. "Well, one thing is for sure, they will never forget it."

"Agreed. Yet I know that Joshua is the right man for Violet. He will treat her right, the way she needs to be loved."

"What about Petyr?"

"What about him?" I said.

Leo scratched his head and shrugged. "I don't know. What do you think he will do now that his father, mother, and brother are all *gone*?"

"Joshua is not gone," I retorted. "He is just getting married. There is a difference."

"The only real difference is that Joshua is not dead. He will have no time for his brother anymore. His priority has changed from being a brother to becoming a husband. Petyr is going to suffer from the change."

I knew he was right, but I did not want to see Petyr as merely another mouth to feed. "He will live with us, then," I said without hesitation. "Doc will raise him as his own, just like he did us."

Leo did not say anything for a few minutes. I grew impatient and blurted, "What is it this time? Why can't he stay with Doc and Grandmother?"

"You and I both know the answer to that question, Claire."

He was right. Doc and Margret were older than when we first came to live with them. They had less vigor, they were fragile, and in a few years they would become unable to support themselves, let alone an angst-ridden teenager. Still, I wanted to believe it was possible.

I told Leo to gather as many flowers as he could, as it was time to head back. We walked in silence the rest of the way home. My heart was heavy at the thought of Petyr being on his own, Doc and Margret dying of old age, and the constant pain of Gabriel leaving me after he had promised so much. I wanted to believe he was coming back, but every day he was gone, my hope dwindled. I just wanted an explanation.

Gabriel

I arrived in Gdańsk six days after leaving Berlin, on the late evening of June 5, almost two full weeks after leaving Claire. I found the address Henning had given to me with ease. The boardinghouse was only a few blocks south of the train station, about a mile from the port, above the local butcher shop. I met my contact outside of the building and introduced myself in the best Polish accent I could muster. The man frowned in disapproval but let me enter his upper room regardless.

"Your Polish is poor," he said as he filled a teakettle with water from the sink. "Henning promised a fluent speaker, and you are but an infant with the language. Nothing will come of your work if you do not know how to speak the language."

"I have been reading and practicing every day since I left Paris. I have improved so much, but that is all I have been able to learn."

The old Pole frowned again and moved to the stove, his feet shuffling with each step.

"I have lived in Gdańsk all my life," he proclaimed as he raised his right hand and set the teakettle onto the stove with his left. "And I know these people. They can tell a true-blooded Pole from a German imposter without even hearing him speak! You are already lost, I'm afraid. There is no hope for your operation now; best you head home instead of wasting my time and yours."

"I am not leaving," I declared. "I was sent here for a reason, and I plan to see it through to the end."

"Why are you here, exactly? What did Henning tell you when he sent you to Poland? That you would be an asset to the Great Reich's hold on the eastern front?"

I nodded and scratched my head in confusion.

"Bah! The eastern front is all but lost at this point! The Russians," he emphasized, "they do not care for you *Germans*. They want to kill you all!" He paused and leaned on the counter. He let out a cough and whispered, "The Russians, they want to kill all of us. Pole, Jew, Gypsy, German, all of us. They do not care as long as we are dead at the end of the war."

I felt the tension pour from his words. I thought about the truth that was weighted in his words, but I wanted to disagree. Henning had warned me about the imposing Russian threat on the eastern front. After the victory of Stalingrad, the Russians were rejuvenated with a vigor and purpose that jump-started their entire country back into motion. Henning called it the "Great Revival" and told me that it would be the end of the eastern front if we did not hold the line in Poland.

"I was sent here for information about a girl," I said, pulling the envelope with the description and photograph from my bag and handing it to the old man. "Henning told me that she had made contact with you a few weeks ago; is that correct?"

He nodded and took the envelope with a steady hand.

"And you told Henning that you knew where she was?"

"Yes," he said as he took a seat across from me. "I do know this girl. I know her well. She visits me often to share and obtain information that is beneficial for each of us."

"You exchange information?" I repeated.

The man looked confused. "Yes, we share information back and forth, and then I share nuggets with the Germans and the Allies. I have become a trusted informant for each party, having no true tie to either, even though I promise that I am loyal to the one in question."

I sat back in my chair and ran my hand through my fresh-cut hair.

"You were never going to tell Henning where the girl was, were you?"

He chuckled. "No, I did not plan to tell you where she was, only that I knew of the girl and that she had passed on key information to me, which is what I told your superior. He took the bait and chased the rabbit down the hole in hopes of cutting off a loose end."

I put my hands over my face and let out a sigh of frustration. "At least tell me what information you gathered from her so that this entire trip was not a waste on my part. Please?"

The old man chewed his bottom lip as he studied the anger and confusion in my face. The teakettle screamed as steam blew from the small spout, and the man removed it from the stove as he blew out the flame. Grabbing two porcelain cups, he brought the kettle over to the table and took his seat once more.

"Tell me, Gabriel," he said as he poured the hot water into the cups, "what do you know about the relocation program set up by the Nazis in eastern Germany and the majority of Poland?"

I gave him a quizzical look and then answered, "It is the program to relocate Jews and other non-German purebloods into eastern Germany and Poland as a safe haven until the war is done. Then they will be given rights to land and settlements so that they may rebuild and repopulate as they see fit."

The old man nodded but did not say anything. His eyes were tired, his posture slouched and uninviting. He looked at the clock and frowned.

"One thirty," he said to himself. "It seems we will not be getting much rest tonight, but you still have much to learn. Would you like green or black tea?"

Eliza

The trip to Gdańsk was more difficult than expected because I had to leave my daughter with Camille. When I left the hostel on the sixth of June, my daughter chased me down the sidewalk for almost a block, shouting for me to stay. When she finally caught up to me, I bent down, hugged and kissed her, and tried to explain what I was going to do. Yet regardless of how I worded my story, she did not understand. How could she? She was just a child.

"Don't worry, dear," Camille said as she picked up my crying child. "We will take care of her until you come home."

I thanked her, kissed my daughter one more time, and then made my way to the train station. I had a copy of my forged citizenship stating that I was not a Jew in my left pocket. I kept my hand on it at all times, hoping that it would bring good fortune in the near future. I would have to display it to the guards at the station and on the train. It had worked for traveling before, but that had been years ago, when I was still pregnant. Perhaps the guards just felt bad for me because I was with child.

I arrived at the station a few minutes after 8:00 a.m. The next train departing for Gdańsk left in an hour, so I took my time in buying my train ticket. There was a small line, but I was in no hurry. I had learned from Iva while still living in Warsaw that it was better to take your time; rushing to get everything you needed drew unwanted attention.

With about thirty minutes remaining before the train departed, I made my way to the line to purchase a one-way ticket to Gdańsk. I kept to myself, looking at the floor so as to not to look unusually anxious or suspicious. Two elderly men stood just in front of me, speaking in hushed Polish with one another. I listened but did not say anything.

"You do not mean to tell me that they are in fact in the war now," the one on the right said.

"I mean just that, Fredrick. They are no longer just involved in the Pacific; they have joined with the British to invade France. Just this morning they invaded the coast of western France in what people are calling the largest sea, land, and air invasion in the world's history!"

Fredrick waved his hand in disapproval. "Bah! The Americans are pacifists. Sure, they are fighting the Japanese on their own terms, but that is only because *they* were first attacked. They would not come to European soil again. You have been hearing far too many stories, Simon."

Simon furrowed his brow and huffed in frustration. "Now see here, *old friend*"—the words came out as a slash instead of a friendly exchange—"the Americans and British have invaded western France, and the Russians mean to move into Poland sooner than we expected. I know my source is credible."

Fredrick grabbed his friend's arm and looked around for any listening soldiers. "Keep your voice down, you old fool! Do you want to be arrested for treason? They'll kill you for saying such things in public."

Simon frowned. "Then I will not speak on the matter any further, for both of our sakes."

The two men minded their business until they purchased their tickets and walked toward the boarding platform. I followed suit, but their conversation pressed in my mind with every step I took.

If the man's testimony is true, and the Americans have in fact invaded, the war will end soon. Yet that also means that the Russians will be moving this way. What does that mean for Poland, my sister, and my daughter? Do I want the end of the war to come just yet? I fear I am not ready.

Yet time waits for no man, and my time was cut even shorter.

Gabriel

The old man stopped talking about the relocation plan around three o'clock in the morning and told me we would continue our conversation in the morning after breakfast.

Around eight o'clock, he woke me and motioned to the table, where fresh eggs, bacon, and toast were waiting for the two of us. I dressed and joined him at the table.

He picked up right where he had left off, explaining the German Relocation Plan. He told me everything that had taken place in secret over the past three years: the sudden rise of multiple concentration death camps across the Polish countryside at Treblinka, Ebensee, Sobibór, Bełżec, Chełmno, Bergen-Belsen, Dachau, Buchenwald, and Auschwitz-Birkenau.

The information that flowed from his mouth made me sick to my stomach. I wanted to vomit as he shared the details of the treatment and extermination of the Jews. Henning had bragged about the relocation program as if it were his brainchild, said it would be the "stepping-stone to a brighter future for the entire world." Looking back, I realized how naive and foolish I had truly become.

"Do you see now why I fear for my countrymen, sir? Do you see why I dare not oppose the Germans and their damned requests for information about their greatest secret in the world? Even *you*, a German soldier, had no idea of the truth." He stamped out his cigarette and threw the butt into the ashtray. "It sickens me to know that even soldiers in the German ranks are not permitted to know what is actually happening here in the east."

We sat for a few moments before I broke the silence once again. "How did this girl come across such valuable information?"

The man rubbed his neck again and took out another cigarette before he answered. "She was a prisoner in Sobibór. She first escaped from Warsaw sometime during the end of the summer of 1940 with other children attempting to flee to northern Poland to escape by ship to Norway. They were captured and taken to Sobibór, one of the extermination camps. The other children and the man who had taken custody of the children were all killed. Your girl, however, she overcame the harsh treatment, and she managed to escape with hundreds of other prisoners in October of 1943. She fled back to Warsaw in search of her sister, but to no avail.

"She was near death when she was taken in by a man named Irek, leader of the Polish underground army in the Warsaw region. She was nursed back to health and soon became a spy for the Home Army. She shared what was actually happening in the camps, thus spurring more revolts and gaining sympathizers across Poland. The Allies were given this same information in turn, but the Germans were informed as well."

"Henning does not care about the information being spilled, then?"

"Oh, he does, yes, but he cannot stop it from spreading like a wildfire. It would be like trying to hold back the wind with your bare hands. No, Henning feels defeated—by a little girl, nonetheless—and wants to dispose of her, though he can't do it himself."

"Which is why I'm here . . ."

"Yes. Sent to murder an escaped Jewish girl who holds the true secrets of the death camps in that little mind of hers? If her story were to go public . . ."

The realization came over me like a tidal wave. Headlines and reporters across the world flashed in my mind: millions dead at the hands of the Germans, millions more in mourning. The importance of this little girl was greater than the information she was willing to share; her story would ripple through history for centuries to come.

The phone rang, startling me back into reality. I watched as the old man walked over to the black telephone, picked up the receiver, and listened to the voice on the other end.

"All right," he said in a hushed voice. "Yes, I will tell him. Thank you."

He put the phone back onto the receiver and turned to face me.

"What is it?"

"There has been an attack," he said, making his way back to his seat.

"An attack?" I repeated. "An attack where?"

"The Allies have begun their invasion of western France. They landed near two hours ago and are uprooting the German hold on the western coast. If it is successful, they will be in Paris within the month."

I covered my mouth and let out a sigh of relief. *They will be in Paris within the month . . . Claire will be safe, and I can go home to her. Thank God.*

Eliza

The train rolled to a stop with an ear-wrenching scream. I left the car and slung my only bag onto my shoulder, making sure to keep my head down as I joined the massive crowd of refugees making their way across the platform. German soldiers were spread across the loading area, checking random citizens and their bags. I spoke to no one, but instead darted for the exit and made my way down the dusty sidewalk leading to the southern end of town, where my sister had last been seen by Iva's informants.

The city was in an uproar. The increasing number of civilian refugees mixed with the already overwhelming number of unwanted German soldiers made me uneasy not only for myself but also my sister. Yet as I thought of her, I had to smile over her cunning ability to survive this long without me.

I pulled out the note from Iva once more and read it with quick eyes, trying to remember where she had said my sister had been last, but a sudden swift wind tore the paper from my hands. I gasped and shuffled after it, chasing it down the sidewalk like a stupid girl would chase a mouse in a field. I stumbled between people walking in the opposite direction, tripping over my own feet and then falling flat on my chest. I gasped for air as I searched for the letter among the trampling feet.

I spotted it and reached out with a trembling hand, but just as I grabbed the edge, another hand descended and pulled it up and away. I yanked at the page, but the paper slipped from my fingers.

I looked up in desperation and saw a man dressed in civilian clothing. He was old, and something about him made me uneasy. His eyes did not fall upon me until he was done reading my letter. When he finished, he folded the paper, placed it in his coat pocket, and then reached out a gloved hand.

I hesitated but allowed him to help me to my feet. He brushed my shoulders off and then looked me over as if making sure everything was in proper place. He then smiled and gave me a firm hug around my sore shoulders.

"It is good to see you, miss. I was afraid that you would not make it here alive."

I was quite confused but said nothing to suggest that I knew not who he was.

"Quite," I whispered as I hugged him back. "It was a long journey, but I am here safe."

He pulled away and then looked at me once more. "You have not changed at all, Eliza," he said with a warm smile, one that seemed familiar from a life long ago, but still I could not pinpoint who this man was.

"It seems age has not done me well," he said with a quiet chuckle. "Eliza, it is me, your papi."

Joshua

The morning of the sixth was terrible. For us French, it meant that the war was coming to an end, faster than we had ever hoped it would, and yet at the same time, the Germans' grasp around our necks grew tighter than ever before. In the days after the first reports of D-day, thousands of troops flooded into the countryside on their way to Paris. Violet and I kept watch on the southern and eastern tunnels to be sure no German patrols in search of supply drops or rain shelters happened onto our cave entrances. Claire and Leo had the northern and western entrances, while Doc, Margret, and Petyr stayed in the cellar, preparing meals and keeping close watch on the house in case any unwanted visitors saw it as a safe place to sleep for the night.

The majority of the time I was on guard duty, I sat just inside the cave entrance, out of sight, waiting as the hours ticked by and my brother brought me food on a small metal tray. His visits were the only human interaction I had for days at a time.

When night came, we retreated to the main compound to eat a larger supper and get some much-needed rest, while Doc, Marcus, or Margret watched the entrances throughout the night.

Days passed, and the German forces grew more hostile with each new day. Violet lost her appetite, though I tried coaxing her to eat something so that she was not operating on an empty stomach. She always refused, and after day three, I let her be.

Later that week, Marcus came back from the city with an update from the local resistance forces.

"It appears that the Germans are being pushed back from the Normandy coast. The Allies are making their move, but progress is slow. The French Forces of the Interior are looking for any help they can obtain."

"What sort of help are they asking for?" Doc said with concern.

Marcus looked at me and then to Leo. "They need fighters. All males between the ages of eighteen and fifty-four are asked to serve in the fight against the Germans."

Violet grabbed my hand and pleaded that Marcus not take me with him, but he waved her away and said, "Anyone who refuses to join the FFI will be subject to trial and perhaps execution for treason against the French republic. Trust me, it is not what I want for anyone, but it is what the resistance demands from us, if we are to remain hidden here and keep the land after the war."

"I will help too," Claire said from the back of the room.

"They only need men, Claire," Marcus retorted as he pointed a finger at her. "You are not fit to fight. You need to stay here and take care of—"

Claire stepped forward and said, "No. I will go with you three. I want to fight."

Marcus frowned. "Fighting the enemy will not bring him back to you. He is a German; he always has been. Odds are he will be out there fighting *against* you. Will you be willing to shoot him when the time comes?"

Marcus and Claire stared at each other with cold, emotionless eyes.

"Yes," she said. "I will shoot any German that comes into my way. Gabriel is nothing to me."

Claire

Doc argued with me all the way to the door, begging me not to go with Marcus, Leo, and Joshua, claiming that he and Margret needed me here. I did not listen to most of his rambling; I was too drained to care what he was trying to tell me. I just trudged up the stairs as I pulled my hair back, tied it, and shoved it into my hat, doing my best to disguise myself as a young man.

"They will not allow you to join them," he said as he ascended the stairs after me. "They will find out that you are a woman, and then they will ask you to leave. Marcus may be willing to take you, but *they* will not allow you to fight. Trust me, Claire, you would do best to stay here with us."

I turned in a fit of rage, my hands balled into fists, ready to hit the old man whom I had called my father square in his face.

"I am not a child anymore! Stop acting like I am weak! I am ready to do something with my life. I have been cowering in this basement for too long; it's time for me to do something worthwhile for my country. The wine trading, yes, it has helped, but that has always been yours—this is my chance to fight for France. Gabriel is gone, most likely dead, and I . . ." I choked on my words. Gabriel's dead eyes flashed in my mind. I knew it was not true, but still I feared the worst.

I gathered my thoughts and said, "And I can't stay here waiting for some sort of fairy tale to happen for me. The war has taken a turn in our favor, and I would be a fool to let it slip through my fingers like running water. I'm going to fight, and you won't be able to stop me."

"Claire," Doc said, sounding defeated, "I just don't want to lose you . . . like we lost your brother."

I released my fists; my heart sank like an anchor. I had overreacted. Doc just wanted me to be safe, and I had treated him like an oppressing parent. I was becoming selfish because of Gabriel, lashing out at those closest to me. I was wrong to yell at him, but I knew that I was right to go out to fight. He knew he could not keep me away from the fight for long, but he could try his best to keep me safe, within his control.

"Doc," I said as I caressed his face. "I love you and Margret. You are my parents. I promise I will come home. And when I do," I said, wiping the tear from his eye, "I will bring a liberated France home with me."

He grabbed my hand, pulled me in, and hugged me with his nimble arms. Then he kissed my cheek and walked back down the stairs to the cellar. I stood there for a moment longer, sighed, and then joined Marcus, Leo, and Joshua outside. Marcus handed me a rifle and motioned for us to follow. We fell in line behind the ex-soldier and made our march to the outskirts of the city. A new day was about to dawn. I just prayed I would come back home . . . alive.

Eliza

My heart sank to my stomach. I wanted to scream.

"How—" I choked. "How did you find me?"

"I saw you on the train, dear. I have been following you since you left Płock. I was with Isabella when she escaped Warsaw. I was unaware that your sister was among the prisoners at Sobibór, but when I arrived at the camp myself, I stumbled upon Isabella and helped to keep her alive."

"You are no hero, Papi," I said. "You whored us as if we were prostitutes, and yet you come here with happy tidings claiming you *saved* Isabella? For all I know, you raped her time and time again in that accursed camp and then left to save your own skin."

"Eliza," he said, trying to calm me down with a hushed voice, "please come with me; it is not safe here. I can help you find Isabella."

I slapped him across the face with an open palm. He rubbed his tender cheek and then turned to face me once more.

"Please, trust me, Eliza. It is not safe for us to be out in public like this. If we are to find your sister, we need to help one another."

"*Help one another?*" I sneered. "It was *you* who caused my sister and me to live in fear every night, wondering if we were going to live to see the next day. You were trusted by my father, your own son, to care for Bella and me, but instead you soiled your own family with your flesh-driven desires. You claim to be an honorable man, that I should hear you out, that you are a changed one after a few short years. You are a devil, Papi, and I suggest that you never show your face around me again."

I turned and took a step away, but my papi's hand seized my bicep. The familiar grip sent a shiver of fear down my spine. He pulled me tight against him and whispered in my ear, "Listen, girl. You will come with me, you will help me find your sister, and then we will go back into hiding just as we were before the war came to our doorstep. Do not think that you will survive this time without me."

"Excuse me, sir," a crisp voice said from behind us. My papi's grip loosened, and he turned to face the approaching man. He wore a German uniform, though one that suggested he was not on duty. "I believe that the woman asked you to leave her alone."

My papi bowed and smiled. "Good day, sir. This is a family matter, and none of your business, I'm afraid."

"Yet it is quite my business, sir," the man said. "Release the woman, else I will take you into custody as an enemy of the state."

My papi did not respond but instead pushed me away.

"Do not make a scene now, sir," the soldier said. "I will take the girl into my custody now, and I will hear nothing more from you."

"I have searched for my granddaughter for these past four years," my papi replied. "I will not let her slip away from me."

The soldier drew a gun from his holster, cocked it, and pointed it at my grandfather's head.

"I will give you one last chance, sir. Release the girl into my custody, else I will kill you where you stand."

Gabriel

I held the gun with a tight grip. I breathed deep and waited for the man's response. I knew that I had no authority to take the man into custody, let alone make him do what I wanted, but I knew this was the woman I sought. Kirkov, my informant, had received a letter from a Gypsy woman still living inside the Warsaw ghetto, speaking of a young Jewish woman who would be searching for her sister as well. Kirkov had not told me of the letter, but I had stumbled upon it while he was out gathering supplies for his shop.

The description of the girl helped me find her quicker than I had ever hoped. I had almost lost her in the bustling crowds leaving the train station, but it appeared that God Himself was in favor of me finding her.

"Very well," the man who called himself her grandfather said as he backed away. "Take her for now. Yet, sir, remember that I will not forget your face. I will find her and take her home with me, along with her sister."

He turned to the woman and said, "Eliza, don't worry, I will come back for you after the war is over. I will come and free you from your hellish prison." He kissed her cheek, glared at me once more, and then stumbled down the sidewalk and out of view.

Eliza watched until he was gone, her eyes on him at all times. She finally broke her trance when I spoke to her.

"Eliza," I said, "Iva sent me to find you." It was my best shot. I had seen the signature written in faded ink at the bottom of the letter, and I hoped that it was the same woman who had helped Eliza to leave Warsaw.

Eliza covered her mouth and began to cry. "Iva, the saint," she said through a cupped hand. "I knew that she would not leave me here in darkness." She embraced me. "I must say, sir," she mumbled into my shoulder, "that I have not trusted German soldiers in the past, but I know that not all are as evil. Please, tell me your name so that I may thank my God above for this blessing."

"My name is Gabriel."

She gasped and gripped my shoulders tighter. "Gabriel, my guardian angel. Please, help me find my sister if it is the last thing you are to do."

"I will help you find her, if it is the last thing I do, miss."

Joshua

We were stationed in the western part of Paris for the majority of the month of June. Sabotage missions were our main form of warfare against the Krauts, hiding in secret, striking from the shadows, and then fleeing back into the sewers from which we'd come. Claire was ruthless and cunning, earning her a high rank in the militia—the same level as Marcus himself. I, however, was not made for fighting and was more a delegate, running messages from safe house to safe house. It was trivial work, but I did not mind it as most soldiers would. They fought with guns and explosives, while my greatest weapon was my voice and my pen upon paper.

"Joshua!" Marcus yelled as he stormed down the sewer tunnel, a rifle in each hand. "Joshua, you are needed up above. Take this and follow me!"

I stuffed the letter I had been writing into my knapsack and slung it over my shoulder. I caught the rifle just as it was about to smack me in my face.

"But Marcus, I am not a soldier! I am only a courier!" I called as I followed him along the narrow canal filled to the brim with sewage. Rats scuttled between my legs, falling into the water as I kicked them out of my way.

"Today, Joshua," Marcus shouted back, "you will be a man among us Frenchmen! Have faith and trust in me!" His laughter was tinged with insanity as he jumped the canal and climbed up the ladder.

I followed him up the ladder and into a space so tight, it seemed to squeeze the air from my lungs. I crawled on my hands and knees to the end of the tunnel, where Marcus had kicked open a small door and stepped through into a dim room.

"Come on now, Joshua," he said as he grabbed my hand and pulled me to my feet. "And don't mind the bones. These catacombs are the largest graveyard in all the world, and they happen to be right under the great city of Paris herself! Brilliant, really. Easy for us scoundrels to move around without being noticed."

The bones embedded in the walls nauseated me, but I pushed on, avoiding the gazes of the millions of skeletons looking back at me.

"Where are we going, Marcus?"

"There is a German outpost near a church not far from here. It is a prime location for us to strike as our Allied forces apply the pressure on the western front of the city. They will be here within the month; best we take out the important hornets' nests prior to our allies' arrival!"

We reached the end of the graveyard and ascended an old, broken stairwell and emerged in an old alleyway off the main street. A blockade of crates and barrels waited for us at the end of the alley, a pair of French freedom fighters hiding behind the small false wall. Marcus slid in next to the other soldiers, and I followed, kneeling next to the men.

"*Bonjour*, Marcus!" they murmured.

"*Bonjour*, comrades. Are we almost ready?"

"*Oui*, sir. We are just awaiting for your signal to move in."

A sudden explosion erupted from the church's bell tower. The obelisk structure crumbled onto the street below, and a hundred screams of civilians and soldiers rang out in terror as the bricks fell like hailstones.

"Damned men can't follow a single order!" Marcus screamed as he jumped over the barrels and fired his rifle in the air three consecutive times, shouting at the top of his lungs, "*Vive la France!*"

The two soldiers followed him into the street and charged to the next available cover. Nearly three hundred French soldiers exploded from hiding and swarmed the church. I gulped, tightened my grip on my rifle, and jumped into the fray with my brothers.

Claire

I charged with my fellow countrymen, my rifle firm against my chest as I jumped over the rubble of the destroyed bell tower. I let off three shots at fleeing Krauts, not hitting a single target but securing passage to the cover of a brick building on the right side of the street.

I had been assigned the command of five young men after proving myself in battle twice before. Rikard, Jacques, Wilhelm, Francis, and Salem all fell in behind me against the wall. I could see the fear in their eyes; they were young, only a few years younger than I, and with so much life left to live. I could see that they did not want to be here; they wanted to go home to their mothers and hide under their white sheets like the cowards they were, but I did not let them know my disappointment in them.

I wondered if they hated taking orders from a woman. But without me, I guarantee they would have been dead before we had even created this band of freedom fighters.

I scanned the street for an opportunity to strike, and before long, one presented itself. A military jeep rolled to a stop outside of the church, carrying three German officers. They scrambled inside and ordered four soldiers to defend the doorway. I saw Marcus to my left, leading a charge on the southwest side of the church, and I alerted my trusted men that it was our turn.

I screamed and charged the southeast side of the building, near the jeep. I took a grenade from my belt, unclipped the pin, and threw it hard at the nearby stained glass window, shattering it on impact. My men followed suit, and the barrage of grenades erupted inside the church, blowing debris through the gaping window.

The soldiers at the front doors opened fire at us, but they were too distracted by the explosions inside the church to aim accurately. I shot three times, dropping one of the closer soldiers. The other three scrambled for cover and took aim against us. Jacques fell from a bullet to the neck; Salem followed as a mounted machine gun sent a dozen bullets through his left leg just above his knee, ripping the limb clean off.

We did not stop the charge and slid in behind the jeep. Bullets ricocheted off its metal exterior, the tires exploded and deflated, and soon we were hiding behind a wall of twisted metal.

"What now, ma'am?" Wilhelm shouted over the clamor.

I searched frantically for an answer. We were in a tight place with nowhere to run. I felt like a rabbit caught in a snare, waiting for the hunter to come and finish the job.

I pressed against the jeep and glanced over the edge, jerking back before it was shot up by what seemed a thousand bullets.

"Damn it," I said under my breath. "Where is Marcus when you need him? Or anyone, for that matter! Where the hell are the reinforcements?"

A roar caught my attention to our left. I turned to see a Tiger tank roll around the corner, aim its cannon in our direction, and fire a massive shell from its metal innards. I cursed and dove as far from the jeep as I could, but the shell struck the jeep, and the explosion launched me into the street. My rifle clattered to the ground beside me, and the moans of my men filled my ears as I struggled to defend myself.

Eliza

Gabriel and I worked for many days piecing together our meager resources on my sister's whereabouts. We met with informants in the cover of darkness, bribed, traded, and even threatened for valuable information. After almost three weeks, near the end of July, we finally hit a breakthrough.

"Gabriel, I fear that we will not be able to find her after all."

Gabriel entered the small back room of the abandoned basement tavern we had taken up as our temporary home. A shell had recently demolished the building above it, and it was the perfect hiding place for the two of us while we stayed in Gdańsk.

"I have a new lead, Eliza," he said as he took his seat across from me. "One of our informants said he saw a young woman matching her description earlier today. I suggest we go after the lead right now before the trail becomes cold."

Something about Gabriel's eagerness made me feel uneasy, but I could not deny the fact that it was the best course of action, seeing that it was our first lead in some time. I shifted in my chair.

"Where did the informant see her?"

"The southeastern side of the city, near the market. She was selling oysters, but before the informant could question her, she abandoned her post and vanished into the crowd of people."

"It is settled, then," I said, rising from my chair. "We will go to the market in the morning. But I must get my rest before we go. I fear that if we are reunited, it will be quite an emotional burden for each of us."

I bid him good night, retreated to my room, and began to pray with such intensity, I could not sleep the rest of the night.

Gabriel

We left the tavern before dawn so as to beat the first patrols. I had observed that they were much slower in Gdańsk than in Paris and especially Berlin. The soldiers were lax, probably because they did not want to be here in the first place. I did not blame them.

We stuck to the back roads and alleyways, crossing the main roads only when we had no alternative. After about an hour of dodging patrols and sneaking between buildings, we finally arrived at the market square in the southeastern district. In my opinion, it was the nicest part of the city. Only one building had been destroyed, and pristine white-and-red-colored buildings framed its crumbled remains and drew the gaze away. If I had not been looking for crumbled mortar and brick, odds are I would not have even noticed it.

We made our way to the small fruit and vegetable stands on the left side of the square. It was still quite early for customers to be out and about, but a handful of early risers were already looking to acquire the day's fresh produce before ravenous crowds picked the shelves clean by ten in the morning. I took Eliza's arm in mine and pulled her along, whispering sweet lines to her as we passed by the food stands. The more believable we could make it that she was my wife, the better chance we had of not being caught by a suspicious guard.

She took the role, even though I could tell she was quite tense. She gripped my hand every time a German soldier passed us, but instead of frowning or biting her lip, she bid him good morning with a sweet smile. Most of the soldiers ignored her happy pleasantries, but a few reciprocated.

"I can't keep this up, Gabriel," she whispered as she leaned in and nuzzled her head on my shoulder. "I am afraid I am going to give us away before we find my sister."

I gripped her hand in mine and said, "I'm sure this young woman would be delighted to sell us some fresh oysters, perhaps some mussels as well?"

I felt Eliza's grip tighten as she lifted her head and searched for the nearby stands. Behind a small counter stood a girl, no more than twelve, with brown hair pulled back tight against her head and a bonnet resting upon her crown. She wore a pair of tattered old pants and a greasy white shirt that was much too large for her petite figure.

"Aye, sir," she said with a wide smile as she cut open one of the oysters with her black-handled knife. "The lady will be given the best oysters in town, I can guarantee that! Just caught this morning, fresh from the harbor."

"What do you say, m'lady? Would you like to see the collection with a better eye?" I said, pulling Eliza to the counter.

She did not break her gaze from the young woman, even when I put a few oysters in her hand.

"Is everything all right, miss?" the young woman said, concerned.

Eliza gave a weak smile and then nodded.

"Yes, these will do quite well."

"That will be ten Reichspfennig, sir," the girl said in a sweet voice, glancing at Eliza with scrupulous eyes.

"You run a high-priced shop here, m'lady," I said with a chuckle. "Yet if you promise them to be the best in town, I can only imagine why."

I handed over my money, and the girl thanked me with a curt nod and bow.

"Is there anything else you need, madam?"

Eliza paused and put her hand over her mouth.

"It is you," she whispered. "I thought I would never find you again. Isabella, it is me, your sister."

The girl's mouth opened, but no words came out.

"Eliza?" she said through trembling lips. "Is it really you?"

Isabella walked around the small stand and reached out to touch her sister's face. Eliza moved Isabella's hands away and pulled her in for a tight hug.

"I thought I would never see you again," Eliza said, her voice trembling. "I have searched for so long to find you."

I let the two girls have a moment, but our sudden reunion was attracting attention. I watched as the soldiers tried to figure out what was going on, but I did not have the heart to break the two apart.

Here she was, though, the girl I had been searching for, the key to my salvation and freedom to get back to Claire. All I had to do was pull the trigger and it would all be over. The girl who held the problems of my life in her hands and did not even know it. I felt the heaviness of my revolver as I began to pull it from the holster. My heart was heavy; the gun weighed near a ton, it seemed. I dislodged it from my hip and held it tight in my hand as I watched the two embrace after long last.

Do it, Gabriel. Shoot her and you are free to go home. It's that simple. Don't worry about the aftermath; just do your job!

"There they are, sir!" a familiar man shouted from the other side of the crowd. "There are the Jewish thieves that robbed me!"

I looked to see a pointing man with a group of soldiers readying their guns. I cursed, grabbed Eliza by the arm, and pushed them away from the oyster stand.

"What is going on?" Eliza screamed as I pushed her and her sister through the produce stands, turning over a few of the tables in our path.

"Your grandfather thought he'd have us arrested, it seems. We are not safe here!"

We ran with such haste that I couldn't even think straight. *I was right there. I had an opportunity, and I hesitated. I could have shot her. Yet I didn't . . . I couldn't.*

Joshua

I heard the tank before I saw it. The first shell blew up a German military jeep to our right, launching shrapnel in multiple directions, striking fighters from both sides. Marcus screamed in agony as the flesh of his abdomen opened just below his right rib, but still he stumbled toward the old church.

We made it to the outside wall and pressed our backs against the splintered wood. I held my rifle against my chest and looked around with frantic eyes for any stray German soldiers filing out of the church.

"Keep your eyes open, boy!" Marcus shouted as he gripped his stomach with a shaking, bloody hand. "The Krauts will be sure to burst from that accursed hovel that they call their refuge."

A side door burst open, and two German soldiers ran from the church, their rifles clattering on the street behind them as they fled. Marcus fired two rounds, dropping both soldiers in the road.

"Marcus," I blubbered, "they were unarmed. They were running from this fight! They were not even going to turn and fire upon us!"

"They are all worth killing, and I plan to do so if given the chance," he boomed. "Now, are we just going to sit here, or are we going to take this bloody church?"

He grunted and stood on shaking legs, one hand on his abdomen, the other holding his rifle against his shoulder, firing wild shots through a broken window just above our heads. I joined him, firing at anything that moved in my reticle, but none of my shots hit the desired targets.

I grabbed a grenade from my belt loop, armed it, tossed it through the broken glass, and watched it explode in a crowd of German soldiers. I gasped at the sight of what I had just done, but still I kept on fighting. Near ten more soldiers burst from the double doors in the middle of the church's main entrance, all trying to flee from the battle; the freedom fighters shot them each in the back, although they were pleading for surrender.

Marcus ordered his forces into the church, and we all followed like sheep after a shepherd. We fired upon the soldiers remaining inside. Left and right, the bodies seemed to fall at our feet. I felt sick to my stomach, but I knew that if I were to stop, I would be killed instead.

Another explosion sounded outside, followed by an eruption of shouts of "*Vive la France!*" and "Victory!" The sudden excitement sparked my enthusiasm and drove me to keep fighting. It took a few more minutes to clear the remaining rooms, and before I knew it, we had assumed complete control of the church.

Marcus had us fan out to cover all entrances and board up the broken windows. At the back of the church, I found a young German soldier cowering behind one of the pews. He raised his hands in an act of surrender, but I did not lower my rifle. I held it tight against my shoulder, my finger on the trigger.

"Get up!" I shouted.

The boy complied and stumbled to his feet. I motioned him out to the middle of the church, just in front of the altar, and then called for Marcus. He approached with heavy footsteps, cursing his entire way to the altar.

"No prisoners, Joshua," he said through gritted teeth. He gleaned a pistol from a nearby corpse and dropped the young soldier with a bullet through his forehead.

Claire

I climbed onto my knees and coughed until I could breathe once again. My groping hand found my rifle, and I rolled onto my side, waiting for someone to be there for me to shoot. My head was swimming, my vision blurry, and my ears ringing like a loud, annoying bell. I screamed, but nothing came from my throat.

In the distance, I saw the grey tank rolling closer on thunderous tracks. I fired my entire clip at the metal hull to no effect. When it was empty, I threw the rifle at the terrible beast.

A powerful blast knocked me back onto my elbows, and when I hoisted myself back up, I saw smoke and flame billowing from the hull of the once ominous Tiger tank. Cries of victory and freedom rang out in the streets as the once entrenched German soldiers fled in haste from their armory. I cheered with the rest of the soldiers as I climbed back onto my feet, shouting in excitement with the little ability I had left.

The church was now ours, which meant that our foothold in the city was growing in scope. If our scrappy warfare could win us a few more battles, the Allies would have no trouble retaking the city once they arrived. For the first time in many years, I was hopeful for the future of our country. The war was coming to an end at last.

Eliza

"Are they still following us?" I said, trying to catch my breath. I looked through the broken window of the abandoned gas station in which we had hidden.

"I'm not sure, but we can't stay here. We need to make it back to the safe house and reevaluate our next steps," Gabriel said as he pulled out his pistol and checked the chamber.

Bella pushed her bangs out of her eyes and sighed. "No. Whatever you called your safe house has already been found, likely destroyed. We have to get out of the city. They know who we are now."

I wanted to protest, but I didn't have the heart to do it. She was a young woman now, no longer the little girl I had known a few short years earlier. So much had changed.

"What do you suggest we do, then?" I said meekly, trying to let her have her own voice instead of overshadowing her as I had done so many times before.

Bella gave me a stern look; my heart ached. I could tell that she was upset with me, but I was not sure if it was due to my four-year absence or the fact that I had disrupted everything she had built up in a matter of minutes, costing her years of progress and trust.

"We need to go west, into Germany. It is the best place we can go at this point."

Gabriel and I exchanged looks.

"Germany?" he said. "That would be suicide."

She shook her head; I could tell that she would not back down from this fight. "No, we go into Germany, or else I am not coming with you."

"Why? What is there that is so important to you?"

She sighed and then looked at me, frowning. "Because the Russians will kill us when they invade. There are plans within Warsaw to incite a riot in the coming months, coordinated with an attack to aid Russian troops. I don't trust them, though. The Russians don't care about us Poles; they want to *rule* us, not save us. The farther we can get from them, the better off we will be."

"Do you think that running into Germany would benefit us more than hopping a ship here, to Norway or Sweden, to be done with it all? We could just stay here for a few days and then, when the city has calmed down, get out without anyone noticing," Gabriel said.

I could see the frustration building in his expression.

Bella laughed. "Are you an idiot? They are watching the docks even more closely now. They have been looking for me for near nine months, and now that they have found me, they want to kill me—or worse, take me alive."

"We can't just go into Germany, though," I said, avoiding eye contact with both of them.

They both looked at me and said, together, "Why not?"

I rubbed my hands together in anticipation. *What will my sister think now that I have a child to care for?*

"I have some precious cargo that needs to be obtained in the south before we can go west."

Bella scoffed. "No, we are not going back south. We *need* to go west, or else we will all be dead."

"What is in the south that is so important?" Gabriel said. "What is it, Eliza?"

Gabriel

"A child?" I shouted. "You have a *child*? When were you planning to tell me?"

"Tell you? When were you planning to tell *me*?" Bella said in a sharp tone.

Eliza began to cry, but she did not cover her face. She just let the tears fall from her eyes. I was not sure if it was the shame of not telling her own sister or the fact that she had left the child behind to find Bella. I was mad, and yet I pitied her at the same time. A mother away from her child in search of her only sister— she was braver than I had ever claimed to be.

"Where is she?" I said in the calmest voice I could muster.

"Płock. Just over a hundred kilometers from Warsaw."

"You realize that is near a three-week journey in the wrong direction?" Bella said. "I don't want to be caught and taken back to that camp, Eliza. Never again."

The camps. So what Kirkov told me was true: Bella had been taken to one of them. I had my doubts, still did, but the girl seemed to be serious about it.

"We will go to Płock, get your daughter, and then make our way westward toward Berlin. I have some friends who would be willing to help us if we made it into Germany without the border control causing too much trouble. It is a risk, but it's the only choice we really have right now."

Bella frowned. "We could bypass Płock altogether and head straight for Berlin, although I think it would be best if we stuck to the coastline. That way, if we needed to hop a ship, it would be easier than trying to make our way through a handful of untimely checkpoints."

I could tell Eliza was upset. It was clear that she wanted to go back to Płock to get her child, but I feared she would lose that argument without my backing. Even though Bella was much younger than her sister, she had been hardened by this war, forced to fight every day and to take the surest, safest route to reduce her chances of getting caught again.

"No," I protested. "We are going to Płock to get Eliza's daughter back. She is your *niece* as well."

Bella frowned at me, her nostrils flaring with frustration. "I did not *ask* to be an aunt."

"And yet here is your own sister in the flesh, willing to sacrifice her child's safety for your own. Are you seriously this selfish?"

"I did not ask her to come save me," Bella retorted. "I was doing just fine on my own before the two of you showed up. She *let* me be taken in the first place. It is *her* fault that we are even here."

Eliza straightened up. Her eyes were wiped clean, and a stern look came across her face. She stood and walked over to her sister, who was still sitting on the ground.

"What are you doing?" Bella said as she looked up at Eliza.

I was paralyzed; I did not know what to do. *Am I supposed to let it happen, or am I supposed to step in?*

Eliza slapped her sister clean across the right cheek, turned, and went back to her spot against the wall, her lip quivering with such ferocity, I thought it was going to tremble off her mouth.

I looked from Eliza back to Bella and said, "We are going to Płock. You can either stay here and die or come with us. At this point, I really don't care what you decide."

"And how would me going to Płock benefit you?" Bella murmured. "I would only slow you down."

I frowned. "If you lead us to Płock, I will give you everything that I own—all possessions."

She scoffed, "You think giving me stuff will change my mind?"

"Bella, please," Eliza pleaded.

She looked toward her sister and frowned. "Why should I come with you, Eliza? Only death awaits us back there."

"Death awaits us anywhere," I said. "South is our best option."

"And how would you know that, Kraut?"

"Because I came from Berlin," I retorted. "I have been to the capital. Everyone is on edge. The guards arresting civilians for appearing suspicious. My superior officer, Henning, he told me when I left Berlin that it was better to go south, to cross the Mediterranean if I could. When the Russians come, there will be no Poland, but when the Allies come, there will be no Germany either."

"But the Allies will help us," she replied. "They will save us."

I could hear the desperation in her voice now. She had been told that the Allies were going to liberate Poland and her people; this was my time to strike the final blow.

"Bella," I said gently, "your sister needs you to help guide her. She can't go on without you. Her daughter, your niece, she needs you. Don't abandon your family out of selfishness. You are the only one your sister can trust besides me."

"I will guide you only to Płock," she whispered. "Then you are on your own."

"Thank you," I said.

"I am not doing it for you, Kraut," she barked. "I am doing it for my niece."

Eliza

We arrived in Płock just under four weeks after finding Bella at the docks. The trip was grueling, but I was happy to be back in Camille's hostel. My daughter had grown so much already that when I picked her up, I could barely hold her in my arms. I had avoided interacting with my sister for the entire trip, but when she saw her niece for the first time, the anger and frustration seemed to melt away completely. For the first time in nearly four years, we were a family again. We did not speak of the trip home, nor did we speak of our papi; we just sat near the fire, holding each other close, until Camille called for supper.

After the meal, we went to the rooms that Camille had furnished for each of us. Since I had left, twelve families had moved out, making their way to the coast for fear of the invading Russians. Warsaw was a mess, and with it came riots and anxious Poles awaiting their final fate as the candle burned from each end. The latest reports claimed that riots had broken out in the central part of the city. The Home Army was at the head of the attacks, but from what I could tell, it was not going well.

"Why is August always so bloody hot?" complained Fredrick, one of the cleaning boys, as we scrubbed dishes after breakfast the next morning. We had been assigned to kitchen duty, and although most hated the work, I found it quite relaxing compared to the other tedious jobs Camille needed done.

"My mother said that if it was a hot August, it would be an even colder December."

Fredrick smiled. "And I bet your mother also told you that when it rained hard during the night, it was cats and dogs falling on your roof that made all the clamor?"

I smiled and agreed. I finished scrubbing the pot, bid Fredrick farewell till later, and made my way back to my room, where Camille stood waiting by my door. A small envelope was in her hand, and when I saw it, I rushed forward and reached for it.

"Iva sent another letter?"

Camille frowned. Her face was grave, tired, and full of pain.

"Camille," I said as I placed my hand on her left shoulder and squeezed ever so softly, "what is wrong?"

She handed over the envelope and whispered, "I read the letter already. I'm so sorry."

Confused, I took the letter and opened it with shaking hands. I pulled out the small note and read the short, scribbled text to myself.

Eliza,

Dear child, it has finally come to this. The rebellion we have been waiting for at long last, but, I must ask, at what cost? It has been a dream of mine since the beginning of this war to see the Germans flee with their tails between their legs, to piss themselves with blood, and to squeal at the sight of a force equal to or perhaps greater than their own! What a glorious day it would be! I must admit, as I sit here writing to you now, that very force is on our doorstep, but I am fearful of what is to come.

I urge you to run far away from here, Eliza. Flee west as soon as you receive this note. The Germans are retreating, yes, but the real threat is the red wave that follows in their wake. I urge you, child: run. Run for your life from the crimson tide! May God have mercy on your soul! I fear this is the end for me. I hear them at the door . . . they are here. I must give this note to my messenger before it is too late.

Remember me in death, Eliza. I love you always.

Iva

Joshua

I stood by Marcus as we watched the Allied tanks roll into the western end of the city. It was mid-August, and the majority of the German forces had been flushed out. The liberation of Paris was well under way. We, the freedom fighters, worked alongside the Brits and Americans to root out the remaining bunkers and machine gun nests until the entire city was back under our control.

When we achieved our victory, the entire city had erupted in excitement. Petyr had joined me on the sidewalk to watch as the massive Nazi flag was cut down from the Arc de Triomphe. The French people gave a glorious shout of victory, and for the first time in four years, I felt at peace. This indeed was the turn of the war for the better. The end was near; I could feel it in the air. I looked up to heaven and thanked God for what He had done for us, his lowly people. I knew that if Mum were here, she would be praising His name with every waking moment.

I grabbed Petyr and hugged him, shouting, "We are free, Petyr! We are finally free!"

Claire

Summer was coming to an end, and the harvest was in full bloom. Doc was the first to the fields; it was as if he were a young man rediscovering an old love long since forgotten. He went out each morning just as the sun came up, strolling among the grapes of various shades of red and green. I watched him from the back porch and wondered what he was thinking through it all.

"He is a brave man, you know," Margret said as she joined me on the porch.

I nodded in agreement. "And he finds time to see the beauty in everything around him."

"A trait most of us lack, I'm afraid," she said. "I know that these past months have been rough, Claire."

I frowned. "Please, I am fine. I should not have gotten my hopes up anyway. It was a fluke. He was German . . . I was just a foolish French girl."

Margret laughed. "If that is all love is, then I was a fool for marrying *him*," she said, pointing to Doc. "Gabriel is a good lad. Do not let your emotions cloud your judgment, Claire; only bad things will come of it. Our emotions . . . they are unreliable at best. To put our trust in them is to say I'm going to hold a match an inch above a pool of gasoline and hope it goes out before it catches. If you are not careful, your feelings will consume you, distract you from what you really want."

"That's the problem," I said. "I don't know what I really want anymore."

"Search your heart, girl, and you will find it."

"What if he comes back? What am I supposed to do?"

She kissed my cheek. "You will know when the time comes. Until then, focus on the now. We have a large harvest ahead of us, and Doc is going to need all the help he can get. He said that this year will be one of the best seasons to date, and I agree."

"Do you think he will come back?"

Margret smiled. "I don't think he left because he wanted to, and if that's the case, he is fighting every day to get back to you, dear. That," she said with a broad smile, "is the mark of a man in love."

Gabriel

"Going? What do you mean you are going? You just got here," I said as I chased Eliza down the hallway into Bella's room. "Eliza, tell me what is going on. Why are you leaving now? It is not even dark outside yet. You would be caught within a few steps of that door!"

She turned and barked at me, "I can't stay here, Gabriel. Iva sent a warning. The riots in Warsaw, they *worked*. They worked, Gabriel!"

I scratched my head in confusion. "That is a good thing. The Germans are retreating to a more fortified position. They will head for Germany. If we were to go with them, it would be an even greater risk now."

"No," she said as she gestured for Bella to fetch a bag from the corner as she stuffed another full of unfolded clothes. "We need to leave now. There is a shipyard in Germany. Southern Germany. They are taking people on the ships, civilians, like us. If we can just get to that shipyard—"

I grabbed her arm and pulled her to face me. She slapped me across the face with an open palm. I doubled back; the stinging sensation burned my cheek, but I deserved it.

"I will *not* let them take my baby and me. I will *not* let them take my sister from me again. I am leaving here with or without you, Gabriel. It is your choice to join us or not, but I am leaving within the hour. The crimson tide is fast approaching, and I do not want to be swept away in the carnage."

The thought of the Red Army sweeping across the Polish countryside caused me to shiver. I did not want to live in that sort of world, especially being German. They might let Eliza, Bella, and her daughter live, but me . . . I was as good as dead already.

"Fine," I said. "I will go with you. We need to head south and then west, like we originally planned. Odds are that the Red Army will move directly to the German capital."

The two of them agreed after a few moments of discussion between themselves, and before I knew it, we were on the front landing, preparing to leave Camille's safety one last time.

Eliza held the old woman tight against her, whispering something into her ear so softly that I was unsure if she had even spoken. Our good-byes said, I opened the door into the muggy August evening air and rushed down the stone steps to the cracked and unleveled sidewalk that stretched in each direction as far as the eye could see.

We crested the hill and stopped, my heart along with us. There, in the middle of the road, was a gigantic caravan of German soldiers ushering people from their houses into large trucks, stripping them of all possessions and threatening them with guns and clubs.

"Damn it," I cursed under my breath. "Quick, back to Camille's house."

We turned, but before we could take a single step, a soldier ordered us to stop. Complying, we turned to face the approaching fox-faced young man in a fresh-pressed uniform. He ordered us to get into a truck, but I snapped back at him that we would not.

He smacked me across the face with his club. The pain from my cheek made my mind go numb, and before I knew it, we were being crammed into a truck bed with nearly forty other people. I feared the worst, but I could do nothing to stop it from happening. We were as good as dead now, and it was my fault.

Eliza

The winter was bitter cold. Many prisoners died of frostbite or hypothermia in the poor living conditions, but I was fighting for my daughter, just to see her again. When the train arrived at the camp, we were shoved off like cattle and channeled into different sections to be sorted by age group. Gabriel and I were forced away from Bella and Emilia, though Emilia cried with such ferocity that it broke my heart. She was sent to the other section of the camp, Cell Block C; I was in A. We were forbidden to travel to other cell blocks, as the soldiers claimed it would boost morale if we saw our loved ones again. I missed Emilia, Bella, Camille, Iva, even my treacherous papi. I wanted to go back to the way the world was before the war, but things were different now.

Months in the camp had taught me that survival was the only attainable goal. The rations were next to nothing, and if you were fortunate enough to obtain some rations, they were far too salty and miniscule to have any benefit. Yet, day in and day out, I fought to stay up on my two feet, to work at my tasks in the camp, and to motivate Gabriel. He had suffered a concussion when we were first taken, and I was not sure that he had fully recovered. His movements seemed slower after that day, but I stayed with him each day throughout the fall and into December and January.

"Eliza," Gabriel said through chapped and bloody lips. "The days . . . they are growing longer. I don't think I will be able to make it much longer."

I put down my shovel and limped over to my working partner. His once-flowing blond hair was gone, leaving a scabbed and bald scalp, same as mine. He smelled of feces, as did everyone, it seemed, and his hands were grimy and bruised. He was subjected to many beatings on my account, always making a stand to prevent me from being tossed from guard to guard for their pleasures.

"Don't say such things," I said as I placed a firm hand on his crooked back. The boy looked to be near sixty now, not twenty-three. What a terrible place this was.

"We will make it out, you will see," I said, smiling.

It was an empty promise. I had little to no hope myself. Every night I would pray, and every night God was silent. We were among thousands of Jews, Gypsies, and foreigners all deemed *unfit to live among the people.*

I looked at my forearm and remembered our arrival, the pain of losing all my possessions, and then being branded with the unsterile needle like a market calf. *499302.* I moved my fingers across the black ink imprinted into my skin. It made me shudder.

"Hey!" a guard shouted from behind me. "What the hell are you doing standing around, you inbred bitch? Get back to digging or I'll beat you till you are bloody!"

I scurried back to my place in the line of diggers, picked up my shovel, and began to tear into the dirt again. The trench was nearly two hundred meters long, already filled with corpses on the far end to our right. They did not say it, but we all knew this was to be our grave when we finished digging it. I did not ever want to finish digging, no matter how cold it was outside.

Gabriel

I tried to force the shovel into the frozen ground, but even with all my effort, it seemed to scrape only the surface. I was beaten for my lack of work, even threatened with death, but I pleaded with the guards to let me live, and for some reason they kept me around. Perhaps it was because I let them flog me without hesitation, cringing each time, only to have more clubs come down on my already frail body.

"Are you not digging like the rest of them?" a guard shouted in my ear as he struck my head. I dropped, my left ear ringing from the smack. "Did you hear me, you mindless Jew? I will hit you again to make sure you heard me if you don't answer!"

I raised my hand to stop him, but instead he took it and broke two of my fingers. I screamed in agony and pulled my hand back against my chest. My ring and middle fingers had been twisted into opposite directions, unnatural positions; they began to throb, and my vision went blurry.

"Get up or I will shoot you here and now!" the guard shouted as he pulled out his revolver and pointed it at my head.

I complied, took my shovel in my good hand, and began to work at the ground again, biting my lip from the pain.

A siren erupted in the distance, growing with intensity as it rotated on its pole. I looked at the guard, but he was too preoccupied by the soldiers running through the camp to pay any attention to the rest of us.

"What's going on?" one of the prisoners whispered to me.

"Shut the hell up!" the guard screamed as he turned around and fired a round into the prisoner's forehead. The man dropped into the trench, his shovel beside him. A small stream of blood soaked the frozen ground around his head with crimson.

"Get to digging or you'll be next!" he shouted as he pointed the revolver at the rest of us, about twenty in total.

Then he ran off after the other guards, who seemed to be in a hurry. Before long, I saw that they were rousting stragglers from their shacks. It began to snow. A northern wind cut across the camp and chilled me to my bones. My black-and-white service clothes were as thick as paper, the wind relentless as it bit through them into my pale skin.

A squad of guards were shouting in German, but I did not look to see what was happening; all I heard was the firing of pistols and automatic guns. I just kept digging. I told Eliza to just keep digging. The twenty of us did not turn around, even when we heard the screams of hundreds of prisoners dying where they stood. Still more were being rounded up by the front gate.

The soldier who had broken my fingers came back to our line and, starting at the far right end, began to shoot the prisoners in the back of the head, one by one. They fell into the pit.

Bang!

Bang!

Bang!

Bang!

Bang!

Bang!

Eliza

Click.

"Damn it!" the soldier shouted as he stood behind Gabriel, his pistol pressed firm against his scalp. He reached into his belt pouch and retrieved a few bullets. His hands shook, but I was not sure if it was from the cold or the sudden murderous rampage he had just forced himself into.

He dropped the handful of bullets and cursed again. I did not hesitate another moment, and before I knew it, the soldier was on the ground, his face bloody and caved in on the right side from a blow from the curved end of my shovel. I kept hitting him with the sharp corner where my heel would go. I gouged his eye out, cut open his cheeks, broke his nose, and did not stop until he was motionless. Blood covered the ground around his bludgeoned head; my shovel was drenched in the crimson liquid.

I screamed as I continued to hit him. It was not until Gabriel grabbed me and threw the shovel out of my hands that I stopped swinging my arms. I let my legs give out, and he held me tight against him. Around us, guards were setting fire to buildings and forcing prisoners into columns and groups to be driven out the front gate and into the oncoming blizzard.

We were left behind with the remainder of the forgotten prisoners. The last two guards pulled the gate closed behind them and secured it with chains and a heavy iron lock. They shot five prisoners who tried to escape, leaving their dirty corpses pressed against the wire fence, their dead gazes watching their fellow prisoners run into the distance, uncertain if it would lead to their death or salvation.

Hours passed like days as the snow fell in heavy sheets across the camp. It was a barren wasteland of death. Gabriel helped me back to our barracks, found three lone blankets, and wrapped us both into them on a single bunk. He held me close to him, but I did not fall asleep for fear that I would not wake back up.

Shouts rang out from the front gate. I roused Gabriel from his slumber, climbed out of our bunk, and walked out into the snow-covered yard. Moaning prisoners filled it, calling out to the strangers outside the gate. The massive force of soldiers in brown cloaks and furry hats, bearing the sigil of the sickle and the hammer, watched us through the fence as if we were in a zoo.

Hundreds of prisoners crowded the gates, pressing in against the barbs until the metal cut their tender skin. Finally, a few of the soldiers barked orders at them, forcing them back as they cut off the large lock and removed the chains. The tall metal doors opened only a few inches, hindered by the accumulated snow. The influx of prisoners pressed closer to the doors, but none left. Instead, they called for food and water, which the soldiers seemed to understand. Within a few minutes, they were distributing handfuls of bread and half-eaten apples to the crowd. They stopped soon afterward, however, as the Russian commander feared that the sudden feeding of the malnourished would cause more problems than it would solve.

Gabriel and I limped forward and met with one of the Russian field doctors. He was gentle, for a Russian; his name was Izzak. He splinted Gabriel's fingers and gave us a small portion of bread to nibble, warning us not to gobble it all at once. We thanked him and were making our way back to our bunkhouse when I heard a weak voice from the crowd.

"Mother!"

I turned and saw my daughter, barely able to stand, on the opposite side of the road. Black ovals shadowed her eyes, and her head was bald, just like mine. I broke from Gabriel's weak grip and staggered over to embrace my daughter with shaking arms.

"Emilia," I cried as I held her against me. "You are alive! I thought I would . . . never see you again."

She pulled away, tears running down her face as she turned away from me. I followed her gaze to the bunkhouse behind her and saw Bella, slumped against the brick wall, struggling to keep her eyes open.

I crawled across the frozen ground and drew my sister's body onto my lap, kissing her pale cheeks with my bloody lips. She had been shot in the abdomen. I tried to wipe the blood from her skin, but it did not come off: it had frozen in her clothes and stained her skin.

"You are all right," I choked. "You are all right, dear. Everything is fine now. We are safe. No more running, no more pain, no more war. We are safe now, dear."

Bella managed a weak smile as she placed her hand on my cheek. I grabbed it and kissed it over and over again.

"Just hold on, okay?" I said as I looked around for anyone to help. "Doctor!" I screamed. "Doctor!"

"Eliza," she whispered.

"Doctor!"

"Eliza. Listen to . . . me."

"You are coming home with me, Bella. I am bringing you home."

She smiled again and nodded.

"I love you, Eliza."

Gabriel—June 1945

"Paris is beautiful," I said. I held Emilia close to my side as we watched the trees pass in a blur. "I miss it more than I do my own home here in Germany."

"Really?" she said, giggling. "When will we get there?"

"Soon." I kissed her forehead. "For now, sleep, little one. You will need to be rested when we pull into the station. There is still much to come."

A few hours later, we pulled into the train station in Paris. Eliza had hesitated to make the trip with Emilia, but I convinced her that it was the best place for us to go now that the war was over at long last. She trusted me, which I was thankful for, but she also knew that I longed to return to Claire.

After we had gathered our things, we made our way through the crowds of returning soldiers, refugees, and civilians until we found a lone taxi outside of the station. I told the driver where we were headed, and he nodded; before long, I could see the dirt road leading to the solitary building tucked into the hillside, massive fields of vines in the background. The green leaves brought a smile to my face. The grapes were once again flourishing.

We got out of the taxi and thanked the driver. A rush of emotion came over me. My stomach ached, my head was swimming, and I was unable to stand straight.

"Are you all right, Uncle?" Emilia said, taking my hand in hers. I smiled. "Quite all right."

"Are you sure they will let us come in?" Eliza whispered. I could tell she was nervous about this new start, but I reassured her it was the best place for us to go.

We walked to the door, and I gave a crisp knock. Footsteps inside made my heart beat faster, and when the door opened with a long ominous creak, I could not breathe.

"Hello? Who is it?" an old man called from behind the door.

"Doc?" I said, my voice cracking. "It's me . . . Gabriel."

Claire

I heard the door open upstairs. Doc answered it, but what I heard after was a shout of glee. I was curious, as were Violet and Joshua, who were sitting across the table from me, eating breakfast. I stood and dropped my napkin on the tabletop, then made my way upstairs to see what the commotion was about.

When I rounded the corner, I stopped in my tracks. Was I looking at a ghost? It was him. It was really him.

"Gabriel?" I said in disbelief.

He said nothing as he ran to me, wrapped me in a hug, and kissed me. I had no time to think; I reciprocated willingly. I had not forgotten the taste of his lips on mine. I held him close and did not let go. We sank to the floor, entwined. *I am in a dream,* I told myself. *He actually came home.*

Gabriel

The happiness I felt with Claire was incomparable, but it lasted only a few weeks. Though we slept together that first night of my return, the atmosphere between us seemed to become stagnant. She was stressed, not herself. We had both changed, and not for the better, it seemed. She had moved on from me; she thought I had abandoned her after that night we shared over a year ago, and even after I explained the whole situation, she could not look at me in the same way. We slept in the same bed, but most nights she would leave and sleep with Violet. I felt alone and broken inside. The woman I loved, the one that I had fought so hard to return to, kept me at arm's length, even though I was here and willing to start anew.

"Are we going to talk about this?" I said as we walked down the dirt road.

She stopped and sighed. "Talk about what, Gabriel?"

I frowned. We were both frustrated, I could tell.

"About us. About where we go from here."

"What is there to talk about? You *left* for a year, Gabriel. How am I supposed to get over the fact that you disappeared without a trace and then showed up again, a year later, with another woman and a child? How do you think I am supposed to react to that?"

I sighed. "You and I both know that Eliza is not my new lover. Emilia was already four years of age when I first met her."

"I don't really care!" Claire shouted. "The fact that you left me that night . . . I just wanted to have you back! I just wanted to have you stay with me. Every single day I waited for you to come home, but you never did. I gave up hope. I thought you had tucked tail and run because you were scared of what could have been. I believed Marcus, you know. He said you were a traitor. I fought him for so long until the day you left and never came back. I *trusted you.*"

I grabbed her hands in mine and said, "Then trust me again, Claire! I did not leave because I wanted to; I was forced to, for your safety."

"My safety?" she shrieked. "My *safety*? You *abandoned* me! You abandoned all of us."

I dropped to one knee and held her hands tight in my own. "Then let me prove that I won't leave you again. I won't ever give you cause to doubt my actions again. Claire, I love you. I want to marry you. I want to spend the rest of my life with you. Please, will you please trust me?"

She pulled her hands from mine. She was crying, trying to hide it, but I knew. She did not feel the same way about me as I did about her. All those months, the turmoil and hardship to get back to her, had it all been worth the struggle?

"I can't," she said. "I can't marry you. I am sorry."

She left me at the crossroads. I watched her walk alone back down the road. Black clouds swirled above me, and a light rain began to fall. I had nothing left here, so I walked home, to Germany.

Part 4—November 12, 2015

Joshua

I heard the car approaching the house before I saw it. My caretaker, Laura, entered my bedroom and said, "Good morning, Joshua. Your son is here. Would you like to come join the rest of us for breakfast?"

I tried to nod, but my rigid neck muscles restricted my movement. I pushed forward on the knob of my wheelchair and made my way across my bedroom. Laura met me in the bathroom to help me change.

As she worked, she told me how exciting it was that my son, Josef, was home to visit. I wanted to contribute to the conversation, but Parkinson's had stolen my speech as well. I was a prisoner in my own body.

When I was ready, Laura wheeled me to the family room where my son, his wife, and their two daughters sat across from my wife, Violet. The mood was somber, and when I entered, the senseless chatter ceased; all eyes turned to me.

Violet smiled and came to give me a kiss on my cheek. I tried to reciprocate, but my lips merely twitched.

"Hi, Dad," Josef said, following his mother's example. "How have you been?"

"We've been quite well," Violet chimed. "Your father has made large strides since the last time you all visited. We are so glad you are home."

Josef smiled at me, but I could see the frustration and concern in his eyes. He was old now, like me. His wrinkled eyes were tired, and his posture was slouched.

"You look well, Dad," he said. It was a lie.

Laura rolled me over next to the couch and put my brake on. I wanted to speak to my family, but my lips trembled instead, my eyes constantly darting. I watched my granddaughters on the end of the couch; they averted their eyes from me. They were young, maybe mid-twenties? I could not remember; it had been years since I last saw them.

"I wish our return had been for a happier occasion, but when I got the call, I canceled all my appointments for the remainder of the week," said Josef, scanning the room with his wandering eyes. "What time is the visitation?"

Violet rubbed her hands together nervously as she mumbled, "At seven."

Josef nodded and spoke to his wife in a hushed tone so that neither Violet nor I could hear him.

She was younger than he was by nearly twenty years. She was vibrant but commanding. I had never been fond of my son's second wife.

I wanted to speak to Josef. In my mind, I screamed as loud as I could, but nothing came out.

"Well," Josef said as he stood, signaling to the rest of his family to follow, "I think we are going to head back to the hotel and get ready."

Violet let out an audible sigh. "Oh," she mumbled, "I thought you were all staying here with us."

Josef looked at his wife. Her gaze was unforgiving, narrow, and stern.

"Why don't you go ahead and take the kids to the hotel?" he said calmly. "I am going to stay the night here with my parents. It has been a long time since I spent quality time with them."

His wife pushed past him in a rush of frustration and anger and stormed out the front door, the two children trailing after her like a pair of ducklings.

I wanted to laugh and congratulate my son for standing his ground, but the only noise that came from my mouth was a low grunt that sounded more like a cough.

Emilia

I arrived at the funeral home an hour before anyone else was told to show up. Mr. Douglas, the funeral home director, greeted me at the door and escorted me into the main receiving hall. The large brown casket drew my eyes immediately.

"Would you like some time alone, miss?" Mr. Douglas whispered.

I nodded and waited for him to leave before I walked any farther into the room. Flowers of all different shapes and colors lined the sides of the casket, gifts from friends and family who thought a few plants could fill the void of my mother's death. It was a nice gesture.

I took my time in approaching the casket, hands trembling the entire way. When I finally arrived, I looked down at my mother's pale, rubbery face. She was gorgeous despite being drained of her normal color. I stroked her face with a shaky hand and prayed over her in a hushed whisper.

"Emilia?" a gentle voice murmured from the back of the room.

I turned to see a handsome gentleman in a charcoal-grey suit holding his tan overcoat over his left arm. Silver-rimmed glasses rested on the bridge of his nose, and his silver hair gleamed in the false light.

"Josef," I said, putting a hand to my cheek. "It is so good to see you, dear."

I met him halfway down the hall and embraced my old friend.

"How was your trip?" I said, pulling away.

He sighed and pushed his glasses up. "Long," He chuckled. "But worth the drive."

"Are your wife and daughters here with you?"

Again, he let out an audible sigh. "They did come with me, yes," He paused. "But I don't think they will be able to make it tonight. Felicia informed me that she has come down with a terrible cold."

"I am sorry to hear that," I consoled him, though I did not feel much sympathy for his wife, as I had never cared for her. "Perhaps she will be able to come to the funeral tomorrow."

He smiled and nodded. "Perhaps."

"Your mother and father," I said, "they are coming, yes?"

His mood changed almost instantly. "Oh yes. They should be here any minute actually," he mumbled as he checked his watch.

I smiled. "Your mother has always been one to arrive far before the designated time."

"It appears I obtained the gene from her. Please excuse me. I am going to use the restroom before everyone arrives."

"Of course," I replied. "I will be here."

Josef

The visitation lasted until about nine. My parents and I were the last to leave besides Emilia herself. With Felicia and the girls choosing to skip the visitation, it allowed me to spend quality time alone with my parents. We exchanged pleasantries and small talk with friends as they came and went, but as the visitation drew to a close, my mother and I wheeled my father to the reception hall to drink some tea and eat the stale crackers left out by Mr. Douglas and his staff.

"Was Emilia surprised to see you?" Violet inquired just before she took a sip of tea.

"Quite," I replied. "It has been . . . five, maybe six years since I have seen her? She looks great for being seventy-three."

Mother batted at my arm, and I pulled away, snickering.

"What are you hitting me for?" I laughed.

She scowled. "You don't need to be saying her age in public, Josef. It is impolite."

I chuckled and nibbled on one of the stale crackers from my plate. "In all seriousness," I continued, "I am glad I came back. It was refreshing to see her after all these years of being away."

My mother smiled and took a long drink of tea before continuing. "Your father has always been fond of her, you know," she remarked.

I frowned. My parents had not only been fond of Emilia but had attempted to coax me into marrying her since I was in my early teens.

"Mother," I replied, "she is my best friend from childhood. Besides, I'm married again, and I'm content."

My mother scoffed, almost choking on her tea. "Let's face it, Josef, you are living in a nightmare."

I squirmed in my chair. "Mother," I whined, "I am almost seventy years old. I have a wife and two children—"

"Who are not your own," she interrupted. "She is only with you for the money."

I didn't say anything. I knew she was right, but I didn't want to admit it.

"I am going to go home," I said sternly as I stood from the table. "I will see you in the morning."

I walked into my parents' house frustrated, threw my coat onto the coat rack, and shut the door behind me. I sighed, leaned against the closed door, and yelled. I let it out, the years of anger and vexation toward Felicia and the kids, my parents, everything in general, it just flooded out of me like a broken dam releasing a massive river. Then I composed myself and walked up the stairs to the second floor, where I entered my room, closed the door, and fell face-first on the bed. I didn't wake up till the morning.

Joshua

I watched as the casket was wheeled down the center aisle, memories of Eliza flooding my mind. I missed my friend dearly. She'd had a full life, especially after the war. I remember when we all first moved to America, the joy that she expressed of finally being free to raise her daughter without the fear of a soldier taking her away again.

The service was quick, at Eliza's request. She had never wanted an extravagant exit. The graveyard was chilly, but Violet had provided my lap with a blanket. We watched them lower Eliza's casket into the ground, and when they finished, the pastor prayed over the grave. There were quite a few people crying and sniffling; I even caught glimpse of Josef tearing up during the prayer.

After the ceremony, many stopped to say hello to Violet, Josef, and me, making an effort to share their condolences with each of us who had been close to Eliza and her daughter. I bobbed my head and mouthed thank-yous, wishing I could stand and shake each of their hands instead.

As the crowds dissipated, Violet pushed me up to the family's tent next to the grave itself, where Emilia was still seated, holding a white rose. Violet consoled her, then Josef. Emilia noticed me and came over to give me a kiss on my cheek and thanked me for coming to the funeral. I nodded, patted her hand in mine, and lay back against my headrest as Laura wiped the collection of drool from my lower lip.

"Will you join us for dinner, Emilia?" Violet said, taking her hand. "I don't want you to be eating alone tonight, especially since Josef is in town. It will be like old times—what do you say?"

Emilia smiled. "I would like to, but I must get things ready at Mother's house for the auction. Besides, Josef's family is here and will be joining you, I'm sure. Isn't that right, Josef?"

He frowned and replied, "No, they went to Felicia's mother's house in upstate New York, only a few hours away. She was quite upset with me yesterday and decided to leave me here until I 'turned myself around,' as she put it. So, I'm stuck here till later this weekend, more than likely."

"Emilia, I insist that you join us for dinner. Joshua and I have missed having you around the house. It will be nice to have you over, like old times."

Emilia smiled at Violet, then Josef, and agreed to dinner with us. I was ecstatic to have Emilia over for supper, but for some reason, I felt uneasy as well. Eliza's voice rang in my mind as I attempted to focus on the conversation.

Joshua, I heard in my mind, *we are old now. You have kept it a secret for so long. You must tell him now; else he will never know.*

Emilia

I arrived at the large white house with the circle drive at precisely 6:30 p.m. The dual lanterns on either side of the doorframe
shined with an inviting hue. I walked up the marble stairs and
pressed the white doorbell on the right. Within a few seconds,
the door opened, and I was met by Josef dressed in a grey suit,
his silver hair combed to one side and his glasses resting on the
bridge of his nose as they usually did.

"You look gorgeous," he blurted. "I mean, good evening."

I blushed and giggled. "Thank you. You look quite dapper
yourself."

He stood there with a goofy smile, as if this was the first time
he had laid eyes upon me. To break the silence, I said, "Perhaps
we can take this conversation inside?"

He apologized and escorted me into the warm house, taking
my coat in the process.

"I brought a pie to share," I said as I led him into the dining
room, where Violet and Laura were finishing the dinner prepara-
tions. "I hope you all enjoy strawberry-rhubarb—it is Mom's recipe."

"What a lovely gesture, Emilia," Violet said as she clasped her
hands together. "I will take it and put it in the kitchen."

Violet and Laura left, leaving Josef and me alone. He was
handsome—he had always been handsome—but something

about him now made my stomach flutter like a young woman in love for the first time. I tried to avert my thoughts from such fantasies, but as hard as I tried, I couldn't seem to stop gazing at the silver fox himself.

"Would you like a glass of wine?" he inquired, breaking my silent trance.

"Red, please," I replied.

He smiled. "I should have known. Burgundy?"

"Lovely," I said.

He walked to the other side of the room and pulled from a tall shelf a bottle of red wine. He blew the dust from the label and red the year aloud: "Nineteen seventy-six. A great year."

"Isn't that when you went with your parents to visit your uncle outside of Paris?"

"That was in seventy-eight. Uncle Leo had been bragging about the seventy-six bottles, though, and claiming it was some of the best he'd harvested in nearly thirty years."

He popped the cork and let the aromas from the bottle fill the room. He closed his eyes and took a long sniff from the open container, producing a broad grin as he pulled it away from his nose.

"Reminds me of France," he murmured. "Oh, how I long to go back again before I am unable to travel anymore."

"Would Felicia ever consider going with you? Not to be rude, but you have the money to do so. Your books have been quite popular these past couple of decades."

He grabbed two glasses from the cabinet, placed them on the table, and began to pour the red liquid.

"Felicia," he said as he finished pouring the second glass, "would not want to travel to France. She is not a fan of planes; hence, we drove here from Cleveland."

"What is that, a nine-hour trip?"

"Just over ten," he said. "Lord knows I was about to kick everyone out of the car at hour six."

We both laughed and took a sip of wine.

"But that is between you and me," he whispered.

"Dinner is ready, everyone!" Violet said as she strolled out of the kitchen with a large plate of turkey. A trail of sweet aromas flooded out of the kitchen behind her, and I realized how hungry I actually was.

Josef

Dinner was delicious, as I had expected, and Emilia's strawberry-rhubarb pie was phenomenal, putting me over the edge with a very full stomach. We retired to the family room, where Laura had already prepared a fire along with five cups of freshly brewed tea. I took my usual seat in my father's old leather chair and gave a loud sigh of satisfaction.

"Well, that was unusually loud," Emilia laughed as she took her own seat across from me. "Was the pie that terrible?"

"Heavens, no!" I quipped. "I am extremely satisfied, that's all."

"I agree with Josef," Mother added. "That was some of the best pie I have had in a long time. Your mother would be proud."

Emilia smiled and took a sip of her tea just as Laura rolled Father into the room. I got up and moved the end table so that his chair could be somewhat close to the fire. He gave a compliment pat on his left armrest, a common sign of appreciation I had come to know over the past couple of years.

"Violet," Emilia said, "Josef tells me that you are you planning a trip to Paris soon to visit your brother. Is that correct?"

"Oh, dearest," she replied with a half laugh, "I am far too old to be planning such a trip. I brought it up once or twice in passing, but I have not really put my mind to actually following through. Leo wouldn't want the likes of me skulking around the vineyard anyway, what with the hundreds of laborers that he has hired on during the busy seasons. I fear I would just get in the way of his operations. He's in his eighties now, but the man still works as if he were twenty! He's a good man, and I'm not just saying that because I'm his sister!"

We all laughed at the comment, though when I looked at my mother's eyes, I could see the emptiness that she felt deep within. She missed her brother; she talked about him more often than she'd care to admit.

"Excuse me, everyone," Mother said, rising suddenly. "I am going to use the bathroom."

No one made mention of her sudden departure. Emilia turned her attention to the mantel above the fireplace and let out an audible gasp.

I turned to follow her gaze and noticed the wine bottle set in the middle on its small holding block.

"I can't believe you still have this," she said, standing to inspect the bottle. "This was given to you by Dr. Reynolds, yes?" She asked it without expecting an answer.

My father moved violently in his chair next to me, letting out a low grunt as Emilia reached out to touch the display. She stopped and turned to face him. I put my hand on his arm in concern.

"Are you all right, Dad?" I said, putting my cup down on the floor in front of me.

"He's fine, I'm sure," Laura said as she walked to his chair and tucked the blanket deeper around his hips. "Just cold, I'm guessing."

Emilia nodded in agreement and turned her attention back to the bottle. This time, she grabbed it by the neck and lifted it off its stand.

My father thrashed his body, nearly knocking himself over.

"What is the matter?" Laura consoled him as she ran her hand over his forehead and cheeks. "You are not running a temp or anything."

Laura glanced at me with concern, but I did not know what to say. I had no background in medicine or even first aid, for that matter. My father again thrashed in his chair, this time throwing his arm forward, his eyes wide and wild.

I followed his gaze and saw Emilia standing with the cork and a handful of papers in one hand and the bottle in the other. Her brow furrowed with confusion.

"What is it?" I said.

"It's a roll of letters."

Emilia

The bottle was extremely light in my hand, and the cork seemed to have been tampered with. I ran my fingers over the top and then the sides of the cork. It was sticking out just far enough for me to get a good grip and tug. Joshua jerked in his chair, but I just pulled harder until the stopper gave, revealing the contents.

I dumped the rolled-up papers into my hand and looked at Josef. He looked to his father, who slumped back into his chair as if he had just been defeated. Violet entered with a small tray of plates and sweet treats, but upon seeing me with the open bottle, she dropped the tray. The plates shattered, and the food littered the floor at her feet.

"Oh no," she whispered to herself.

"What is this?" I said.

"Please," Violet pleaded, "put them into the bottle and put it back where you got it."

Again, I insisted, "What is this?"

Josef stood and looked at his mother with scrupulous eyes. "Mother," he whispered, "answer the question."

Violet covered her mouth and began to cry. She shook her head, but again Josef demanded she answer the question.

"No," she whimpered, "not yet."

Josef interjected. "Not yet? What do you mean, not yet? What the hell is a note doing in the precious wine bottle that you forbade anyone to touch?"

"Josef," I mumbled.

He turned on me and shouted, "What?"

"It has your name on the top," I began. "It is addressed to you."

"What?" he scoffed. "What do you mean it's addressed to me?"

I handed him the notes and watched as his eyes scanned the old pieces of onionskin paper, his face shifting through a multitude of different emotions.

When he finished, he looked to his mother, his eyes filled with tears, his face contorted in anger.

"Is this some kind of joke?" he whimpered. "Is this some kind of sick joke?"

Violet remained silent, her hands over her mouth and tears staining her rosy cheeks.

"N-no," Joshua croaked from his chair. He was sitting straight, his head against his headrest and mouth gaping slightly.

"What does the letter say?" I whispered.

He turned to me, tears in his eyes. "I'm adopted."

Josef

A rush of sorrow and betrayal filled my heart and mind as I read the collection of notes aloud after taking my seat again in the old leather chair. The room was silent except for my voice, which seemed to blast like thunder as I read.

> *Dear Josef,*
>
> *If you are you reading this letter, that means that your mother and I are already passed on, and this priceless bottle was left to you in our will. Although we told you from a young age that the bottle upon our mantel contained the greatest secret known to the world, we never allowed you to peek at it for fear of your finding this letter inside. I regret to say that your uncle Leo in Paris is holding the bottle passed down from the late Dr. Reynolds for you. Enclosed within my old cigar box, under a false bottom, is enough money for a one-way trip to Paris whenever you are ready.*
>
> *Before I continue, however, let me preface the following with the promise that I love you and always have, since the day you were born. Do not*

let this message make you think any differently of Violet and myself, as it was for your own good that we followed through with our plans to keep you safe.

Violet and I are not your real parents. Please, take a second to let this sink in. The secret of your past has weighed on our hearts and minds since the day you were born. Your mother, Violet's sister, was named Claire Decroix. She died in the spring of 1946 after complications from your birth. Her last request to Eliza, Violet, and myself was to take you and Emilia to America to begin a new life together. Eliza became your surrogate aunt, while Violet and myself became your parents.

Before we left Paris, however, we deeded to you a plot of land, approximately seventy acres in total, of the finest vineyards in the world. They are priceless. Leo is the current caretaker and has been anticipating your return to obtain the inheritance left by your mother.

You are probably wondering about your father, and rightly you should. His name is Gabriel Schroder. After the Great War, his father opened a tailor shop in Kehl, Germany, and when the Second World War began, Gabriel was drafted into the German army and stationed in France. He met your mother and served the French rebellion well until he left us for Poland on a secret mission from his superior. When the war ended, he returned with Eliza and Emilia but did not stay long, per your mother's request.

Soon after he left, your mother learned that she was pregnant with you. She chose not to tell Gabriel and forced each of us to swear that we would not reveal this secret to anyone until all of us—Violet, Eliza, and myself—had passed on. You may not understand our reasoning for never telling you—Lord knows I wanted to tell you long ago—but we each promised your mother.

I write this letter with a heavy heart, as it is with great sadness that you must learn the truth this way. Do not hate your mother for her choice to keep this secret from you, as she wanted the best life for you, knowing we would raise you as our own son.

We love you, Josef.

Sincerely,

Joshua, Violet, and Eliza

I let the letters fall from my hand; they dropped noiselessly to the ground. The room was silent. All eyes were on me, but I had nothing left to say.

Emilia

I left shortly after he finished reading the letter. I drove home in silence, and when I arrived, I crawled under the covers and lay awake, staring at the ceiling. I traced the tattooed ink on my right forearm, *943398*, my constant reminder of my mother's sacrifice to keep me alive while in the concentration camp. I never talked about it, but neither did she. We didn't talk about Europe unless someone brought it up in conversation, and even then, we avoided detail.

However, as Josef read the letter, I was drawn back to the underground bunker that I had called my home for nearly a year. I remembered Claire, only slightly, but I could not remember her being pregnant. I had been told since I was a little girl that *Violet* had Josef and that Claire had died of sickness due to the long winter. I was so naive.

I traced the number on my arm again and thought about my mother. *What else did she lie about to keep me safe? Who was my real father?* She never told me anything about my biological father, though I had inquired quite a few times throughout her lifetime. Her only response was, "Oh, your father, he was a gentle man with a beautiful voice. He was killed in action in Poland, long before you were born."

I wanted to know the truth about my own father, but my only source, my mother, was gone now. At least Josef's parents had the decency to share some of the details of his mother's life prior to us coming to America.

Sleep escaped me, and eventually I found myself holding my phone, scrolling to find Josef's number in my limited contacts list. I found it and called him, even though it was three thirty in the morning.

The phone rang twice before I heard a hoarse voice on the other end.

"Hello?" he grumbled.

"Josef," I said.

"Hello? Who is this?"

I sighed. "Josef, it's me, Emilia."

There was a pause on the other end before the voice returned. "Emilia, it is almost four in the morning. Why are you calling?"

"I can't sleep," I confessed. "Your letter, it is keeping me up."

"My letter?" he repeated. "Why is my letter keeping you up?"

"I just . . . I just want to know the rest of the story. I want to know why your father left your mother. I want to know why they kept it a secret from you all these years. It just . . . it just doesn't make sense, you know?"

"What are you suggesting we do, then? Go to Germany and try to find my father?"

I didn't answer, though that was exactly what I thought we should do.

"Josef," I said sternly, "you may never get a chance again to go and *potentially* meet your biological father. You can't replace your father."

"Apparently, my mother thought so," he said coldly.

The comment was brass but true. "Josef, you can't hold this above your mother's head until you find out the real truth of what happened between them. Please, go to Germany with me?"

Another long pause. Then, "Let me at least sleep on it?"

"Call me tomorrow," I said. "Good-bye."

Joshua

Laura was feeding me my morning oatmeal when Josef entered the kitchen with his cell phone pressed up against his ear with his shoulder. He was buttoning up his white shirt and attempting to tuck it into his black slacks while staying focused on his conversation. It was quite comical, to be honest. I laughed in my head, but only a low drone came from my mouth.

"Excuse you," Laura quipped as she wiped my lips clean with a napkin. "I thought you were always one for manners, Joshua."

"Look, Felicia, I know it's short notice, but—" he said before he was cut off yet again. "No, I am not doing this to make you angry— No, I am not running away with some other woman—I told you why I'm going—Wait, can we at least—Felicia, just listen—please."

Removing the phone from his ear, he let out a frustrated sigh. He set the phone on the counter, his shirt still half-buttoned and half-tucked-in. He looked like a mess. Then again, I didn't blame him for being so frustrated, and that woman was a nightmare, to put it politely.

"Laura," Josef said, "may I have some time alone with him?"

Laura looked to me, then back to Josef, and finally to me, but she left the two of us in the kitchen to talk—well, for one of us to.

Josef pulled up a chair opposite me and sat down as gentle as a feather—not making a single noise in the process. He cleared his throat and began, "I want to be mad at you and Mom, you know." His voice was strained as he held the tears back. "You lied to me for sixty-nine years. Sixty-nine."

I wanted to tell him why I did it, why I kept quiet, even before my condition got worse. In my mind, I was screaming louder than ever, *I am sorry! I never meant to hurt you!*

"But despite that," he continued, "I can't blame for you being an honorable man to my mother. I respect you too much to hate you, Dad. You are always my dad. Even if you aren't my biological one, you will always be my dad. I just—" Tears dripped down his cheeks now. "I just wish you would have told me. I had . . . I had a right to know."

I tried to speak, but tears only welled up in my eyes. The inability to console my son was worse than any pain I had ever experienced before. I wanted to tell him everything, the reason why, the truth, but I couldn't do it. It was right there on the front of my mind, but I sat instead, staring like a vegetable in the hospital, waiting for my clock to run out.

We were both crying now. Josef got up and wrapped me in his arms, and he whispered into my ear, "I'm going to Germany, to find my father. Pray that he is still alive. That is my last request from you, Dad."

With every ounce of strength I had left in my frail body, I lifted my left arm, placed it on my son's forearm, and squeezed.

He pulled away, tears in his eyes, and whispered, "I love you, Dad."

I patted his arm and croaked, "I love . . . you too . . . son."

Satisfied, he kissed my cheek, grabbed his phone, and said farewell to my wife and caretaker. As I heard the car roll out of the rocky driveway, I wept alone, knowing it was the last time I would see my adopted son.

Josef

I made my way to Eliza's home, not Emilia's. We decided the best place to begin our search would be Uncle Leo's home on the edge of Paris, as the letter indicated that he would be expecting me when I inherited the bottle with the letter.

Within three hours, we were on a flight to Paris. I did not bother to call my wife. I had nothing more to say to her, though I knew that the divorce papers would be arriving in my attorney's office within the next few days. So as to not cause him trouble, I called him to briefly explain the situation. He was not happy about it, but I was paying him to take care of it all for me until I got back to the States.

We touched down in Paris after one in the morning, local time, and I arranged a taxi to bring us to my uncle's cottage on the edge of town.

"Sir," the driver said, "that is nearly an hour's trip south due to the intense traffic flow. Are you sure you wouldn't rather just take the bus instead?"

I handed the man a couple of hundred euros and asked him if he would be willing to drive us. He complied with a genuine smile, and before we got out of the lot, Emilia and I were asleep in the back seat.

It was nearly three in the morning when the driver woke us, and I jumped out of the cab, nearly forgetting my luggage altogether.

I headed straight for the beautiful wooden porch that wrapped around the entire house, about to knock with such fury that it would wake the entire countryside. But just before I struck the door with my fist, I turned to see Emilia standing just off the main road, admiring the cottage.

"I remember this place," she whispered. "I was here . . . with my mother and Gabriel," She looked around and murmured, almost to herself. "We rode in on a cart . . . from the south, down that road," She pointed. "Gabriel, he was driving the cart, and my mother and I were nervous that Doc wouldn't allow us to live here."

She retraced her steps up the old dirt walk to join me on the porch, her eyes wide with excitement and wonder. "I had repressed so many memories about this place, about the war," she continued, "but now that I am here, it is all coming back. I remember your father. He was kind and gentle. He helped us survive the concentration camp."

The door opened suddenly, and an old man with a crooked back, leaning on his cane, stepped out of the dim entryway and onto the main porch. His wiry hair was messy atop his head, and his eyes showed hints of cataracts.

"If you have come to rob me, I have nothing of value except my grapes," he growled.

"Uncle Leo," Josef said calmly, "it's me, your nephew, Josef."

Leo turned his cloudy gaze toward me and straightened up as best he could. "So you know, then," he replied. "You've come to take what is rightfully yours."

"Well, not exactly," I said. "I am coming to ask you about my father, Gabriel."

Leo nodded in agreement, his bottom lip fat as if he were constantly pouting. "Come inside, then. We'll speak about such things in the morning. For now, I'm going back to bed. Find a spot on the couch, Josef, and your wife can have the spare bed."

I looked at Emilia and opened my mouth to say something, but just smiled instead as I followed my uncle into his cozy cottage for the night.

Emilia

The next morning, Josef and I joined Leo for breakfast and began to inquire about the history of Josef's real father.

"So where did my father go after the war ended?" Josef said, pouring more coffee into his mug.

"Your father," Leo began, "left us after your mother decided it would be better for him to go home to Germany. He did not say good-bye; he just never came back here."

"I remember Claire coming home that evening," I interjected. "Vaguely, but I do remember asking when Gabriel would be coming back."

Leo nodded in agreement. "Yeah, Claire had always been fond of the man, but even when she found out she was pregnant, she did not care to reach out to him for help. Your mother was always stubborn."

"And what about after the birth?" I said. "I know that we left quickly, and even when we arrived in America, we did not talk about France or Gabriel. In fact, I think my own mother made it a point to rid my mind of him, as if to keep me safe from some hidden harm that might come with knowing him."

Leo's face was stern, his lip curled slightly in disgust. "Aye," he growled. "And a good thing she did that for you too. Danger always follows when a Nazi forgets his priorities."

"What does that mean?" Josef said.

"Exactly what you think I mean," Leo barked. "Gabriel was a Nazi, there was no secret about that. When he came home with Eliza and you," he said, pointing at me, "he brought trouble."

I was taken aback by the comment. "Are you implying that my mother and I were not actually welcome?" I countered.

"That's exactly what I'm saying!" he shouted, rising slightly from his chair. "You are the reason why Claire is dead!"

"I was a little girl! How did I cause her death?"

"Because you lived, damn it!" His voice cracked. "You and your mother were supposed to die in that concentration camp, but you survived. Eliza's bloodline survived. When you came here with Gabriel, you endangered everyone. Just because the Nazis lost the war didn't mean that their operations were not still in effect. They needed to tie up loose ends. Gabriel was a loose end, and with him, you and your mother."

"What do you mean, he was a loose end? Why did they want to kill him?" Josef said.

Leo turned to his nephew, his frown deepening. "Because," he growled, "he failed to follow through with his first mission by killing Eliza's sister, Isabella. The man who put the bounty on Isabella's head decided to mark the remainder of her family as retribution," He motioned to Emilia. "Gabriel claimed he only knew of Isabella's assassination, but when the first sympathizer showed up here asking questions about our dealings with Gabriel, I knew it went deeper than that."

"Sympathizer?" I said.

"Yes," he replied. "Loyalists to the Nazi party, dedicated to fulfilling Hitler's greatest mission—to kill the entire Jewish population."

I laughed in disbelief. "My mother was not Jewish. She was Catholic."

"No," Leo said. "You were not taken to that camp because you were just Polish."

Another lie, I thought. *My mother always commented about how loyal she was to her Catholic faith. How much of my life has been a lie?*

"I'm sorry you had to learn all of this just now," Leo mumbled, taking a sip of his coffee. "The truth is not always forgiving."

"The sympathizers, though," Josef said, breaking the short silence. "How many came here?"

"Just the two," Leo said. "The first asked about your father but did not push the situation when Doc Reynolds claimed he had never heard of the man. Gabriel left soon after the first confrontation. Claire was heartbroken by her decision to ask him to leave, but she knew it was the best for the rest of us. Then she found out that she was pregnant with you, Josef. Nearly a year later, Gabriel returned and demanded that he be allowed to speak to Claire. After much debating with myself and Doc, Claire was allowed to meet with him, though the secret of your birth remained hidden from him."

"Why did he come back?" I said.

"That's the mystery," Leo replied. "No one knows the real reason because Claire died with the secret."

"Wait," Josef interjected, "my mother died in childbirth."

Leo's eyes filled with tears. "No, Josef," he rasped. "Your mother was murdered."

Josef

The news hit me like a truck to the chest. First I had been told that I was adopted, my mother having died giving birth to me, and now *this*.

"What?" I choked out.

"Aye," Leo said. "Killed in the streets of Paris while shopping for fresh produce. She was caught in the crossfire when an assassin attempted to shoot your father and killed her instantly."

The story just continues to change around me. When will I actually learn the truth of my past?

"He was the second sympathizer to visit, wasn't he?" Emilia whispered.

Leo nodded but said nothing.

Emilia's eyes grew wide. "I remember him. I was in the kitchen helping Margret with the baking when I looked out and saw the man on the porch. He was not dressed like a soldier, but when I saw him, I knew he was dangerous. He was tall and slim, with short blond hair and a crooked nose. His left eye socket was distorted and scarred. He did not see me in the window because I scampered away from the counter and down the hallway. The memory of him, though," she said slowly, "is clear as day as I talk about it."

"I never saw the man," Leo said, "though Doc told us that he did not trust him based on first sight. He attempted to coax

Doc into letting him stay here, claiming he was a weary traveler, but Doc saw through the lie and turned the questions back onto him. He left soon after, but when the reports of a gunman running rampant in Paris came to us, Doc immediately contacted the authorities, and they arrested a German soldier about a mile west of the city."

"So this man," I said, "he was the one who killed my mother?"

"I know it was him," Leo growled. "I have no doubt in my mind."

"And where is he now?"

"Six feet under," Leo said. "And good riddance to him too. Someone killed him shortly after he murdered Claire as he was trying to flee the police. No one knows who shot him, but I applaud whoever did the deed. Knowing the police, it would have been years before they reached a verdict on his sentence. Better to just rid the world of the filth when you can instead of letting him fester in a prison cell."

My view of my uncle had changed significantly from what I first remembered of the old man. I had once thought him to be gentle and pure of heart, but hearing him speak made me wonder what my mother had been like when she was alive—my hope was that she was not as gruff and unforgiving as her younger brother.

Emilia cleared her throat and said, "So, since this gunman is dead, who can help us to find Gabriel now?"

Leo rubbed his chin and leaned back in his chair. He closed his eyes and began to hum to himself as if ignoring us. I was about to tap him on the leg when he answered, eyes opening slowly, as if he had been napping. "There is a private investigator by the name of Langston Drudgestein," he said. "He lives in Munich. Here is his card." He said pulling a card from his pocket with Langston's information printed across the front. "I sought him out a few years ago after one of my workers decided to steal from me and then hop the country with nearly a thousand dollars' worth of wine. Langston later informed me that he had caught the culprit on the outskirts of Berlin attempting to sell the wine to a secret buyer, but was thwarted before the deal could be made."

"And this Langston," I said slowly, "we can trust him to find Gabriel?"

Leo frowned. "Why do you think I would encourage you to contact him if I didn't believe he could actually do it?"

After a few more days with my uncle, we took a train to Munich to meet with Langston. He was exactly as my uncle had told us and agreed to help us for a hefty price.

Emilia

The search for Gabriel was more tedious than either of us had hoped, but after nearly three weeks, Langston hit a lead and was hot in pursuit.

"Can we go with you?" I called from the next room as I stuffed my suitcase with wrinkled shirts and other assorted dirty laundry. "Josef and I have been itching to get out of the city."

Langston hobbled into the bedroom, his cane scraping the floorboards. "No," he growled. His bushy black eyebrows danced above his beady eyes whenever he spoke. "I am not even sure this lead is credible, let alone worth my time to pursue. I've been searching for Gabriel for nearly three weeks, working tirelessly to find just a shred of information about him, but the man is a ghost."

"But you said this lead was a solid one."

Langston raised his cane and pointed it at me. "I say a lot of things. You two have given me quite a lot of grief lately, so I had to give you something to hope for."

Anger boiled inside me. "What?" I barked. "You mean you have been lying to us for these past three weeks, making us pay you for nothing? What a lousy investigator you are!"

"It's not my fault that the man has not been seen by anyone for nearly twenty years! The only solid lead, as I have informed you—and yes, I have not been working nearly as hard as I usually do, due to my age—is a somewhat decent start."

I was fuming at this point, my words sharp as daggers. "Well, you'd better start pulling your weight, or we will demand all our money back and bring you to court for false practice!"

"Now, now," he said, "let's not get too hasty here. Investigator work is not that easy, especially at my age."

"Not that easy?" I repeated crossly. "You have everything you could possibly need to find anyone, and yet you can't find an old man who is probably confined to a wheelchair!"

Josef entered the room, and my anger quickly subsided into embarrassment.

"We are not firing him," Josef said sharply.

Langston turned his attention to Josef behind him. "I'm glad that one of you has some sense—"

"Do not think that I am taking sides in this," Josef interrupted. "I am paying you more than you deserve, so you had best start performing at the level for which I hired you. Otherwise, as Emilia said, I will find someone more capable."

Langston's brows furrowed, and his postured straightened. "Now see here," he boasted, "there is no investigator greater than Langston Drudgestein."

Josef stepped closer and looked down on the portly fellow, his voice dropping to a hoarse whisper. "Then prove it."

Josef

My confrontation seemed to inspire Langston, who doubled his efforts and expanded his network of connections to aid him in finding Gabriel within a week. According to his sources, Gabriel had retreated to the coastal city of Marseilles on the bank of the Golfe du Lion. Langston gave us the address, wished us the best of luck, and saw us off as we boarded the small plane upon the tarmac runway.

The flight was bumpy, to say the least. Emilia fell asleep almost immediately, but I was so nervous, yet excited, that I couldn't rest. We were about to find my father, at long last. *What will I say to him? What will he say to me? Will he be excited to see me, or will he deny that I am actually his son?*

The restless thoughts bounced through my mind for the entire four-hour trip, until we were landed safely at the Marseilles airport. We ordered a taxi and immediately headed to the location on the card, even though I was extremely hungry after skipping lunch due to a sudden change in departure times.

The taxi rolled up to a small residential area with simple, square buildings and red tile roofing. The houses were nearly impossible to tell apart, save for the numbers that hung just to the right of each front door. The house marked 210 had a forest-green door and a crooked black knob.

"Are you ready?" Emilia whispered as she placed her hand on my arm. I hadn't realized how violently I was shaking till she touched me.

I looked at her with wide eyes and nodded.

We were halfway up the sidewalk before she stopped and motioned for me to continue ahead of her. I took her hands in mine, leaned in, and kissed her on the cheek.

"Thank you," I said with a faint smile. "I couldn't have done this without you."

She nodded and again motioned for me to go to the door. After a few seconds of catching my breath and calming my nerves, I made my way to the large door. I gave a firm knock on the center and took a quick step back.

After about a minute of waiting, I moved in for another crisp knock, but then heard the slight click of a latch on the other side, followed by the slow turning of the old knob. The door groaned loudly as it opened, revealing an old man with round glasses and short white hair on the other side. His hand trembled slightly as he pulled the large door open, revealing the rest of his body.

He was shorter than I had expected, but I could tell that his posture was still upright, regardless of a slight lean due to age. He licked his lips and said, "And who might you be, lad? I am not looking for anything to buy today, sorry. Though I believe that Ms. Kirkov down the street here would be interested in hearing what you have to sell."

I cleared my throat and said in the most confident voice I could, "Are you Gabriel Schroder?"

The old man's eyes searched me again, then Emilia on the sidewalk. "What's this about?" he said sharply. "What do you want with him? Gabriel has been gone for nearly fifteen years. Died of pneumonia in a hospital bed. He is long gone. Best you go back to where you came from." He began to push the door closed, but I grabbed it and held it open.

"Let go of the door," he growled desperately. "I don't want any trouble, but I will call the police if I need to."

"Sir, please," I said. "We just need to talk to you."

"I don't want your business here. Have a nice day now!"

"Josef," Emilia said, "tell him why we are here. Tell him who you are."

The old man relaxed his grip on the door, suddenly, and I grasped the frame firmly, as much to steady myself as to keep it open.

"Gabriel," I panted, "I am your son."

Gabriel

"My son?" I repeated in disbelief. "Sir, I have never had a son. I fear you have mistaken me for someone else. Please, leave me be. I am quite busy today."

"Gabriel," the man said, still struggling to hold the door open, "you were a German soldier in the war. You are from Kehl, but when you were drafted, you got stationed in Paris. You then met Claire Decroix, with whom you soon after fell in love. You spent three years living with her and her adopted family just outside of Paris, where you helped keep the underground wine network intact despite the raging war around you. You then were called on a mission to Poland to find and kill a girl, yet you couldn't do it. Instead, you saved her, and her sister and daughter, bringing them home from Auschwitz to Paris. Claire asked you to leave, and you did not argue, but you came back a year later and witnessed her murder. You've been in hiding ever since."

My heart sank, and my lips trembled. "How?" I whispered. "How did you know all of that?"

"Because I am your son," the man repeated.

I looked past him and motioned to the woman behind him. She was fair despite her age. "And her," I said, "who is she?"

She walked up to the door and pushed gently past the man. Grabbing my hand, she brought it to her lips and kissed it softly.

"Gabriel," she said with tears in her eyes, "it is so good to see you again. It's me, Emilia."

I gasped. "Emilia," I repeated as I grabbed her hand and pulled her into a hug. My arms were frail and shaky, but I held her tight against my chest, and she reciprocated.

"I have not seen you since . . . since you were only four years old!" I cried. "Oh, how I have missed you, dear. Look how you have grown!" I kissed her cheek and took a step back to marvel at the woman. "Such beauty, just like your mother." The sudden rush of memories flooded my mind—Eliza's sweet voice, innocent and full of love.

"Your mother," I said, "is she . . . ?"

Emilia's face fell as she shook her head. I had feared such a fate would befall Eliza in this old age, though Emilia later informed me that she had gone peacefully into the night.

I looked back to the man who had claimed to be my son. I studied him—his face resembled many features of my youth, and yet I could see Claire in his eyes as well. *Could this actually be my son? Did Claire protect him from me for fear that they would come after him once they finished me off?*

"Your name, please," I said to the man.

"My name is Josef," he replied.

"Josef," I repeated. "Please, come inside. I think we have much to discuss."

Josef

I could tell that Gabriel did not yet trust me, and I didn't blame him—I would not trust an older-looking gentleman coming unannounced to my house, claiming to be my son. Still, a part of me believed that he would soon believe it. It had taken me weeks to truly wrap my own head around the idea, so I was willing to give him time to understand and cope with the truth—it was the least I could do.

"You have been living in America all these years?" he said, looking over his glasses.

"That's right," I replied, setting my cup on the table in front of me. "Joshua and Violet took me as their adopted son. I graduated high school at the top of my class and then went on to study at Boston College, where I received my first degree in journalism. After that, I worked for a newspaper in Vermont before I went back to school again, this time at New York University, to get my master's and then doctorate in creative writing with a certification in copyediting—I'm a full-time author today."

Gabriel nodded, his eyebrows raised in surprise as I listed my multiple accomplishments off as if I were some highbrow person. I hated talking about myself. If I could, I would always divert the conversation toward the others, as I was far more interested in hearing from them than blabbing about me.

"My son the author," Gabriel whispered before taking a sip of tea. "Quite remarkable." He chuckled and leaned forward on the edge of his seat. "So, what sort of stuff do you write, then?"

I was surprised. Usually people already knew what I wrote about, seeing that I had publications in more than fifty countries, including France—though, to give him credit, he would have never known to look for my name in a bookstore or best-seller list.

"Uh," I said, "primarily historical fiction, but I also focus a lot on essays and commentaries. I have been writing a blog for about ten years—it is quite successful."

"And you also lecture throughout the world," Emilia quipped. "You aren't always just sitting in your study, thinking of the next great novel to come from your keyboard. From what you've told me, you are quite active for a sixty-nine-year-old with a wife and two kids."

I felt my cheeks getting warm as red color flushed up my neck and around my face.

Gabriel sat up straighter still—any farther and I was afraid he'd break his fragile back like a toothpick. "You are married and have children? I have grandchildren?" His eyes grew bright, and his smile widened.

"Well," I said, "not exactly anymore."

The hope in my father's eyes died out as quickly as it had been sparked. "What do you mean by that?"

"My wife—well, my second wife—was not fond of me coming in search of my parents after Eliza's funeral. In fact, she filed for divorce the day I left for Europe. When I get back, the papers will be waiting for me in my mailbox."

He frowned. "And your children? What will happen to them?"

"They aren't technically my own children. They are my step-daughters. Felicia, my now presumably soon-to-be ex-wife, had the two girls before she met me. They are in their midtwenties now—I don't see them much as it is, anyway."

"I see," he replied. "It's too bad that you did not have a stronger relationship with the three of them. Much the same that I wish I would have had with your mother."

"Will you tell me about her, the truth of her? Especially what happened that day she was killed? I need to know."

He nodded in agreement. "I will tell you the whole truth, but I will also tell you that this story is not for the lighthearted. Can you handle that?"

"Of course," I blurted out.

He smiled, poured another cup of tea for the three of us, and then began to recall the memories from the beginning, starting with the day he met my mother on that lone road leading out of Paris. While he spoke, I could see the passion, the courage, the *love* that he had for my mother, for his friends, for his honor as a man and soldier. It was truly inspiring, and the story was . . . *beautiful.*

Gabriel

As I retold my son the story of my journey—well, all our journeys: Claire, Joshua, Eliza, and even Emilia at times—I remembered the massive sacrifices that had been made, the heroes who gave up their lives, and the passion and love each of us had for one another in those days. At the time, I had not truly appreciated my circumstances—I saw the war as a nightmare, a hell that I could never escape, and yet years later, here I sit, retelling those same horror stories to my own son and a woman who had been there, though her age had hidden the truth of what was going on. As I told the stories, she smiled and nodded, even adding significant details that I had misplaced or forgotten.

I spoke for nearly four hours before I finally finished at the crossroads where Claire and I parted ways.

"When I left your mother there," I said as the tears filled my eyes, "I could not think of anywhere else to go. My home was there with Doc, Margret, Joshua, Petyr, Violet, and Claire for years—with the addition of Eliza and Emilia after our return from Poland in nineteen forty-five. When she asked me to leave, my heart shattered. I thought we would get married, settle down, have a few children, and live in peace with one another till we passed from old age."

"Where did you go, then, if not back to the cottage?" Josef inquired.

I sighed. "I went back home to Kehl to work in my father's tailor shop. My parents took me in, praising and thanking God for my safe return. They had received a letter from my field commander stating that I had died in action on the front lines in the east in the fall of forty-four, when, in reality, I had been taken to the camp at Auschwitz. I never told them what had actually happened, always taking care to cover the hideous number on my forearm. I stayed for nearly a year and then moved on again. I said that I was restless, but in truth, I was still in love with Claire.

"I hopped a train and rode up to Paris in hopes of finding her again. Since I was traveling illegally, I had to hop off the train nearly ten miles from the capital and walk the remainder of the way into town. The city, when I arrived on the outskirts, had changed dramatically in the last year. The construction activity was astounding—if it was your first visit, you would have never known that the city had been under occupation for four years."

"So you just went straight into the city and found Claire, then?" Emilia said in disbelief.

I laughed. "Heavens, no! The city is gigantic, and she is just one person. No, I went to cottage first, but I made sure that I was not seen. I waited in a neighboring field for nearly an hour, but no one came or left. Then, when I was about to give up and head into town, a man arrived—who, to be honest, I found quite peculiar. He was tall and thin, blond, wearing regular civilian clothes, but I could tell by his short hair and extremely stiff posture that he had a military background—and he was tense, ready for battle. Though I couldn't hear the conversation directly, I did get a good glimpse of him as Doc turned him away. His left eye socket was distorted, as if it had been caved in, and the skin around it was scarred and quite hideous."

I watched as Emilia and Josef exchanged uneasy looks.

"What? Is it something I've said?"

"Only that we've heard of this mystery man before," Emilia said. "Josef's uncle, Leo, whom we visited before we found you, told us only a piece of the overall story—though he mentioned the killer only briefly, your recollection of this man matches the exact description that Leo gave us, as well as what I remember."

I nodded. "That makes sense. After I watched the stranger walk down the road and out of sight, I rushed to the door and called for Doc until he answered. When he threw the door open, I was met by a rifle in my face—though once he recognized me, he dropped the gun and embraced me joyfully, as though I were the prodigal son returning home. I told him that I suspected his visitor was a German spy, and he told me where Claire was. Knowing the dangers of the road, I walked through the countryside to the market she was shopping at. When I initiated contact, I made sure to keep her moving, not allowing her to stop and ask me questions until we were out of the busy market—your mother was always stubborn, but this time she did not question anything, not even me being back in the city.

"'Gabriel,' Claire murmured to me as I hurried her out of the marketplace, 'Are you being followed?'

"'There is someone searching for me,' I whispered as I looked back over my shoulder. No one seemed to be following us yet. 'I came to see you, but we are not safe here.'

"We rushed out of the market and down the sidewalk, rounding the corner at the local café. There she pulled her arm free of my grip and stopped me on the sidewalk with a firm hand on my shoulder. 'I have something to tell you,' she said.

"I told her, 'Claire, we have to keep moving. It is not safe here.'

"I turned to look for any assailants, but just as I moved, a shot rang out, followed by a thud. I searched desperately for the gunman, but all I could see was the crowd of terrified civilians running in horror from the scene.

"Claire's grip loosened, and her hand slipped from mine. I tried to catch her, but it was too late, and she dropped, dead, to the sidewalk. I had no time to think, no time to react—I just ran as fast as I could, away from the shot. Another shot rang out, but the bullet didn't find me.

"As chaos erupted behind me, I cursed myself for coming back."

Josef sat back in his chair, his hands over his mouth, and I could see the tears falling from his wet eyes.

"So that's it?" he said. "That's how it happened? You just *ran?*"

I sat straight again, though my lower lip trembled. "I could not have done anything for her. She was dead before she hit the ground."

"But you ran from everything, from everyone. The least you could have done was go back and tell them what had happened!" Josef's voice cracked as he yelled.

I remained calm, but my voice was stern. "If I had returned to the cottage, everyone there, you included, would have been killed. I ran because I had to, not because I wanted to."

"You abandoned me!" he cried. "You left me here in France while you ran!"

"I didn't even know you were alive!" I retorted. "If I had known that you were alive, that you were at the cottage, I would have come for you, but I had no idea. Son, I am so sorry, but I didn't know. I swear."

Josef

The sincerity in his voice was genuine. I had pushed too hard, had broken my father's heart to the point of feeling betrayed. It was the only way I could tell if he was being truthful about the entire situation—I pushed, and he broke.

Emilia went to comfort my crying father in his recliner; I stood and left the room. My emotions were high, my anger still building, but pity for my father also stirred in the pit of my stomach. Had he come back for me, we might indeed have been killed by the assassin—though I couldn't get over the fact that no one had told me the truth all these years.

Do I hate my father, or was it my adoptive parents who caused me the most grief? Each played a part in keeping me alive, but still my heart grieves.

I splashed water onto my face and took a deep breath, attempting to control my emotions and frustration. A sharp knock on the doorframe broke my mental spiral.

"Josef," Emilia said gently, "you can't be mad at your father for what he did."

"Then who should I blame for all of this? My adoptive parents? Myself? Who?"

"I can't change what happened to you," she replied, "but I do know that you can start over with him, right now. However, you have to be willing. I know that he is, but the real question is, are you ready to forgive him and start over?"

Water dripped from my face, or perhaps it was the fresh tears—regardless, I was a mess. I cleaned myself up with the towel on the wall, took a deep breath, and rejoined the two in the living room. Gabriel had a large notebook on his lap, his hands resting lightly on the cover, as if not to press too hard. I took my seat again.

"I am sorry for being mad at you," I whispered. "You did not deserve that. I am sorry that I was not patient with you, that I felt abandoned, when in reality you had no idea I was alive. That was not fair. I am not sure what I want right now, but I do know that I want to start over with you. Right here, right now."

Silent, he nodded. He ran his hands over the notebook's leather cover and opened it carefully.

"Then I will give you this," he said. "It has everything I have collected over the years about the war, the people I encountered, stories from your mother, Joshua, Eliza, and myself. I took down each account and put them all in this book. The truth, it is all here."

He handed the book to me with gentle caution. It sat heavy on my lap. I ran my fingers over the leather cover and opened it to the first page, which was blank.

"Why is this page blank?" I inquired.

"Because I could not think of a title for the contents. Though, I'm sure you will think of something."

I smiled and nodded as I thumbed through the old book.

"Gabriel," Emilia said, "I have to wonder, whatever happened to the real bottle of wine that Doc Reynolds supposedly kept hidden?"

Gabriel smiled. "Ah, the drink worth more than gold." He chuckled. "Doc told me about the very bottle you speak of, even showed it to me at one point, but he never let me hold it, never let anyone touch it."

"Why?"

"There was no bottle of wine, dear."

I looked up in confusion. "You just said you have seen it with your own eyes. You said Doc kept it very close to him at all times."

"And what about the bottle in your parents' house?" Emilia interjected. "That was supposedly the same bottle, but when the seal was broken, there was nothing inside but a note."

"There was no bottle," I repeated softly. "You saw it, but you never touched it. Why?"

"Because the bottle was a metaphor for something greater than itself. It was a symbol for those of us who remained loyal to the cause of preserving the wine, the hundreds of bottles containing our history and culture. Doc always showed the bottle to inspire us all to keep fighting for something. We looked to the bottle for a sense of hope, to keep us focused on why we were fighting to keep the traditions of France alive."

"Then what about the other bottles? Why make them?" I said.

"As a distraction, should the Germans have stumbled upon one. The bottle is only a face; its contents are where the real treasure lies. Doc did not fight to save the wine; he fought to keep a dream alive—a dream of a future for each and every one of us. And when you were born, Josef, he made every effort to keep that dream alive and out of the way of danger. You are, in a way, Claire's treasure, one that survived the test of time—a gift worth more than gold itself."

I leaned back in my chair in disbelief. It was all making sense. The bottle on the mantel, the note inside preserving my past until I was ready to hear it, the entire journey home to find my father, and here, on my lap, was the culmination of the entire story. This was my purpose: to publish this story for the world.

"You must finish it," he said, looking over his glasses. "My story has already concluded; it is time for you to write yours. I left a few pages at the end for whomever inherited it after my death. I'm giving it to you, son. Finish it, for your mother."

Epilogue

Both of my fathers passed away in the late spring of the following year, Joshua first, and then Gabriel. I spent much of the winter with Gabriel, combing through the pages and asking the questions that only he could answer about the stories. Emilia stayed too, keeping my father as healthy as possible up until the day we left.

Their deaths marked the end of an era that would never be forgotten, thanks to Joshua's story and my father's diligence in writing everything down. Though it took almost three years to finish the manuscript, the book was a best seller almost overnight. It was the fastest-grossing book I had written in my entire career, but I could not take credit for the contents, for I merely told the stories of those who had already passed.

I received many awards for the book, was invited to speak at panels and seminars, and was even granted an opportunity to review the final script for the motion picture that was in production after the book's enormous popularity. It was a change of pace, for sure, but after long discussions and many hard decisions, I decided to draw the curtain on my writing career.

Though Emilia and I never officially married, we moved together to the Vermont countryside, where we bought a house on a lovely farmstead atop a hill that overlooked a large river valley. Though the divorce took most of my initial income, the royalties coming in from the book and, eventually, income from the vineyards I inherited and the large inheritance that my parents left for me, we settled into a quiet, yet comfortable life.

The story was finished, the truth completely told, and as I sat on the porch swing, watching the sunset, with Emilia cradled in my arms, I closed my eyes and felt peace in my heart for the first time in my life.